Forever Your *Heart*

Mary Whitney

OMNIFIC PUBLISHING
LOS ANGELES

Omnific Publishing
1901 Avenue of the Stars, 2nd floor
Los Angeles, CA 90067
www.omnificpublishing.com

First Omnific eBook edition, April 2014
First Omnific trade paperback edition, April 2014

Library of Congress Cataloguing-in-Publication Data

Whitney, Mary.
    Forever Your Heart / Mary Whitney – 1st ed.
    ISBN: 978-1-623421-27-4
    1. Contemporary Romance — Fiction. 2. First Love — Fiction.
    3. New Adult — Fiction. 4. Washington, DC — Fiction. I. Title

10 9 8 7 6 5 4 3 2 1

Cover Design by Micha Stone and Amy Brokaw
Interior Book Design by Coreen Montagna

Printed in the United States of America

*I'm not sure when my love of all things British began.
It may have started when I was very young as my mother watched
every episode of* Upstairs, Downstairs *on* Masterpiece Theatre.
Or maybe it was when I was eight and devoured
Charlie and the Chocolate Factory *and everything else*
Roald Dahl *ever wrote. Regardless, it was in high school and college
when I met all those Byronic heroes in my English classes
that I became an Anglophile for life.*

*So this book is dedicated to Mr. Darcy and Mr. Rochester
because there wouldn't be an Adam without you.*

Prologue

Adam Kincaid

Blokes don't cry, at least they're not supposed to, but it didn't stop me that steamy Texas morning in 1993. Bawling like the teenage baby I was, I'd crouched down on Nicki's driveway as pure anguish knocked the wind out of me. I must've been a sight for her to run out of the house for another goodbye. She made me smile, but it didn't change anything. She loved me, but she didn't want to have anything more to do with me, and my dad's job was taking us back to England. Her goodbye was for forever, and I had to leave.

I ran down the row of suburban homes, simultaneously berating myself for fucking everything up whilst selfishly hoping distance might make it better. After all, she was stronger than me. She'd proven it time and time again. But when she was at her weakest, I'd caused her irreparable harm — more than once. What I didn't know then was that I'd scarred myself for life as well.

At the time, I'd tried to justify what I'd done. She'd hurt me also. Terrified of any more pain in her life, she'd pushed me away even before I ruined everything. So hadn't she played some part in what I'd done?

With each passing year, however, I realized that even if the answer was yes, it didn't lessen the guilt I felt or how much I missed her. A decade and a half later, we were now going to see each other again. Could she ever forgive me?

Do you forgive yourself when you hurt someone you love?

You don't have to answer now, because I've jumped ahead of the story. Pardon me if I tell it out of order. We do that with our wounds. The memories jumble together, and we revisit them over and over as if the years might change our perspective. I can't start at the beginning, though. You might not forgive me if I did.

Chapter One

London, UK
July 1998

Five years after returning to England, I could go days, even a week or so without a thought of Texas and Nicki. I lived in the present rather than dwelling on the mistakes of my past. In the words of my father, I had a bright future ahead of me—the start of an impressive career, and a beautiful girlfriend with a pedigree and résumé to match my own. All in all, everything in my life had been going splendidly until I got the email. Nicki's best friends were planning a visit to London and wanted to get together while they were here.

The evening we'd agreed to meet, I was late—uncharacteristically so, sign enough that I wasn't ready for what lay ahead. As soon as I stepped onto the street from the tube, I ran to the pub. I'd catch hell from David for being late, so every second counted. Though when I arrived at the Barnfield Arms, I wondered why I'd hurried.

Far at the back, David seemed to be enjoying himself and clearly was not worried about me. He leaned back on the bench, occasionally taking a swig from his pint of ale as he checked out the girls standing around the noisy bar. He was my cousin and best friend, and I knew exactly what he thought as he gawked at a blonde with huge knockers.

"David, put your eyes back in your head," I said as I took a seat. "They're on stalks."

"Piss off. You were looking, too."

"It's difficult not to notice that one." I chuckled, taking another glance at her.

"You're late. I thought we said half past six. It's almost seven."

"I…er…got caught up at the studio."

"Right." He rolled his eyes. "You're late on purpose because you're nervous as fuck."

"Maybe…a little bit."

"You're only seeing her friends again—not her."

"I know, it's just weird—know what I mean?"

"I suppose, but you've got a serious girlfriend now, bucko. Shouldn't you be—"

"Let's not talk about Muff." I rubbed my forehead in frustration. I was tense, and I shouldn't have been snipping at David. "I'm sorry. I'm being an arse. It's just that they're different."

"Yeah, they're different. Muff's not Nicki. That's your problem, cuz."

"We've been through this a million times. What do you want me to do about it?"

"Can't say. I'm not you." David shrugged. "No one gives a flying fuck about what I do or where I live. I don't have a family bloodline to keep up." He sipped his beer as if toasting to the fact. "Thank the fuck."

"I'll drink to that," I said, raising my glass.

"So does Muff even know about Nicki?"

"No, and she never will."

"You're a bloody nutter. What does it say if you won't even tell your girlfriend about her?"

I flashed him a look, and I felt badly as soon as I did. Why was I mad at him when I was really mad at myself?

Then his tune changed entirely. "Well, look at what's walked in—our little American birds. They're even prettier than I remember."

I craned my head to locate Lisa and Rachel. "That's because at the time you were looking at Nicki."

"Well, someone needed to." He nudged me with his elbow. "Anyhow, it got you off your cowardly arse."

"That it did."

If David hadn't made me jealous as hell, I might never have asked Nicki out. I'd already hurt her once, and she'd run away from me like I was the devil himself. Well, when David had made his move on her, I couldn't have that. She was mine, not his, and even he'd known it. That's what had got my arse in gear.

As Lisa and Rachel walked toward our table, we both stood and donned smiles. David's eyes glittered as if he'd struck gold and would now have his choice between Halle Barry and Heidi Klum. If he only knew.

"Which one do I pick?" he said breathlessly. "You don't suppose I could have them both."

"Fat chance. If you're lucky, maybe Rachel." I doubted Lisa had changed since secondary school, and back then, she'd been formidable. There was no way she was going to give my cad of a cousin the time of day.

On the other hand, the way Rachel sashayed through the pub indicated a romp in the hay with a Brit was just what she'd had in mind for her European holiday. During my year in Texas, Rachel had been a devoted girlfriend to my best mate, Tom, but they'd long since broken up and were now only friends. Tom had warned me Rachel had mentioned David more than once before her trip.

"Hello, Lisa. Hello, Rachel," I said, stepping aside from the table to greet them.

"Hi, Adam. Thanks for meeting with us," said Lisa. Five years later, her tone hadn't changed with me; it was still friendly with a hint of skepticism. She gave me the kind of perfunctory hug I'd seen my sister, Sylvia, give to our creepy Uncle Willard. To David, Lisa simply extended her hand for a quick handshake.

Rachel's vivaciousness made up for Lisa's coldness. She gave me a warm but platonic hug, along with additional greetings from Tom. Turning to David, she said coyly, "I remember you."

"And I remember you," he said with his arms open.

Accepting his invitation, Rachel hugged him, which caused her blouse to rise. Since his hand was at her waist, it wandered onto the bare skin of her back, where it resided long enough to signal a very promising night was ahead of him.

After we saw to it that our guests had drinks and were comfortable, we began to exchange information about our lives in the last five years. With her eye on her prize, Rachel asked the first question. "So, David, the last time I met you, you were traveling the world. What are you doing now?"

"I'm an investment banker at Barclays, based in the City."

"You're an investment banker—like a stockbroker?" Lisa asked a little incredulously.

David shrugged. "I've always been a good gambler. Now I get paid to gamble with other people's money. It's the best of both worlds."

Lisa turned to me, and the friendly interrogation I'd braced myself for began. "What about you, Adam? Where did you go to school?"

"I graduated from Oxford, and I've just started working for the BBC…you know, training to be a journalist."

"I've thought about going into journalism also," Rachel said. "I majored in mass communications, but I really have no idea what I'm going to do next. Tom even suggested I meet up with him in LA and start going to auditions. I told him I can't act, but he said that doesn't matter."

David's eyes scanned Rachel's generous breasts and said, "I have to agree with him on that."

I snorted but quickly covered it up by asking Lisa, "What about you? You always did well in school."

"I'm pretty boring. I went to Columbia and majored in chemistry. Now I'm at Johns Hopkins for med school."

"It's kind of sad," Rachel said. "I don't think Lisa, Nicki, and I will ever live in the same city again."

My eyes flashed to hers upon hearing Nicki's name. I thought it would take longer for her name to come up, but here it was so soon. Taking a deep breath, I asked the question everyone was waiting for me to: "So, how is Nicki?"

Lisa answered immediately, "She's good. She says hi."

I nodded, trying to maintain some inner calm as my heart thumped at the idea of Nicki telling me hello. "What has she been up to?"

"Well, she graduated from University of Chicago, but she first went to school at UT. She wanted to be close to her grandma, who was sick for a while. When her grandma died, she left Austin and moved north to be near her dad. Her mom had already moved out of Texas when she remarried."

Another death for Nicki? She had just lost her sister in a car crash when I'd known her. Nicki and her mom lived. Her sister hadn't. Riddled with grief and survivor's guilt, Nicki's own scars from the accident were a constant reminder of it. Now the grandmother she'd always spoken of so fondly was gone. A pang hit my heart as I remembered holding her in my arms as she'd cried for her sister. Really, it was the pain in her life that had brought us together.

This time, had she grieved alone? Did she have another guy there to hold her? It gutted me to think that someone else had taken my place, even though, realistically, I knew it must have happened.

I'd surmised from the addresses on her letters to Sylvia that Nicki had moved around, and now I had an explanation. My smile had long since faded when I said, "That's awful. Please tell Nicki I'm sorry to hear about her grandmother. I know how much she loved her."

"Um. Sure." She gave me a perplexed look, and after a moment of awkward silence she added, "Anyway, Nicki did really well in school. She majored in history and English and graduated Phi Beta Kappa. Her dad was all set on her going to law school, but I don't think that's going to happen now."

"Why not?"

"She caught the political bug. She interned with a few elected officials during college, including her state senator, James Logan; she also worked on a few elections, so she held off filling out her grad applications. Now Logan is running for governor, and she's helping run his campaign's field operation. If he wins, I bet she'll go work for him — not like a big job, but something. Logan thinks she's super smart. I don't see her going to law school when she can work for the governor of Illinois."

"Really?" That I was not expecting. The budding journalist in me took over as I began to configure Nicki's story. She'd always known what was going on in the world and was thoughtful about it. She had a lot of opinions and was shrewd. I could imagine her involved in politics. And as a future member of the press, I loved politics, so I started peppering Lisa with questions. "So this James Logan. Is he a Democrat or a Republican?"

"Democrat."

"Conservative or liberal?"

"Moderate...I think."

"Really? How so? On what issues?"

"I don't know." Lisa shrugged. "That's just what Nicki said."

"So does Nicki consider herself a moderate?"

"I have no idea. I don't even really know what that means. Frankly, I don't care about politics."

"What does she think of this mess about President Clinton and Monica Lewinsky?"

Rachel chimed in. "Oh, I can answer that one. Nicki's worried about what it means for Democrats in the next election, but she still laughs about it. I mean…how could you not? The president got a blowjob from an intern right there in the Oval Office. That's pretty funny."

David looked to Rachel with raised eyebrows and seductively said, "Indeed."

Ignoring the eye-fucking that commenced between the two of them, I went back to my questioning. "So does Nicki have any interest in foreign policy or just domestic issues?"

David interrupted his stare at Rachel to look at me. I could easily guess his thought: *Ask her yourself, you tosser.*

Lisa and Rachel caught each other's eye and exchanged knowing looks. At once, I knew I'd gone too far and quickly changed the subject.

For the next hour, we chatted, having a good time. Lisa and I both watched with amusement as Rachel and David inched closer to one another, never missing the "accidental" opportunity to touch. I also kept my eye on the time. I'd scheduled a date with Muff just so I could have a quick exit, but regretted it now because I wanted to stay and see if they disclosed another tidbit about Nicki.

Seeing me check my watch a third time, David asked, "Time to leave?"

"Pardon me." I smiled apologetically to Lisa and Rachel. "But I must run. I have an appoint—"

"A date," said David.

The words jolted me at first, but I realized I needed to man up to the situation.

"With who?" Rachel asked innocently. "Can she come here?"

"I'm seeing my girlfriend. Muff." It sounded altogether wrong. Rachel and Lisa's presence reminded me that my girlfriend's name had been Nicki. Then I saw Lisa's incredulous face. Was she angry with me?

"Excuse me? What's her name?"

"Uh, Muff. It's a nickname. Her given name is Mary."

"Oh." Lisa kept a straight face, but she didn't appear upset. Then her lips skewed as if a smile was trying to force its way through.

"I'm sure she's a very nice person." Rachel giggled. "But in America, 'muff' means…"

"It means the same thing here." David smiled at her in admiration. "The posh types are so inbred that they don't know better. They give their children ridiculous nicknames."

Rachel snickered. "So does she have a sister named Theresa who they call Twat?"

The table erupted in laughter, except for me. I only mustered an anxious chuckle. As the giggles died down, I became even more uncomfortable. I needed to leave, but I didn't want to, and I was unsure what to say to the girls about Nicki. Eventually, I reminded myself that I'd set the date up with Muff just to avoid the situation I now found myself in.

I looked over at David to make sure he was all right being left with the girls. He grinned, indicating he was chuffed to have the job of entertaining the ladies for the evening. Seeing that was covered, I glanced at my watch yet again, which confirmed my dithering had made me very late. Now I felt like a coward with Nicki *and* a heel with Muff. Without another word about Nicki, I swiftly bade them goodbye and fled the pub.

As I walked away, I heard David say, "What? What are you two thinking?"

Rachel's distinct Texas drawl answered, "Awkward…"

Over a long dinner with Muff, I managed to remove Nicki from the forefront of my thoughts. Hopefully by the next day, she'd be back to her proper place, buried in memories I did my best to avoid.

In the meantime, I spent the evening focused on Muff, who couldn't have been more different from Nicki. Muff was a tall, willowy blonde with perfectly coiffed straight hair falling below her shoulders. Nothing about Muff's appearance or her life was ever out of place. If I couldn't have Nicki, Muff's consistency was at least reassuring.

As I guided her out of the restaurant, she went on about a wedding we were to attend together the following weekend. Muff liked talking about weddings, and the hints weren't lost on me. They just weren't persuasive. I hoped she would eventually figure that out.

I then heard my name called from behind. The American accent threw me off at first, but I recognized the voice soon enough. Apparently, the universe wasn't going to let me out of the evening so easily. I turned to see Lisa and, consciously or not, removed my hand from Muff's lower back, where it had been resting. I called back, "Lisa."

Noticing I'd stopped touching her, Muff gave me an alarmed look for paying attention to a random American girl on the street. I tried to restore her confidence by steering her over to Lisa.

"Muff, please meet my friend from America, Lisa Roberts. Lisa, this is Muff Selbourne."

Muff gave Lisa a not very discreet once-over. I could tell she judged her to be a stereotypical, poorly dressed American backpacker and thus no competition for her. Of course, that didn't mean Muff didn't view Lisa as a threat. When she greeted her, her voice held the effortless insincerity of the British upper-class. "It's a pleasure to meet you, Lisa."

Lisa didn't respond well to being appraised by a snooty Brit. I wondered what she would say. It wasn't in her nature to be insincere.

I watched as she nodded with a slight snarl. "Yeah. Hi. Adam mentioned you." Lisa then raised her eyebrows at me. She wasn't impressed with my choice of women, but when she spoke, her voice was friendly. "Adam, I'm glad I ran into you. Can I talk to you for a sec?"

"Certainly," I said, though terrified at the thought. I turned to Muff to confirm it was okay. She dutifully smiled and walked a respectable distance away.

After a last glance at Muff, Lisa wasted no time in putting me on the spot. "Do you have anything to say to Nicki? You left before I could ask you."

I stared blankly at Lisa as her question reverberated in my mind. I had so much to say to Nicki, but would she listen?

I could hear Muff's voice in the far background and turned to see her. With her mobile to her ear, she chatted away. I considered her for a moment. She was a good girlfriend, my father adored her, and we had a great many friends in common. As the daughter of the Earl of Selbourne, Lady Mary Selbourne was considered a special girl.

But she didn't make me laugh. She never caught me off-guard. She never tripped me up. There was never a time when she was the absolute first person I wanted to tell a story to. Muff was special, but she wasn't special to me. As David had said, she wasn't Nicki.

I focused on Lisa, someone who had always been skeptical of my intentions with her friend. Yet here she was, asking to deliver a message to her. After what I'd done to Nicki, I couldn't request anything of her. She needed to come to me, and I'd learned to live with the fact that it wasn't going to happen.

My voiced tightened as I said, "Please…just tell her that I miss her." I gulped hard and added, "I really do."

Lisa waited a moment before speaking, no doubt deciding whether or not I meant it. I searched her eyes, willing her to believe me. Soon a slow nod seemed to signal she thought I'd spoken from the heart. "Okay," she said, releasing a breath. "I'll be sure to tell her."

"Cheers for that. Thank you."

"No problem." She looked at her watch and said, "I've gotta get back to the hostel."

"Have a good trip."

"Bye, Adam."

"Goodbye, Lisa."

She whipped around to leave, so I joked, "Do you want to say goodbye to Muff?"

Lisa snorted, turned back around, and smiled. "Not particularly."

"I thought that might be the case." I grinned and pointed to the road ahead. "Now get on with yourself."

After she sped off, I walked back to Muff, who gave me a cheeky smile. "Is everything okay with America?"

"Er, yes. Fine. She just wanted to talk about a friend."

Muff put her hand on my bicep, giving it a possessive squeeze. "Shall we go back to your place?"

I should've just said yes. Nothing had changed. Nicki was still living her life on another continent, and I was living mine on an island. But there were too many thoughts of her right then for me to be with anyone else. I knew Muff would soon be back in my bed, but that night I just couldn't. So I patted Muff's hand to reassure her as I gave her my answer.

"Not tonight. For some reason, I don't feel very well."

Chapter Two

Washington, DC
November 2008

Though everyone knew it was coming, I'd been waiting for the official announcement. Yet I was still struck by surprise when the press release appeared on my computer screen, probably because it was so unfathomable.

Nicki and I were going to be living in the same city. I read the email over and over again, skipping the first few more senior names and focusing only on hers.

WHITE HOUSE COMMUNICATIONS AND PRESS SECRETARY POSITIONS ANNOUNCED

NICOLE JOHNSON, DEPUTY WHITE HOUSE PRESS SECRETARY

Nicole Johnson currently serves as the deputy communications director on the Logan-Grady Transition Team, a position she also held on the Logan-Grady presidential campaign. Prior to her work on the campaign, she held communications positions with President-Elect Logan throughout his career in public service, beginning with his early years in the Illinois State House and continuing through his time as governor of Illinois. She also has worked on several electoral campaigns and spent two years working for the Peace Corps in Mexico. A native of Texas, Johnson is fluent in Spanish. She pursued a double major in English and history from the University of Chicago, where she graduated Phi Beta Kappa with a bachelor's degree.

Would I ever see her around town? She had to know I lived here. Should I give her a welcoming call, or would that be unwelcome after what I'd done to her? I leaned back in my chair and took a deep breath, searching for the answer and the memory that had been repeating itself in my mind since Logan had won the election. It was a vivid night of two teenagers lying in each other's arms, when Nicki's practicality had fought against my optimism.

"Nicki, will we ever speak to each other again?"

"I…don't know. I guess never say never, but it's kind of unlikely. Our lives are going to be very different. I mean, we really do live a world apart. An ocean apart, anyway." She was silent for a moment until she added, "Maybe. Maybe, if we were living in the same city."

"As you said, that's probably not going to happen." At that time, it seemed impossible.

"Probably not."

I looked down at her arm resting on my chest and caught sight of one of her scars. Most would describe it as ghastly, but to me it had become just part of her, part of her history that made her so strong. Realizing this would be the last time I held her, my mind began to grasp for a future together, even if it was impossible. "But what if…what if I was thirty-five and still single? Could I contact you then?"

"In the highly unlikely event that was the case, I'd say sure."

"Really?"

"You've got to admit, it's probably not going to happen."

I happily kissed her nose. "Maybe, maybe not."

What a foolish lad I'd been. Life wasn't so easy. There were wrenches in our situation that a wiser person could have easily predicted long ago.

Out of the corner of my eye, I saw a framed photo of my on-again-off-again girlfriend, Felicity. I kept the photo for the spectacular view of Chartres in the background rather than Felicity in the foreground. Still, she was there smiling at me. I half expected the picture to turn into one of those photographs in *Harry Potter* that comes to life. It was as if I feared her expression might change to a scowl at any second before she demanded, *"Remember me, you sodding bastard? You haven't called in a week!"*

Losing all sense of reality, I quickly grabbed the picture and tossed it in the back of a desk drawer. *There. Now I can think.*

Having once been the BBC's White House correspondent, I knew the job Nicki was about to take. Deputy White House press secretary was a huge role in a presidential administration. I was now an editor, so even though I would be intimately involved in the BBC coverage of the White House, I wouldn't be the one interacting with her. This was good because, given our past relationship, there would be ethical questions about our objectivity in our capacities as reporter and White House official.

I remembered her final words to me fifteen and a half years before: *"I'll always love you, Adam. Remember that."* If either of our bosses knew we'd once confessed our undying love to one another, we could both be reassigned to other posts where we'd never interact professionally. I could end up in ruddy Manchester covering the local government, for Christ's sake.

I stared at the press release on my computer screen. So this would be how our lives would turn out. We'd end up in the same city, working in the same field, but only seeing each other at the occasional cocktail party. My heart sank at the thought. I'd spent the last decade with this woman in the back of my mind, and she was going to end up just another old girlfriend I bumped into now and again? What a sad joke life would be if a relationship I'd never got over had such an anti-climactic and unresolved ending.

This was the way things happened, though, wasn't it? We didn't always get what we wanted. This was why Brits had a stiff upper-lip. There was no reason to get too emotional. It was a given that life would let you down.

That should've been the end of my thoughts on the matter, but it wasn't. Instead, a burst of irrational hope exploded in my chest, and my mind did a one-hundred-and-eighty-degree turn that was both self-serving and self-destructive. What if I forced the issue? If I was the White House correspondent again, I'd see her every day.

Then I really went off the deep-end of foolish hope. *Maybe seeing each other in a professional capacity would be good for us. Maybe it would help make things normal between us again. Maybe she could forgive me. Then I can move on.*

So I picked up the phone and lied—to myself and, more importantly, to my boss in London.

"Yes, yes," I said when he didn't believe me. "I don't think of it as a demotion. It would be a real treat to cover the White House during the start of a new administration."

"No, no," I said when he reminded me he needed an experienced editor in Washington. "I don't have to do it for very long."

And as I closed the call, I added as nonchalantly as possible, "Oh, and by the way, one of my old school chums is Nicole Johnson, the deputy press secretary."

I hadn't said anything contradictory to the truth, but the amount of information I'd withheld was tantamount to a lie. I considered my breach of ethics and panicked for a moment, but I soon justified my actions.

After all, I was interested in a different assignment, and I'd disclosed all the facts to management. The emotions that accompanied those facts weren't facts themselves and, thus, not necessarily material. I felt safe in my denial, though it was utter bollocks.

January 2009

I was certain I could do my job with a clear conscience, but a few days after the inauguration, I walked into the White House press briefing room and my lies hit me again.

"I heard you might be here," said an exaggerated baritone voice.

I looked to my right to see Dan Roark, ABC News White House correspondent and all-around American arsehole. He eyed me suspiciously.

"I missed reporting." I shrugged. "And these are interesting times."

"Hmm." Dan raised his eyebrows. As he walked to his prized seat front and center in the room, he said, "*Very* interesting times to bring Adam Kincaid out of his ivory tower."

Wanker, I thought. I began determinedly scrolling through the messages on my phone to regain my composure. When that didn't work, I checked the Premier League results, but Dan's remark haunted me. *He's right. Really, why am I doing this? Does she wonder as well?*

As the noise in the room diminished, I looked at the podium. Standing in front of the iconic blue and white oval sign with an illustration of the most famous white house in the world was Matthew Foster, press secretary for President James Logan.

Still high from the inaugural honeymoon, Matthew smiled as he cleared his throat before greeting the room. "Good morning to you all. Welcome to our first official press briefing. I'm sure we'll soon get sick of seeing one another every day."

Laughter at the joke reverberated through the room, but my attention was focused on finding her. A minor player in American media, the BBC shared its seat with *The Baltimore Sun*, far back in the steerage of the room. When the *Sun* reporter arrived, I nodded for her to take the seat today. No doubt she thought I was a chivalrous Englishman, but really I wanted to stand for a better view. Unfortunately, my height wasn't helping me. As I searched for her, I began to doubt myself. *Do I no longer recognize her?*

My frustration ended when Matthew spoke again. "Before we get started, I want you to meet our team. First, I'd like to introduce you to our deputy press secretary, Nicole Johnson. If you were on the campaign trail with us, you know Nicole well." Then he motioned toward a small crowd of men behind him, saying, "Nicole, get out from behind Jeff so you can say hello."

She emerged from the collection of men's suits, smiling and with a small wave of her hand. Taking to the podium with confidence, she addressed the audience, and her soft Texas twang warmed the room.

"Hello, everyone. Being new in town, it's nice to see some familiar faces from the campaign. And I'm looking forward to getting to know those of you I haven't met yet."

My eyes never left her as she moved to stand not far from Matthew's side, and I didn't exhale until Matthew spoke again. Forgetting all of my professional responsibilities, I stopped listening to Matthew. My focus was on Nicki because she was the same — just the same.

Physically, she was as beautiful as I remembered her. She only looked different to me because I'd never seen her in a suit before — but why would I have? She wore her dark hair up at the back, and I knew that look on her; occasionally, she'd worn her hair in a ponytail. Her figure was just as enticing, petite as she was, and accentuated by a jacket belted at the waist. But it was those dark eyes that I couldn't stop staring at.

My colleagues battered Matthew with questions, and he blathered on about the economy, health care, energy, climate change, the Middle East — all the news of the day. But I took in none of it. I noticed Nicki's small hands, which she clasped in front of her skirt.

It came to me that I knew that woman the way no one else in the room did. I knew how her hands felt when you walked hand in hand with her and when you held both of them in your own. Moreover, I knew how those hands felt on my body—when they tickled the back of my neck or stroked my chest. Or held my dick.

I knew her. I looked around the room and saw all the men who wanted to know her—Dan Roark being one of them. Obviously checking her out, Dan ogled her lean legs. Did he see her scar, I wondered?

Her scars. I knew her scars. I'd never forget them. I still could picture many of them, and my mouth remembered kissing the brownish purplish lines, wishing I could make all of her pain disappear. I wondered what they might look like now. Were they just faded ghost lines crisscrossing her torso? Maybe the dark memories had faded as well.

I kept a steady gaze on Nicki's face. Her skin was bright as ever, and the small indentation between her eyes was most likely only noticeable to me. When we had been together, it would appear when she was serious or concerned or sad. But sixteen years of life had fissured her otherwise flawless skin; like a river creating a canyon, sorrow had eroded a tiny crevice where none should be. At once, I felt sick to my stomach because I'd had a part in the cutting of that line. I'd caused anguish that had torn at both our hearts. *But why does hers have to be visible?*

In the back of my mind, my reporter's sixth sense kicked in, telling me now was the time to ask my question. I raised my finger to Matthew, who I already knew.

"Adam," Matthew said with a nod.

"As a candidate last autumn, the president made lukewarm comments toward the relationship between the United Kingdom and America. Is the Logan Administration going to mark a new era in the two countries' special relationship?"

Dutiful to my job, I scribbled some notes as Matthew answered my question, saying the "special relationship" was as strong as ever and comments during a campaign had to be taken with a grain of salt. As I wrote, I thought Nicki had to have seen me; she had to have at least had a glimpse of me.

With my question and answer over, I allowed myself to look at Nicki again, who now had that Jeff character at her side. They were talking quietly as the press conference continued.

Why isn't she looking at me? Is it on purpose? Or does she simply not care?

When the briefing finally ended, I casually but quickly made my way to the front, occasionally greeting a friend but never stopping for conversation. Matthew was backslapping the inner circle of America's Fourth Estate, whilst Nicki answered a few reporters' follow-up questions.

Soon, Matthew started to head for the door. He caught my eye. "Welcome, Adam. I hear you're going to be with us for a while."

"Yes, thank you. I'm looking forward to it."

As soon as I replied, Nicki turned to face me. We stood only a few feet apart as our eyes met. Instantly, I felt like I was being pulled toward her, but soon I knew something was wrong. My heart caved as I realized there was no reciprocity. She only gave me a blank stare.

Doesn't she feel anything for me?

"Nick—"

I only wanted to say hello—or anything that might give me some insight into her—but I was interrupted by Matthew as he said, "Nicole, we need to move on."

And then everything changed.

Nicki stopped for the briefest moment and peered over her shoulder, wrenching my heart again with another indifferent stare. But this time, her mouth twitched ever so slightly, just like it always had when she was anxious. A shy smile crossed her face, and without a word, she turned back around and quickly exited the room.

Late that evening, I arrived at the expat pub inside the British Embassy. It was easy to spot David sitting at the bar, engrossed in a rerun of Sunday's Liverpool-versus-Manchester United match on the TV. Since the bar was filled with mostly government types, David stood out like a sore thumb. His designer suits were noteworthy, but it was his thick Cockney accent that made him most noticeable.

Whilst the rest of the room cheered and booed with some decorum at the match, David was apoplectic over a decision the ref had made. "A fucking yellow card? Jesus H. Christ, bloody referee! Do you have shite for brains?"

David was never one to completely forget his surroundings. Sitting next to him was an older expat. The genteel-looking, tweedy man obviously wasn't accustomed to such pro-Liverpudlian outbursts. He looked at my cousin like David was a hooligan who had escaped from the terraces at Millwall and now terrorized America. The poor old guy appeared to be in fear for his life.

Noticing the uneasy expression on the face of the man beside him, David's entire demeanor changed. He saw me walking toward him and smiled. Then he began to smooth things over with the old gent using the extra reserve of Cockney charm he kept for moments just like this.

"I do beg your pardon, sir. I know I was being an arse. Sorry about that. I got a little carried away." He extended his hand, "My name is David Bates."

The older man shook David's hand and hesitantly smiled. "Hello. Malcolm Fields. I work in the archives here at the embassy. Pleased to meet you."

David gestured to me. "This is my cousin Adam Kincaid. He works for the BBC."

"Hello. It's nice to meet you." I offered my hand to the wary man. "Please excuse my cousin. He's quite a vocal fan."

Shaking my hand, Mr. Fields said something I heard almost daily. "It's a pleasure to meet you. I've seen you on the telly."

"Thank you. It comes with the territory."

Still not quite understanding David's combined appearance of expensive suit and foul mouth, Mr. Fields turned to him. "And what is it that you do, Mr. Bates?"

"I work in international finance at Barclays," said David with mirthful pride. He loved that no one could ever decide what to make of him. "I sometimes help with the regulatory work. I'm based in New York, but I quite often find myself in Washington."

"Lovely. Ah, well, I'll let you spend time with your cousin." Mr. Fields rose, offering me his barstool. "Please, take my seat."

When I objected, he pointed to an empty table. "I'll sit over there. It's better, really." With a grin, he added, "I'm a Man U fan, after all."

As soon as Mr. Fields was out of hearing range, David turned his full attention back to the match and muttered, "Poor deluded old bastard."

"Can you keep it down? I'd like to keep my invitation here." I was pleased to see they had a guest bitter I loved, Adnams Broadside, on tap. As I ordered my pint, I became as engrossed in the match as David, albeit in a much more orderly manner. When Liverpool was two up with six minutes to go, David rightly sensed that I was ready to talk. He briefly looked away from the screen and said, "So, you saw her."

"Yes." I took a long swig to ease the conversation.

David gave me a side-eye. "How did she look?"

Images of my morning encounter with Nicki flooded my mind. There she was, gorgeous and poised, simultaneously looking both everything and nothing like I'd imagined. I was matter-of-fact. "Beautiful."

Usually, I had a blurred vision of Nicki. There were a few snippets of memories stored in the back of my mind that I'd go to on occasion when I wanted to think of her. The first mental picture that always appeared was one of Nicki with her head turned toward me. The angle of her face showed the pretty architecture of her cheeks, with her eyes meeting mine and her smile beginning to bloom. I always felt like I'd earned those smiles. After all, I'd made a great effort coaxing them out of her, especially in the beginning when she was so sad and I was such an arse.

The memory made me sigh. "Just like she used to."

"Were you able to speak to her?"

"Not really."

"What the hell does that mean?" David's usual frustration with me about Nicki was showing.

"It means I tried, but she appeared to be busy and walked away." I frowned. "I think she did it on purpose."

"Well, of course she did." David rolled his eyes. "She's the White House deputy press secretary. She hasn't seen you for almost sixteen years, and you just show up—"

"I know…believe me, I know. I turn up out of the blue on one of the most important days of her career." I shook my head and laughed aloud at my stupidity. "In the fucking White House with the entire Washington press corps around us. I'm an arse."

"You are, but it is what it is," David said with a shrug. "You need to make the most of it. So tell me, did she acknowledge you at all? Or just ignore you?"

"She sort of nodded at me. Then she…" *Fuck. Do I tell him all of this? Oh, why the fuck not? He knows everything anyway.* I pointed to my lip for a second and said, "She bit her lip like she used to do when she was anxious. God, I remember that so well." But the more I spoke, the more I realized how ridiculous I sounded. "Oh, hell. I'm a fool. I sound like a silly girl. Why am I doing this? It's ridiculous."

David was quiet as he seemed to assess my predicament. Glancing at the screen once more to make sure that Liverpool was still ahead, he finally said, "I think that's a good sign. You know…like she still feels something. If she didn't care anymore, she might try and chat you up because she wouldn't feel awkward at all. Or if she's spent the last sixteen years hating you, she'd stomp off or give you the evil eye." Then he smiled. "I think a nod and a little bite of the lip is good. Pretty hot, too."

His words rang true. "Well, to be honest, that was my gut reaction as well. That there's something still there—although I suppose it could still be hate."

"Hate? Nah. If she hated you, she'd never have kept in touch with Sylvia."

I'd always wondered if Nicki's correspondence with Sylvia was her odd way of communicating with me. For years it hadn't made sense to me that she never wrote me, but she always responded to Sylvia, letting her know her whereabouts. As time passed, I began to hold a pathetic hope that she was signaling to me that she was keeping up her end of bargain—we wouldn't talk, but if we were ever in the same city again, then maybe…

David had always had a way with women, so I humbly asked for direction. "So what do you think I should do next?"

"Oh, you've got to take this one slowly. This is delicate. But not too slow. Not like last time." Puffing his chest up and sitting a little straighter in his seat, he acted like the cocky bastard he was. "Don't make me have to step in again and get things going for you. I can't guarantee I'd stop this time. I remember she was a little minx and—"

I punched his arm hard. "Don't even think about it."

"It was a bloody joke," he said, rubbing his bicep.

"It wasn't funny."

"Come on, Adam." He shook his head. "You should be prepared that she's probably seeing someone else. Pretty little thing that she is, she's probably got a boyfriend. Someone like her isn't going to be single."

"I know." I looked at my beer, contemplating the thought I hated.

"And you've got Felicity. Whatever the status is of that relationship."

"On hold while I'm out of the country."

"You haven't lived in the UK for three years."

"It works for us right now. She can date whomever she wants."

"But when you're in London, you fuck like rabbits."

"We see each other sometimes." I tried to say it with a straight face, but a smile betrayed me.

"Sometimes?"

"I try not to let that happen *too* often. It makes things messy."

"There's a reason why we're cousins," he said with a laugh. Then he leaned back in his chair and crossed his arms. "Back to Nicki. If I were in this situation, I'd play it cool but not cold."

"How does that work?"

"You need to approach her casually…take the pressure off. You'll be seeing her every day, right?"

"Professionally, yes. Every day. And when the president travels, we'll be on the same trips."

"All that time together makes it even more important that you don't rush things."

"Rush things? I can't rush things." I lowered my voice. "Remember, it isn't ethical that I'm even thinking of doing this."

"*Thinking* of doing this? You *are* doing it."

"Maybe so," I grumbled.

He acknowledged the gravity of the situation by lowering his own voice. "But isn't it an ethical issue for both of you?"

I nodded. As usual, David saw through it all, and a wave of guilt hit me as I reconsidered the dilemma of pursuing Nicki. I was romancing a source — or at least I wanted to. My producers would deem it a breach of the journalists' code, as I could easily go soft on my reporting of President Logan in an effort to win Nicki's favor. And for Nicki, it was an issue with the president because she might pass on information to me that she wouldn't give to others.

David continued, "So you've downplayed your relationship with her to your boss. Doesn't she have to do the same? What if she tells her boss about how close you were?"

"She could. It's a gamble on my part." Jesus Christ. I was risking my career, and for what? Forgiveness? A clear conscience? A rekindled love? Everything seemed so far-fetched, at least for an innately pessimistic English journalist like me. What was I doing? Maybe I had been in America too long.

Sighing, I tried to put the topic to rest. "I just don't want to worry about it until something happens…if something happens."

Taking pity on me, David gently slapped my back. "Something will happen."

"How do you know?"

"I couldn't tell you. The conditions seem right — too many things converging not to notice." He grinned. "If you two were corporations, I'd buy your stock because it looks like you might merge."

I gave him a half-hearted smile. "So I should be cool, but not cold, and above all, it can't be obvious to anyone or I'll get sacked. Not an easy task."

"No. Not easy, but it can be done. I think in a few days…whenever it feels right…you should ask her out to lunch. Reporters take long lunches, right?"

I liked the idea. "A perfectly acceptable request on my part. It's something I eventually would do anyway — regardless of who had her job."

"Just make me a promise."

"What's that?"

"Don't turn into serious and moody Adam on her. Keep it light. Don't scare her off." He winked. "And tell her I said hello."

The next morning, the White House briefing room had the same air of excitement as the very first day. There was a cordial atmosphere as everyone was still getting to know one another. The questioning remained tough during the actual briefing, but the jokes were plentiful, which eased any tensions.

Except for me. I was still tense. I tried not to be obvious as I stared at Nicki — hopefully not noticeable to her or anyone else. Fortunately, as his deputy, Nicki stood off to the side as the White

House press secretary, Matthew Foster, fielded questions. I doubted she could see me, although I could see her perfectly. Most of the time she was in silent communication with the other White House staff as they quietly assessed how their spin was playing with the crowd of reporters.

I kept busy, scribbling away on my notepad, but I found myself often forgetting where I was. After gazing at her for a while, my pen would twitch, wanting to draw her profile. It was like I was seventeen again, with an enormous crush on a girl who wouldn't even talk to me.

Even if I hadn't been stuck in Texas the year we'd met, I would've found Nicki interesting. She was quietly pretty and very clever with a wicked sense of humor. What I had really admired, though, was this strength she'd had about her. She had lived through a hellish accident and lost her only sister, but she'd remained stoic and moved about her day like anyone else.

We'd become friends, yet sometimes through our flirting, I would catch a glimpse of how broken she actually was—like a beautiful but cracked china doll you want to pick up but don't because you're afraid you might break it even more. No wonder that when we had finally got together I'd eventually bollocksed the whole thing up.

In a lot of ways, she was the same girl as back then. She was attractive but mercurial, and as much as I was drawn to her, she also scared me. But now I had a job to do. We were much older now and in a professional setting. Yet we never made eye contact. In fact, it seemed like Nicki looked everywhere but at me.

Later that morning, I finally got through to her. Calling upon the Univision reporter, Antonio De La Fuente, for the first time, Matthew listened to his heavily accented and testy question about when President Logan would visit Mexico. It was plain that the question was designed to elicit the relative importance of Mexico and the rest of Latin America to the foreign policy of the new administration. Everyone in the room knew the reporter wouldn't like the answer. Whilst the previous president had made Mexico his first international trip, President Logan planned on mending fences with "old Europe" first, and he wasn't traveling at all until the American economy was on better footing.

After hearing the Univision reporter's loaded request, Matthew pleasantly dismissed him, using Nicki as a diversion. "Antonio, I think I'll let Nicole answer that one."

Nicki took to the podium with a smile and began rapidly speaking her fluent Spanish. I didn't need to understand the words — which was good, because I didn't. Between their facial expressions and body language, I could fully comprehend what was going on. Nicki easily wooed the fierce reporter into submission with her looks and command of his mother tongue. Wearing a dark red wide-collared shirt with a black jacket and trousers, Nicki looked gorgeous and in control, and with the Spanish rolling off her tongue, she was sexy as hell. I glanced over at Matthew, who was grinning with satisfaction at what was bound to be great coverage of the White House in the Spanish-speaking media.

Even with my ten-word Spanish vocabulary, I understood the final words they exchanged. It was quite apparent that Antonio was fully satisfied with her answer and gushed over her accent. She gave him a professional nod and thank you, but not before I saw the old Nicki I knew come out from hiding. All of his compliments made her cheeks blush the color of her shirt, and she wore a sheepish smile.

She then spoke to the rest of the room. "Antonio can fill you in on the details, but in general, President Logan considers Mexico to be both a good neighbor and friend of the United States, and one of our closest trading partners."

A practiced public speaker, Nicki made eye contact with the entire audience when she spoke. After two days of nothing from her, I didn't expect her to look at me, but she did. Whether it was on purpose or not, she ended her remarks with her eyes on mine, saying, "We also share many pressing issues. As soon as his schedule allows, the president will visit the country."

Did she mean that for me? Was it code? I studied her, looking for a clue. As she moved back to her place with the rest of the White House staff, I considered the eye contact. Something told me the time was right to talk with her. We'd connected visually, and I needed to make my move.

After the briefing ended, I couldn't get to the front of the room fast enough, but Antonio had already cornered her. They were speaking in Spanish again, and for all I knew he was inviting her for a weekend in Paris. The only thing that tempered my jealousy was the wedding ring I noticed on his left hand. His wedding ring might not mean anything to him, but I knew that Nicki — at least the Nicki I had known — would never cross one. Despite that reassurance, I didn't like her talking to him for so long. I made myself less conspicuous by grabbing another Logan staffer and asking a follow-up question that I already knew the answer to.

As soon as Nicki began to extricate herself from Antonio, I placed myself about five feet away from her. She said goodbye to him, turned around, and our eyes met. Still smiling from her conversation with Antonio, she held her expression but softly exhaled in surprise.

I hadn't really thought of what I might say to her when we finally talked. If I had, I would've probably botched it anyway. The nervous knots in my stomach were in full force. I needed to break the ice for both of us, so I tried a roundabout approach of self-deprecating humor.

"I only speak English."

"Really?" she asked, her smile growing.

"Maybe a bit of French."

"I think I remember that." Her voice was almost coy.

Nicki had done it. She'd brought back our past and put it in our present — right in the middle of the fucking White House. And she'd done it with a smile. I was encouraged.

"Hello, Nicki. It's so good to see you again."

"You, too, Adam."

"Your Spanish sounds lovely. Where did you learn to speak it so well?"

"Over the years, and then I…and also my…" She glanced down for a moment, looking as if she was debating her words. When she lifted her head again, she said, "We should probably go for coffee one day, don't you think?"

"Yes, that would be nice." I could tell she was trying to end the conversation because of where we were, but I didn't like the idea of thirty minutes in a Starbucks. I countered, "But how about lunch instead?"

She gave me a slow nod in agreement, so I added, "I dare say you're busier than me. So you tell me when."

"Oh, I think it's always going to be crazy for me around here. We can go whenever."

"How about tomorrow, then?"

"Sure. So far I've only eaten lunch at the White House Mess. I've seen a salad bar around the corner not far from Blair House."

A short lunch at a crowded salad bar with stale fried chicken and lousy curry was not what I had in mind. I shook my head and suggested a respectable, public place that still satisfied my purposes. "The White House Mess? You need a proper lunch, then. Maybe the Old Ebbitt Grill?"

"It's not too far away, right? I don't know my way around DC yet."

"Just a few streets over."

"Is one o'clock all right?"

"Certainly." Feeling like a teenager once again, I repeated something I'd done long ago. I ripped a page from my notebook and began writing. Handing it over to her, I said, "Here's my mobile number in case you need to get hold of me."

Nicki took the piece of paper and blinked twice, perhaps recognizing my handwriting. She looked up again and, with a half-smile and her thoughts seemingly elsewhere, she said, "Thanks. There shouldn't be a problem, but it's good to have. They've handed out my number, right?"

"They have." It was true I had both an office and mobile number and an email address for her, but they were all for her work. I was a little hurt that she didn't offer up her private information.

"Good." She looked around what was now an emptying room. "I've gotta go. I'll see you tomorrow, okay?"

After such a cryptic yet powerfully quiet conversation, I wanted to acknowledge everything that we'd left unsaid. With my full intent, I gazed at her. She stared back, yet I couldn't pinpoint what her dark eyes tried to communicate. If I had to make a guess, I'd have said they were caring but also apologetic. I wasn't sure that I wanted to hear what she was sorry for.

I softly said, "Tomorrow, then."

"Bye, Adam," she said in an equally quiet voice before walking away.

Chapter Three

The following morning, the thought that there was a flicker of hope with Nicki carried me through the briefing, though she'd reverted to ignoring me. It was frustrating, but I realized that I was stupid and selfish to expect more. The rap on Nicole Johnson was that she'd worked for James Logan for over ten years. Despite being younger and outside his most senior staff, she was a still a close confidant of Logan's and had become a friend of his family. Nicki's silence toward me for nearly sixteen years had shown her steely character; she was stubborn and unwavering in her ability to put her emotions aside. There was no way she would let her high school crush get in the way of her responsibilities to the president of the United States.

After the briefing, she sort of waved to me, which seemed to convey that our lunch was still on. I arrived at the restaurant early enough to make sure we had a relatively private table. The place was crowded, loud, and full of the K Street crowd, making it one of those occasions when I truly appreciated the effects of my accent on a young hostess. They always found me the seat I wanted.

Nicki arrived five minutes late, apologizing profusely, but I brushed it off. How could I not when she sat before me looking so bloody beautiful? Had she remembered that I'd always liked her in purple?

The first few minutes were taken up with discussion of food and drink, and we ordered quickly. Afterward, Nicki looked at her phone and again said, "I'm sorry. I know it's rude to check my phone all the time, but I have to keep up with what's going on." She shrugged shyly. "It's my job."

"No worries. I have to do the same."

Nicki genuinely laughed but then stopped as if something had just occurred to her. She seemed perplexed and a little nervous. "It's funny that we ended up sort of in the same field," she said before taking a drink of her water as if to steady herself.

"Well, I was always going to go into journalism. That's rather boring. How you got to the White House is a far more interesting story."

"I really don't think it's interesting at all." She shook her head. "It's sort of by inertia that I'm here."

"Inertia? What do you mean?"

"A body in motion stays in motion along a straight line, right?"

"So you started doing one thing—working for James Logan—and didn't stop?"

"Pretty much. I was in school at UT for a couple of years—"

"UT?" As soon as I asked, I remembered. "Ah. The University of Texas."

"Exactly." She gave me an approving smile. "You remember now."

"Oh, I remember."

I hadn't spoken with any force or any real intent beyond that I remembered the name of the university, but those three words hung in the air with the weight of everything that had happened between us.

Her eyes widened, and she was quiet for a moment before she spoke quickly as if dismissing the thought entirely. "When I was a sophomore at UT, Mom remarried. His name is Bill Delano, and he's a successful school superintendent. He really turned around the Houston schools, so he got the opportunity to move to take over the Los Angeles school system. He and Mom moved to California while I was in college. I decided to transfer to the University of Chicago, near my dad. That's where I started interning with President Logan when he was a state senator. He was friends with my dad."

"When did you practice your Spanish?"

"The Peace Corps."

"Really?" I played dumb so she didn't know I'd stalked her online.

"It was actually at President Logan's urging. After college, I'd been working for him in the governor's press office for a few years.

He suggested I go in the Corps, so I joined and was in Mexico for two years. I came back to work for him afterward."

"So you were in the Peace Corps." I leaned forward. "I thought you wanted to go to law school."

"I always expected to — my dad pretty much demanded it, but once I was working in politics, I didn't want to. President Logan had been in the Peace Corps when he was young and recommended it. For me, it was an amazing experience."

I kept my expression placid, though I became suspicious. It seemed contrary to what she'd told me long ago. I distinctly remembered her saying she couldn't be far from her family. That was one of the reasons why we hadn't kept in contact. I tried not to be accusatory as I asked, "What made you want to live out of the country?"

"The time was right for a break. Mom was in California, and Dad had married his long-term girlfriend, Michelle. Anyway, it felt like it was time for me to do something on my own." She shrugged. "And it was only Mexico. It's right next door. I got to go back home during the year, and both my parents came to visit."

On a whim, I decided to expose that I had kept track of her a little bit. I pretended to snicker. "Hmm. I don't remember Sylvia ever saying you lived in Mexico."

There it was, out in the open. I had talked with Sylvia about her whereabouts, and I could tell Nicki caught on immediately. She searched my eyes for a moment before mumbling, "I kept my apartment in Chicago as my permanent mailing address since I was coming back there anyway."

I nodded and moved on. "So your time in Mexico is where you got your impeccable Spanish?"

"I wouldn't call it impeccable. It's really only passable, but it's enough to get me around."

"Antonio seemed impressed."

"That's because I have a Oaxacan accent. He's from there." She smiled. "Anyway, enough about me. Tell me about your family. I know that Sylvia is in New York."

"Yes, working as an editor at a publishing house that specializes in art books."

"You know, I've never asked her, but does she still paint?"

"A little. Not a lot. About halfway through art school, she said she learned enough about art to know that hers sucked compared to everyone else's." I raised a brow. "So now she's a bloody critic and thinks she knows everything."

"Hasn't she always been that way?" Nicki smiled.

"Why yes, she has." Laughing with her, I felt once again the sheer fun of being with Nicki. The laughter continued as I told her about David and his jet-setting ways between London, New York, and DC. I didn't tell her that he used my flat in DC as a crash pad and occasional love shack, but I did decide to tease her. "He says hello, by the way."

"Please tell him hello for me, too." Her voice rose as if she'd flashed back to that night she and David had snogged while I'd stewed in much deserved jealousy.

"I will," I said, pleased with her reaction. She may have been thirty-three, but she still got embarrassed like a seventeen-year-old.

"And how are your parents? Is your dad still teaching at Cambridge?"

"No, not anymore." It was inevitable she would ask about my parents. I talked about it easily every day with many people, but I'd feared that speaking about it with Nicki would be different, and I was right. The seriousness of the situation hit me hard. Wincing a bit, it was my turn to take a drink of water to find some grounding. "He's actually rather ill…with pancreatic cancer. My mum spends her days taking care of him."

"Oh, Adam…I'm so sorry." Her eyes were so sincere and sad that I had to fight getting choked up. When I didn't respond, she asked, "When was he diagnosed?"

"A few months ago. The outlook isn't good."

I felt Nicki's hand on mine before I saw it. In fact, her hand felt so natural that I clutched it without thinking. A few seconds passed before I realized we were essentially holding hands. When I looked down at them, she must've felt uncomfortable, because she withdrew hers at once.

The atmosphere lightened as our food arrived just at that moment, and the conversation then became more fun. Talking to Nicki, I saw once again all the things I used to love about her, but there were also moments when I saw someone new who was even more interesting than the friend of old.

Occasionally, her lips caught my eye. I wondered what it would be like to kiss her again. *Would it be the same?* More than once, my gaze also wandered to her chest. Her blouse was sheer enough that I could see a slight outline of her lacy bra, and I thought back to what she looked like topless. My thoughts drifted soon enough, remembering our past. *God, we fucked a lot—in her bed, on the sofa, outside, in my car…*

I couldn't say for certain, but it felt like Nicki was having as good a time as I was. I got her giggling so hard at a story about a fellow reporter that she started to cry. As she dabbed her eyes, she saw her phone flashing and checked it immediately.

"Is everything okay?" I asked.

"Yeah, I just need to deal with it when I get back. It's going to be another long day and not much sleep tonight."

"So where are you living? Have you found a flat yet?"

Nicki continued to stare at her phone for a moment without saying a word. She then looked at me and swallowed hard before forcing a smile. Whatever was coming next was going to be bad.

"I'm crashing with Lisa right now. She's doing some post-doc work at NIH and has a place up on Van Ness."

"Lisa? That's nice that you're in the same city again. Do you plan to get a place of your own?"

"No, I…" Her eyes hardened, and her tone became resolute. "I'm moving in with my boyfriend."

Intellectually, I'd been prepared for it, but emotionally, I wasn't. *A boyfriend. Nicki has a boyfriend, and it's not me.* She might as well have plunged a knife in my heart. The apologetic look in her eyes told me she knew it.

I was a reporter, though. I was trained to hear shocking information and not give away any hint of reaction. My eyes might have already told her what my heart felt, but I was matter-of-fact as I questioned her. "So tell me more about this boyfriend. What's his name?"

"Juan Carlos Jimenez. We've been together about a year."

Juan Carlos Jimenez. The Cuban-American mastermind of President Logan's election campaign. He was now a high-paid political consultant, and several women in my office bloody swooned all over him. Prior to this moment, the attraction had made sense. But now, hearing he was with Nicki, I didn't understand at all. I picked the man apart and found the easiest thing to judge him on: he was short. I kept it to myself, though, and was pleasant.

"Really? Juan Carlos Jimenez? I can't say I've met him, though I know of him, of course. Did you two meet on the campaign?"

"Yeah, and we decided to live together last month."

"So why aren't you already moved in?" I regretted the question. It came out terse, and Nicki responded by shrinking in discomfort.

"Just busy. He's traveling a ton, and I have no time. We'll make it happen, though."

I looked down at my food, which had become completely unappetizing to me. My head shot up when I heard her say, "So what about you? Who are you dating? You have to be dating someone."

"There's someone." I didn't know how much I wanted to tell her, so I was vague. "Back in London."

"Someone?"

She stared me down, unsatisfied with my answer, so I answered in a clipped manner, "Felicity Chambers. She's also with the BBC."

"I think I've seen her on TV. She seems like a good reporter."

I almost snorted because Felicity was actually a crap reporter. The BBC hired her for her looks and blueblood lineage, and everyone knew it. She'd say it herself.

Then Nicki said a little sourly, "And she's beautiful."

Now what was I supposed to say to that? If I agreed, it might kill things with Nicki from the start, and it would be dumb to disagree. Felicity *was* a beauty. I examined Nicki's tight expression. *Is Nicki jealous?* It was only a feeling, but I was a reporter and my instincts were usually good. Considering I would have to get used to Don Juan Carlos, her jealousy made me happy. "She's nice."

"Are you two serious?"

"Serious? Not at the moment. We've been seeing each other for a while, but now that she's back in the UK for good, we've put things on hold, so to speak." If Nicki was indeed a little jealous, it was partially her own doing. I couldn't help but twist the knife a bit and remind her of why she'd dumped me the first time. "You know. Long-distance relationships are difficult."

I'd only wanted to tweak her a bit, but when her doe eyes first widened then sadly drooped, I knew I'd been unnecessarily mean. Feeling like a complete arse, I couldn't continue looking her in the eye, so I glanced around the room, searching for a new topic.

Luckily, her phone buzzed, and she immediately took the call. On the phone, she was back to being professional Nicki, whilst I sat recovering from the shock of it all. I did catch a few bits of her conversation, which was something about Congress.

When she got off the line, she placed her napkin on the table. "I'm very sorry. I need to get back to the office. Something's happened."

"Anything I might find interesting?" It seemed like she did want to tell me more about the subject of her phone call, and if I'd been there with any other member of staff from the White House, I would've probed in all seriousness. But with Nicki, I couldn't. It would ruin everything. "That was a joke. I don't want it to be like that between us. You don't have to tell me anything if it will make you uncomfortable."

She snorted.

"What? What did I say?" I asked.

"Like some of the conversation today hasn't already been uncomfortable." At least she'd found some humor in our situation.

"I'm sorry." I laughed. "That wasn't my intention."

"I know, and I don't want it that way either." She bit her lip and grabbed her bag. "Sorry. This isn't the best time for me to leave, but I've got to get back."

I couldn't let her go just like that. We had to talk or things would never be normal between us, not to mention I needed some information from her so I didn't get sacked. "Nicki, before you do, I need to know something. Please. It's important."

"What's that?"

"Well, when I took this assignment, I told my boss in London we were once school chums. I left it at that, though. If I told them anything else, I might not have been allowed to take the position. So I need to know…what have you said?"

Normally I was good with words, but not that afternoon. She wasn't thinking about what she said because whatever *I'd* said pissed her off. Her forehead crumpled, and she became curt. "I told Matt I knew you in high school and that we went out. Juan Carlos knows as well. I agree it's not something we need gossip about."

"Precisely."

She gave me a stern look, and I grasped for something to salvage the conversation. Instead, her phone buzzed again, and she practically spat out, "Thanks for lunch. I'll see you tomorrow."

"Yes. Tomorrow." Thank God there would be a tomorrow because I knew I'd somehow fucked it all up again.

Around three o'clock every afternoon, I'd call Mum to see how Dad had fared that day. Everyone in the office thought I'd taken to having tea at that time. Rather, I always headed over to the steps of St. Matthew's, the Catholic cathedral not far away from the BBC offices. It was a nice location to make the call home. No one bothered me, and though I wasn't exactly a believer, somehow having a church close at hand was a comfort.

I chose the middle of the afternoon because of the time difference and Dad's health. If he'd had a good day, he'd still be up in the late evening, and I could talk to him. If the day hadn't gone well, he'd be asleep and I'd talk with Mum. As it was a Monday, Dad was still recovering from the effects of the chemo from Friday. I didn't expect him to be awake.

Despite my camel hair coat, the January chill made the concrete steps bloody cold under my arse. I stared out onto the busy DC street, waiting for Mum to pick up the phone. She knew it was me when she answered. "Hello, Adam."

"Hi, Mum. How are things?"

"A little better than this time last week. I think he's getting used to the new chemo treatment. He tried to stay up, but he was too exhausted. He really wanted to talk to you today."

"Why?"

"Well, we watched your bit on the telly on the lunchtime news, like always, but Dad almost jumped out of his chair. Why didn't you tell us that Nicki Johnson was working at the White House? Of all people! What a coincidence!"

I grimaced, having figured my parents would see Nicki's name in the paper or catch her on television soon enough. That morning, Nicki had covered the second half of the press briefing by herself—not long after I got my question into Matthew about the effect of the financial stimulus package on the global economy. I was both relieved and disappointed that I hadn't had to ask Nicki the question instead—relieved because I might have mucked it up, and disappointed because I would've loved to hear her answer. She had ignored me the entire briefing. After our lunch on Friday, I'd thought that I might at least get a hello, but I was wrong. She'd avoided looking at me altogether, whilst I had stood there dying to know what she was thinking.

Because Nicki had answered half of the day's press questions, there were a number of clips of her laced into various stories the BBC had been running. I'd seen a few of them, and she looked lovely and spoke brilliantly in each piece. Given the amount of television my parents now watched, it was inevitable they would see the reports, too.

"I thought you knew," I said, telling a white lie.

"No." She used the same disapproving and disbelieving maternal voice that I'd heard my entire life when I fibbed. "We didn't know. Why would we?"

"She worked for Logan when he was governor. You knew that."

"But I didn't know she followed him to Washington and had such an important position in the White House."

"Well, she does."

"Your father and I were gobsmacked to see her. When we first recognized the name and face, Dad jumped out of his chair to look straight in the TV screen to confirm it was her. And then she did so well. She could speak on any subject they threw at her. She's so mature and poised."

I shook my head. Parents were parents regardless of our age. "She's thirty-three. She's an adult now, Mum."

"Oh, I know," she said, brushing my reminder aside. "We were just so impressed by her—what she's made of herself. And she's turned into a beautiful woman. Dad was especially taken with her."

Pinching the bridge of my nose, I took a moment to take in what I had heard. *Oh, the irony.* Sixteen years ago, Dad had seen Nicki as an ordinary American girl. He hadn't disliked her—in fact, he'd been rather fond of Nicki—but he hadn't seen anything special about her. Now he thought she was a catch. She only had to become a press secretary for the president of the United States, the leader of the free fucking world, for him to change his mind.

Dad bore some responsibility for my current situation, but I'd never held it against him. There'd been too many other things conspiring against Nicki and me when we were seventeen—both my own arsehole behavior and her terror of being hurt again.

"Adam, what is going on here?" Mum's demanding tone brought me back to the present. "You didn't really want to go back to reporting, did you? Is Nicki the reason why you changed jobs?"

"No. Well, yes, but…" I didn't know how much I wanted to tell her. Then I realized Sylvia would blab everything to her anyway; I might as well tell the truth. "I mean that it's very interesting to witness firsthand the start of a new presidency, but, yes, if I must admit it, I wanted to meet Nicki again…just to see if…"

"And?"

I scowled. "At the moment she has a boyfriend."

Then instead of my mother, Dr. Judith Kincaid the psychologist replied, "And how does that make you feel?"

"How do you think it makes me feel, Mum? Bloody jealous."

"Now, Adam…"

How many times had I heard that in my life? When I was younger, I'd have grunted and shut up, but I'd become soft in my old age. I knew she was being kind. I succumbed to becoming her patient. "Nicki and I had lunch last week. It seems like she's in a serious relationship. But…and this is going to sound ridiculous, but I hope there still might be something there between us."

I thought back to the lunch — how Nicki had alternated between being an assertive, accomplished woman and the contemplative, slightly awkward teenage girl I'd known…how she'd laughed with me…how she'd touched my hand. We still shared something — of that, I was confident.

Even with the little information I'd given her, Mum still had enough to elaborate on my life. "Well, you two weren't together very long, but you were *very* close. That was such an intense time for her. You were there when she was grieving the most, so seeing each other must bring out many emotions for both of you."

The cold stone steps numbed my arse, but the conversation was becoming even more uncomfortable. I stood up and said, "I'll call a bit earlier tomorrow. Oh…and can you send me some HobNobs?"

Mum understood my signal. An out-of-the-blue request for my favorite chocolate biscuits was a sign I'd had enough of the long-distance shrink session. She was quiet for a moment, but she mercifully let me go. "Certainly, dear."

Just because I cut Mum off didn't mean I didn't stop hearing her thoughts. Nicki and I had only dated for six months. We would've had more time together if I had picked up on her cues earlier, but I was a stupid boy. I'd been shagging a girl named Meredith every afternoon whilst spending most of my day fascinated with Nicki. Granted, I hadn't thought Nicki wanted to have anything to do with me, but it was still my fault it took so long for us to get together. That was the first time I had hurt her so much that she'd run away from me.

As I walked back to the office, my mind was far away from the streets of downtown DC. I was back in Bellaire, Texas, sitting on a curb with a drunk seventeen-year-old Nicki.

Nicki placed her head between her knees, trying to steady herself so she wouldn't vomit. The glare from the streetlight made the golden notes in her otherwise dark hair sparkle. For months, I'd stared at her curly hair, wondering what it felt like. Was it coarse or soft? I had my chance to finally feel it, and with a hesitant hand, I reached over to find out.

I smiled when my fingers first brushed against her curls. They were as soft as her heart. The whole experience was so tantalizing that I couldn't stop. She was vulnerable at that moment, and I was happy stroking her dark tendrils. I always loved the feeling I might be soothing her a bit. So I was shocked when she asked, "Adam, why are you always so nice to me?"

Huh. Wasn't it obvious? I tried to look her in the eye, but her head was turned. I stopped touching her hair for a moment and let my hand rest on her back. "Well, I want to be your friend. I like you, and…" I was hesitant to say more because it would just bring up her sister. She always talked with me about her, though, so I decided to go for it. "I wish you were happier."

"You're being too nice."

"Really? How so?"

She snapped her head to stare me in the eye. "You have a girlfriend. So stop it. Stop being like this with me."

At first, I only focused on the first two things she'd said. Like a thief, I'd been caught red-handed, only I wasn't stealing. I was lying—lying to Meredith. Nicki was right.

I grumbled. "I know. I should…" But as I thought about it, I realized she'd said something else, which was even more disturbing. "Wait." I looked her in the eye. "What do you mean 'stop it'?"

Her dark eyes welled with tears as she gasped out, "I can't. I can't do it anymore."

It was a shitty thing to make any girl cry, but to do it to Nicki was unconscionable. My heart beat double-time as I comprehended what I'd done to her.

When she rose from the curb, I was already in a panic. Despite the tears rolling down her cheeks, she demanded, "Please just leave me alone." She turned on her heel. "I'll walk myself the rest of the way."

I couldn't have Nicki turn her back on me. This was not supposed to be happening between us, so I grabbed her arm. "Please, Nicki. Don't go. I'm so sorry—"

She jerked her arm away in a huff, but that was no deterrent to me. I placed my hand on her shoulder, hoping to calm her down. Maybe I could find the right way to explain myself. "Nicki, please. I've wanted to be your friend since I moved here. I like being with you…so much. And you…you seem happier when we talk. You actually smile, and when you smile, you're even more beau—"

She flinched from my touch, causing my hand to drop. Her tears were quickly replaced with fire in her eyes. "So I'm a pity project for you? The Make Nicki Happy project?"

"No! Not at all. Please believe me. I care for you, but I haven't known if you're—"

"Care for me?" Now she was livid, and her lip curled in disdain. "Right. I'm sure you think about how you care for me when you're fucking Meredith."

Like a slack-jawed idiot, I'd just been slapped in the face to wake up.

"Now leave me alone," she said and stomped away.

I hadn't followed her, but the next day I'd tried to speak with her, only to be rebuffed again. After that, fear and guilt had kept me away from Nicki, but not for long.

Whatever I'd said at our lunch together caused Nicki to ignore me for weeks. It was ridiculous. You'd have thought I was a random reporter from a backwater paper in Mississippi rather than the White House correspondent for the primary news outlet of the United States' closest ally. She did her best not to look me in the eye, and if I had the chance to ask her a question, she always gave the podium over to someone else. After a few weeks, I was determined to get some kind of acknowledgment from Nicki that she knew I was in the room every morning. One Friday, I was thoroughly frustrated because I couldn't even get a glance out of her. So I decided to force the issue.

After that day's press briefing was over, I walked straight over to Matthew, figuring Nicki would have to see me if I stood there talking with her boss. I could see her standing off to his side, talking to that tosser, Dan Roark, who I was sure was flirting with her.

When Matthew turned around from a conversation, I piped up. "Matthew, do you have a minute? It'll be short."

He smiled at me. Like most press secretaries, Matthew was a likable chap. He was jovial with everyone, even if he felt your reporting was less than fair. With a back slap, he said, "Sure, I'll talk today, but we should probably get coffee or something soon — and definitely before we head overseas."

Quickly glancing toward Nicki, I could swear her head was slightly tilted toward Matthew and me. *She must be listening for something.* I jumped on Matthew's invitation. "Wonderful. I'll speak to your assistant to arrange a time. I need some immediate help, though."

"What's that?"

"I'm working on a story on the new administration and China. I was wondering who the best person is to talk to about the Administration's position that China devalues its currency. Is there someone you recommend at Treasury?"

"Now, Adam, don't put words in our mouth. I don't believe the president has made any official comments about the value of China's currency."

"Ah, that's part of my story. The president mentioned it during the campaign as a major economic issue for the US."

"I gotta tell you, this is not at the top of Treasury's mind right now. Hell, we're still working to get the Secretary confirmed by the Senate." He looked over his shoulder and said, "Let me see what I can do for you. How about talking to Nicole? She handles all the wonky stuff."

Nicki turned around, but not before quickly sending Dan the twat on his way. He gave me a dirty look as Nicki asked Matthew, "Excuse me? What do you need me for?"

"Adam here needs some background on the president's thinking about the Chinese currency." His eyes darted over to me as he added, "I believe you two know each other."

Before I could reply, Nicki answered tersely, "Yeah…" The old Nicki came out as she became furtive, unsure of what I might say. I wondered if Matthew could see that she was nervous. Maybe it didn't look like it if you didn't know her, but I could tell. It was funny that she ended up in a profession where she had to skirt around the truth all the time. She'd become very good at lying; had talking to me become difficult for her?

Trying to calm her down, I stated a vague but indisputable truth that she could feel at ease with. "Yes, we've known each other for a while."

"Great. No introductions are necessary," Matthew said, slapping my back. To Nicki, he signaled toward the door. "Nicole, I need to leave. Can you make sure to cover that meeting for me at noon?"

Nicki said, "Sure," as he walked away, and then she looked me in the eye. With a small smile, she greeted me warily. "Hi."

"Hello. How are you? Shame we haven't been able to talk this week."

I almost laughed when her eyes widened as though she'd been caught in the act. It was proof she had been avoiding me on purpose.

Once again, though, she recovered and answered me forthrightly. "Yes…it's been busy. Is there something you needed besides this China question?"

I inwardly shook my head and fidgeted with my pen in lieu of answering. Her brow furrowed. Was she confused by my silence or disappointed that I hadn't offered anything special to talk about? I was just about to ask her what was wrong when her face became all business again. She looked at me directly and commented as if speaking on the record.

"As a candidate, President Logan often spoke of his belief — a widely held belief, I might add — that China artificially manipulates the yuan in order to unfairly bolster its exports."

"It's not so widely held. The Chinese government disagrees."

"And your own government agrees. Great Britain has long concurred with the assessment that the yuan is undervalued."

"Yes, the British government agrees, but that doesn't make it so. If it's such a pressing issue, why isn't President Logan working on it right now? What does he plan to do?"

"At the appropriate time, no doubt, the president will address the issue again. When that will be or what it might look like, I don't know."

"Does he believe that China's currency manipulation is contributing to the global recession?" The question popped out of my mouth just as it would've were I asking any government official, and Nicki responded in kind. She spoke to me like I was any reporter in the room — although most members of the lousy American press would never ask the question. Dan Roark certainly never would.

"There are many factors that have created the recession. The president is simply concerned about any effect China's monetary actions are having on American jobs. The trade deficit impacts the lives of working men and women by sending production overseas."

"With regard to China, what is he planning to do?"

"President Logan will always act to save American jobs."

"Does that include trade protections that the WTO might take issue with?" I grinned as I asked, wanting to show her that I knowingly goaded her.

Thankfully, I brought a laugh out of her, and she was coy. "I think I told you I don't know what the president will do."

She wore her hair in a loose knot at the base of her neck. I wanted to gently tug at it and watch her hair fall around her shoulders so I could see her as I'd remembered her for all these years. With the smile she had on her face at that moment, I was sure she'd look the same. Her brown eyes were warm as she awaited my response. It felt so good seeing her like that, I kept quiet for a few seconds longer just to enjoy it.

"It looks like we've both done our jobs," I finally said.

"What do you mean?"

"I asked the tough questions, and you responded that you don't know when clearly you do."

"What do you think I know?"

"You tell me." I smirked. "I'm not sure."

I continued gazing at her, which seemed to have the exact opposite reaction I hoped for. She became unsettled, and her smile faded.

"I have to go," she said. "I'm sorry that I wasn't more help. I'll have someone follow up with you. Bye." Then she scurried out of the room.

What just happened? It was such an odd ending that I decided to walk back to the office rather than get in a cab. I wanted to think, and I couldn't do that in a minging DC taxi.

Walking north from the White House, I ruminated on talking with Nicki. She seemed to have several general reactions during our conversations. The first was utterly professional; you'd never know that at one time she'd sat in my lap, wrought with grief and crying over her sister. It killed me to think she might not care about me anymore. Yet when she laughed with me, I felt what had once been between us. There was also a glimmer of what fun we might have together now. Her final reaction was confusing, though. She seemed unsure and distressed. *But why?*

It hit me, and I abruptly stopped on the street. High school was happening all over again.

She doesn't know what to think!

I started walking again, confident in my conclusion. It made sense. My own uncertainty had to show through my actions. I thought of my attempts to lighten things up between us compared to when I'd bluntly asked her not to tell anyone about our past.

Oh God. Nicki might think I'm screwing Felicity, but that when I flirt with her, all I want is access and information. Surely, she wouldn't think that of me, would she? She wouldn't think I was a slimy arse?

Well, of course, she would, you fool. You've done it before.

Panic came over me as I realized that I needed to set things straight with her and I needed to do it quickly. But when? And what on earth would I say?

Chapter Four

On Saturday night, fate must have been at work, because I got my chance. David had taken a late flight from New York that evening. The reason for the trip, a meeting with the SEC, wasn't until Monday, but he'd flown in early for a football match. Sometimes we played five-a-side on Sunday afternoons. The matches were great fun—as long as David didn't have a hangover and play like shit or get in a fight because he'd hit on someone's girlfriend.

The prospects of a Sunday morning hangover for David were high that night when he demanded that we go out for tapas. His favorite tapas place was a restaurant in Adams Morgan that had plenty of black-haired beauties who went there for the dancing. Neither one of us could dance a salsa to save our lives, but we made the most of the bar.

When we walked in, the place was crowded, and the music loud. I ignored the dance floor at the back and instead scoped out the bar to see if we could find a seat. I was about to nudge David over to an open spot when I heard him say, "Well, it's been a long time, but I'd say that's your bird."

"What?"

"Over there. Dancing. With that short-arse."

As soon as I focused on the dance floor, I saw Nicki. There she was, in a slinky green dress, dancing with Juan Carlos fucking Jimenez.

They were laughing as he spun her back and forth in his arms. Her dress clung to her body, showing it off nicely. When they switched to moving their hips together, Juan Carlos looked straight down at her pelvis with a leer. There was no doubt about it. The man was thinking about having sex with her, and I wanted to kill him.

"Those are some nice moves she has. I like the hip action." David chuckled. "Looks like her partner is thinking the same thing as me. Got some competition there, Adam."

"Fuck you."

Motioning to the dance floor, David retorted, "No. Fuck her. Before he does."

"He already has," I said, feeling the heat rise on the back of my neck. "That's her boyfriend, Juan Carlos." I hated saying the words. Watching Nicki act so happy and carefree with him made it even worse.

"Juan Carlos. Huh." Never afraid to size up the competition, David gave an appraisal. "He's a handsome son of a bitch. Still short, though."

"So is she."

"But you said that Nicki's keeping everything about you two quiet, right?"

"Yes, for the most part. But she told him."

"Doubtful she shared everything. And a bloke like that wouldn't feel threatened by a childhood boyfriend. That's good. Work it to your advantage. You've gotta get in there, mate. Dance with her."

"Salsa? Are you kidding me?"

"Wait for something slow." David shook his head disapprovingly. "It's a miracle you ever had a shag without me." Then he snickered. "Though it's been a while…"

That deserved a slug in the arm, but the music changed to something softer, and David patted my back. "Sorry, cuz. Forget about what I said. It's time to make your move."

At once, I looked over to Nicki. Overheated from the dancing, she fanned herself and wiped her brow with the back of her hand. Juan Carlos had his goddamn hand on the small of her back. It appeared that he was asking to dance again, but she shook her head no.

"Now's your chance." David nudged me forward. "Don't worry. I'll cover you."

I nodded even though I wasn't certain what he meant or what I was about to do. Yet I quickly walked over to Nicki and Juan Carlos as they started to move off the dance floor. Maneuvering myself directly in front of them, I first smiled at Nicki, whose mouth had gaped open.

"Hello," I said to her. I turned to Juan Carlos and offered my hand. "Adam Kincaid. You're Juan Carlos Jimenez, correct?"

"Yes," he replied in his deep, slightly accented voice. He shook my hand. "It's nice to meet you. The BBC, right? I've seen you before."

"Yes, I'm with the BBC."

"I believe you and Nicki know each other," he said, touching her protectively. So much for not feeling threatened. I already didn't like the guy, but I had to admit he was perceptive.

Nicki was once again struck with that same furtive, lying look, only this time she seemed bewildered. I took that as a very good sign and tried to calm her by repeating our downplayed truth. "Yes, we've known each other for a while."

She smiled at that, though she still seemed anxious. "Hi, Adam."

I grinned, and with all the courtesy I could find, I asked Juan Carlos, "Do you mind if I have a quick dance?"

Old JC narrowed his eyes like he was sizing me up. Would he sniff out that I was up to no good? Even if he did, he probably knew better than to say no and look like a paranoid, possessive arse. Eventually, he shrugged and turned again to her. "Nicki?"

Not breaking her smile, she was nonchalant. "Sure." She pointed over at a corner and told him, "I'll meet you back at the table in a minute."

Juan Carlos gave her hand a quick squeeze but must've decided there was nothing wrong, because he patted my arm. "Join us when you're done."

"Thanks," I said. "I'll do that."

As he walked away, I gently took Nicki's hand and pulled her into my arms. The look on her face was priceless. At that moment, there was no veneer at all. She was all shock.

The music was a slow, romantic song, so the dancing was easy. I greeted her with all the warmth I felt. "How are you?"

"Good. Who are you here with?"

"David. I'm sure he'd like to talk to you."

"Of course. David," she said under her breath as if her night was getting worse.

"He's in town for a meeting at the SEC on Monday."

"Where are you two sitting?"

Scanning the room, I soon spotted him at the table in the corner with Juan Carlos and a large group. Ever my wingman, David was already sitting with them, right next to a beautiful black woman. I hadn't seen her for ten years, but she had to be Nicki's friend Lisa. She was looking directly at me but then snapped her head to glare at David, who'd just stretched his arm onto the back of her seat.

I raised my eyebrows. "It looks like we're sitting with you now."

"What do you mean?"

"David appears to have joined your table."

"What?" Nicki tried to look around, but she was too small and there were too many people dancing around us for her to see. A short and seated Juan Carlos likely couldn't see us either. I liked that.

"He's sitting next to Lisa. I apologize in advance if he makes a pass at her."

"Are you crazy? That's the last thing I'm worried about. What is he going to say?" Then she shook her head at herself. "What is *she* going to say? Oh my God."

"Don't worry. David won't cause a scene. He's got things under control." I looked back to where he was holding court with the table. Everyone appeared to be having a good time—except for Lisa. She surveyed everything going on around her as if on guard, probably because David hadn't removed his arm from her chair. I reassured Nicki. "He'll take care of Lisa. I'm sure he's laying on the Cockney charm and everyone's getting on just fine. I see Juan Carlos is laughing."

Nicki gave a quick smile and then withdrew it in silence. The quiet built up between us, and I was about to make a comment about the weather when she smiled again and announced the obvious. "We're dancing."

"Yes, we are." I took a breath before reaching into our past. "I don't believe we ever did that."

"I don't think so either." She actually giggled.

I arched a brow, suggesting all the things we did do together. She immediately looked down. "Nicki, you're blushing. I think I know why."

"Why?"

"Because you're thinking what I'm thinking."

The redness didn't leave her cheeks, but she sighed as if in surrender. "In an effort to keep things from being awkward between us, I'll say those were fun times."

"I thought so." I waited a few beats before I splayed my hand across her back, trying to tell her that it had been more than just fun for me.

It worked. Her smile vanished, and her gaze intensified. When her lips parted, I was overcome. In any other place, at any other time, I'd lean down and kiss the gorgeous woman in my arms. I swore she was asking for it, but I couldn't do it.

As if on cue, the song ended. Nicki looked like she'd been saved by the bell and mumbled, "I should get back. Thanks for the dance."

I wasn't about to let her go. The DJ segued into another slow song, so I demanded, "I think I get another dance since I only got half of the last one."

The same stunned look as when we'd first started dancing came across her face, but she didn't walk away. Instead she begged breathlessly, "Adam, what are you doing?"

"To be quite honest, I'm not sure."

"Why did you take the White House job?"

"Why do you think?"

"I don't know. I can't tell."

I'd been right. I'd given her mixed messages—some of them intentionally, some not—and there was one I needed to dispel immediately. "For the record, it definitely wasn't because I thought I might get some kind of special access to the Logan administration because of you."

"That thought really never entered my mind." She shook her head. "You wouldn't do something like that."

"You know me well." Emboldened, I pulled her closer to me, enough that I felt her heart beating double-time.

At once, she jerked back. She seemed fearful and swallowed hard. "I have a boyfriend. Here. In this room."

"I know." Silence and reality loomed. Looking for a way out, I said, "Yet surely we could be friends again."

"We were never *just* friends."

With those few words, the emotions of sixteen years ago surfaced. I felt them all once more and tried to work through what was then and what was now. "No…we weren't, but we could give it a try."

Not giving me an answer one way or another, she announced, "I should go back."

Her hand dropped from mine, and she walked with determination to the table. I followed and cringed when I saw Juan Carlos's smile as she took her seat next to him. Luckily for me, David was going full throttle as I sat in a chair beside him. He was in the middle of a story, and no one was minding Nicki's and my arrival. Or so I'd thought until I spotted Lisa, who gave me a most suspicious look.

After he finished his story, David smoothly introduced me to her. "Adam, Dr. Lisa Roberts. You remember her, don't you?"

How she reacted to this charade would be interesting. I was friendly. "Hello, Lisa. I believe I last saw you in London."

She practically rolled her eyes in disdain. "Hello. It's been a while." Then she stared at Nicki with a clear what-the-fuck-is-going-on expression.

Nicki looked uneasy and took a gulp of sangria.

A Hill staffer next to me introduced himself just then, and apparently seeing an opportunity, David moved his body just a tad to cut me out of further conversation with Lisa. I wasn't offended; David obviously wanted to pursue her, and his effort was amusing if a little nauseating.

"You know, Lisa," I overheard David say, "you're beautiful—like a Nubian princess."

"You have got to be kidding me."

"Not at all."

"Do you even know where Nubia is?"

"Africa, I suppose."

"You say it like it's a small place. Africa is a friggin' continent."

"What does it matter? It's a compliment, princess."

"Princess? I bet that's something you call all your women."

"Only if they're gorgeous like you."

"And the black ones are Nubian princesses?"

"Not all of them. You're special."

I stopped listening when the young staffer started lobbying me to do a story about his incredibly boring boss. Matters only became worse when a friend of Juan Carlos's sat between us. Bursting out of a tight red dress, Maria Ines had great tits, which I did my level best to completely ignore as she purred to me in her thick Columbian accent. The problem with not looking downward was that I had to look her in the eye, and she eye-fucked me the entire time. I got so annoyed with her that I paid more attention to the staffer. That led to actually agreeing to include the dull senator in a piece I was doing on the new Congress. It was a small price to pay to keep Maria from thinking I had any intentions toward her. She was pretty, but my mind was elsewhere.

Sadly, Nicki didn't look at me for the rest of the night. I took some comfort, however, from seeing that she didn't talk much to anyone. There were a lot of people at the table, and Juan Carlos, who had a big personality for such a little guy, talked with everyone. He would speak to Nicki in Spanish occasionally, which drove me insane with curiosity. I wanted to think she only gave him short, polite replies, but I had no way of knowing.

When it got close to two in the morning, I started to feel sick. It was coming to the end of the night when Nicki would most likely go home with Juan Carlos. I didn't want to stick around for that. I nudged David, and he nodded. Overhearing him ask for Lisa's phone number, I craned my neck to see her response.

David must've made some headway because she looked like she was debating her answer. When she saw me, she yawned before saying, "Adam is a reporter. He should be able to track it down."

"Still playing hard to get?" David smiled.

"Oh, I'm not playing at all," she answered. "I am hard to get, especially for you."

Leaning over, he pecked her cheek. It was good that he then got up quickly—she looked like she was going to deck him.

As we said our farewells, everyone was polite. Maria gave me one last leering look, and the staffer gave me his card. Since he'd been the hit of the party, David got more than one invitation to come back another night, which made Lisa sneer at Nicki like it was all her fault.

When Juan Carlos and I shook hands goodbye, he was perfectly congenial with me. He wasn't properly minding his date, though.

He missed it as Nicki barely acknowledged me. I said to her, "Good night, Nicki. I suppose I'll see you on Monday."

She smiled but looked askance. "Yes. Monday. Good night."

I uneasily walked toward the restaurant exit, not knowing what the night had meant. Hoping I might get a clue, when we got to the door, I snuck a peek back at the table we'd just left.

There was Nicki, looking straight back at me.

Chapter Five

What made me pull back, I didn't know. Yet from the moment I had left the restaurant that night, I sensed I should give Nicki some space, and I really needed to sort out what in the world I was doing as well. It was all too much too soon, so I retreated. For weeks, I still saw her every day at work, but I was simply cordial with her. Though I thought about her all the time, I didn't seek her out. I had barged into Nicki's life, and it was unclear if I was welcome.

Late one evening, I was watching a football match that I'd recorded earlier. When my mobile rang and I saw it was my sister, I paused the program. "I'm watching football. Is it about Dad?"

"No, it's not about Daddy, and you can stop your bloody match for a moment. It's not like it's live."

"Well, what do you want then?"

"What are you up to this weekend?"

"Not much. I need to do some research for work, and I was hoping to play football on Sunday, but it looks like it might snow. What's up?"

"I've got a trip to DC for work. I just want to make sure I can stay with you. David won't be there, right?"

"No. I think he's in Singapore."

"And no Felicity either?"

"You know she's rarely in the States."

"Good. I still don't know what you see in her."

"Well, right now I'm not seeing much of her. We live in different countries."

"Are you dating anyone else?"

"Not at the moment." I sneered at the wall. "Anyway, what does this have to do with you coming to visit? Yes, you can stay here. Is that all?"

"It was just a question…you're so touchy sometimes. But thanks for letting me crash with you."

"Can I get back to my match now?"

"No. I have one more question."

"What?"

"I'm sure you have Nicki's number by now. May I have it? I'd like to see her when I come down."

"Really?" I was intrigued. Sylvia knew that I was still interested in Nicki. How couldn't she when I'd begged her for any scraps of information about the woman for the last decade and a half? I still didn't tell my sister everything, though. It was far too embarrassing. "You want to see her?"

"Yes. I thought we might have brunch."

"What are you going to say?" I slapped my forehead for sounding like a fourteen-year-old boy.

"Blimey! I think I can fill the conversation without talking about you, though I know what I should say."

"What's that?"

"That you're still the same sweet but cowardly boy she knew in secondary school."

"I'm not a coward."

"Oh yes, you are. She's been in Washington for months now, and you still haven't gone out."

I straightened my back as my voice rose. "Our jobs won't allow it. Not to mention she has a bloke, even if he is a short-arse."

"He's short? What does it matter if he's short?"

"Oh, nothing." I wasn't about to tell her the universal truth that tall men considered short men slightly inferior. It may have been irrational, but it was instinctual.

"Regardless, those are excuses."

"And then there's Felicity."

"Admit it, Adam. You don't want Felicity. You just like having her around."

"You don't know that."

"That's what David says, and he's an expert on stringing women along."

Was I stringing Felicity along? *Nah.* If I was, she was doing the same to me. "Moving on, then," I announced. "Get a pen, and I'll give you her number."

"Thank you."

After she wrote everything down, she said, "One more thing."

"What now?"

"Whilst I don't plan on talking to Nicki about you, how about the three of us go to a museum together afterward? We could visit the Sackler. I've been working with the director there on a book of Asian art."

Though my heart jumped at the thought of spending an afternoon with Nicki, I remembered the times Sylvia had hung around us when we were in school. It was really fucking annoying. "She'll probably have to work," I said.

"Well, we shall see. I need to say goodbye and get to bed. I'll get to your flat around two on Saturday afternoon. Can you make sure you have some food in the house for once?"

"I'll try," I said, rolling my eyes at my demanding but useful little sister. "See you on Saturday."

On Sunday afternoon, I waited outside the modern building that housed the Sackler Gallery. It was next door to the old Art Deco structure of its sister Asian art museum, the Freer. The white flurries falling around the two distinct buildings made for a beautiful scene. Sylvia and Nicki were late, but I blamed that on the weather. DC taxis were crap in the snow.

When a taxi pulled up and the two got out, it was a sight. They couldn't have dressed more differently. Sylvia was in her usual black garb, only that day it was the Manhattan/London winter-weather version and far too flamboyant for stodgy Washington.

On the other hand, Nicki looked like she was from middle-America, wearing jeans and a ski jacket. I was dressed similarly in jeans and a parka, which made me happy. I grinned as they walked toward me, and I realized something else about Nicki's appearance. For the first time, she looked entirely like my Nicki—the girl I'd left behind. I'd only seen her dressed up and in heels for the past month. In snow boots and tight jeans, she seemed more petite, and her colorful wool hat made her look young.

As they approached, we exchanged hellos, and I could see Nicki's cheeks had reddened in the cold and wind. She looked too bloody cute. Without thinking, I reached out and tousled the bobble on top of her hat. She met my playful gaze with a pensive one, and her face became even pinker as she whipped the hat off.

Her blush told me something that rang in my heart. It was happening all over again with Nicki. Well over a decade had passed, yet there we were again—I liked a girl so much that I couldn't help but react like a little boy and tease her. Without a doubt, she felt something, too, but was so scared that she was flummoxed by it.

With that realization, I knew I had the upper hand on everything standing between us. A boost of confidence shot through me.

After saying hello to Sylvia, I opened the museum door. "Shall we?"

Nicki smiled and went in first. Sylvia followed, but not before giving me a pinch on the arm. She'd seen what had happened between Nicki and me. She loved being right, and it drove me nuts.

Nicki and I were both quiet as Sylvia spoke with a woman at the front desk. She had already contacted the director of the galleries, who'd arranged for us to have a special viewing of some works not on display, but we started our tour walking through the museum by ourselves.

At the first Hokusai print, it was clear there was no need for me to make conversation with Nicki. In fact it was impossible for either of us to get a word in edgewise, because Sylvia had begun her art-expert routine. That garnered her a crowd, and soon there was a motley crew of strangers following Sylvia from one piece to another, listening to her expound upon the details of each one. She took the small crowd in stride, as if this happened to her all the time. She always loved being the center of attention.

After being dragged around by Sylvia for long enough, I saw her tour as an opportunity to have Nicki all to myself. Pointing to a bench, I asked her, "Do you want to sit this one out?"

"Sure." Sitting down, she said, "I love Asian art, but I've seen a lot before."

"How come?"

"When Logan was governor, we traveled a few times to Asia. You know, trade trips and stuff."

I had asked the question, yet I'd known the answer. Over the years, I had received scant information about Nicki's life, but I *was* a reporter. A few times, I became so curious that I would do a Lexis-Nexis search of her name in the papers. I had rarely done it because it really wasn't healthy behavior. It only made me feel like a fucking loser of a twat. Yet I'd learned a few new things about her — like that she'd traveled across Asia with then-Governor Logan. Illinois had trade ties to Japan and China, and she'd gone on a few trade missions with the governor. I often found her in the background of photos of prime ministers and premiers.

Occasionally, there had also been photos of her at campaign events. Those were the worst ones for me to see. She was always smiling and often had a man's arm around her. I knew all the pictures couldn't just be Nicki and another campaign official congratulating one another. She had to have been going out with some of them. That made me feel like shit.

I nodded, pretending it was news. "It sounds like you've traveled a lot, then. You did when you lived in Mexico as well, right?"

"Oh yeah, I did a lot there, too — throughout Central America. And then with Logan, a little in Europe."

The thought of Nicki being in Europe piqued my interest. She'd been on my side of the Atlantic and never contacted me. Had she been to the UK?

She must've read my mind. Her eyes darted around, and she quickly added, "But never to England. Only Berlin and Brussels."

Bobbing my head, I conceded that as fair enough. "The president is going to Berlin again next week for the summit."

"Hopefully I can get away for an hour. It has some great museums."

I'd be with her in Berlin covering the president's trip. I knew what David would've said next: *Maybe we can slip out together?* Unfortunately, I couldn't say it. He'd also told me I had to take things slowly with Nicki, and after my realization of what was going on between us, I understood we had a delicate dance ahead.

I casually said, "That sounds like fun, and it would be nice for you—to get a break from the stress."

"Yeah, my job is stressful, no doubt about that, but it's also amazing and rewarding and can be a lot of fun."

Just as I was about to suggest she take some time off, Sylvia reentered the room with her impeccably bad timing. She was happy after being the center of attention. "Sorry about that. I should've warned you. It happens a lot. I just can't help sharing with people everything that I know."

"Can we get on with our own tour now?" I asked impatiently.

We strolled through more of the gallery and then wandered over to the Freer to see its collection as well. Even though we were in the splendid Peacock Room, I'd had more than my fill of Asian art and Sylvia's lecturing on it. Nicki seemed a little weary, too, and asked if we could sit a minute.

When Sylvia instead declared it time to go back to the Sackler for our private showing, I racked my brain for a reason to skip it. "What exactly are we seeing? I'd like to sit down for a few minutes as well."

"Oh, it's wonderful stuff that no one gets to see." Sylvia brightened. "Since the galleries are part of the Smithsonian, they're government-funded. There are pieces the museum has in its holdings but never displays because Americans are such prudes." She turned to Nicki and said, "Your crazy right wing would go mad."

Nicki cocked her head in question. "So it's political art?"

"Oh no. It's *Shunga*. Japanese erotic art." Sylvia smiled as if she'd just as well said they were still-lifes of flowers in cheery English kitchens.

My eyes flashed at her the question, *What the fuck are you thinking?* She was clearly nutters if she thought porn was my path to Nicki's heart. I looked at Nicki, who appeared completely taken aback.

"I'm sorry, Sylvia," she said. "It's nice of you to arrange it, but as you said, Americans are prudes, and I work at the White House. I'll stay here."

"Indeed," I said, glaring at my sister, who was doing me no favors. "The deputy White House press secretary probably shouldn't be on a private tour of hidden erotica at the Smithsonian. I'll keep her company. You go ahead."

Ignoring my stare, Sylvia huffed in annoyance. "Oh, you two have always been such duds. I'll go by myself and meet you back here in half an hour or so."

"I hope she's not upset," Nicki said after Sylvia left the room.

"Who bloody cares? That's not something I want to see with my sister."

Nicki giggled, which brought out her prettiest smile. Once again, I was struck by what David would've immediately followed up with at that moment: *That's something I'd like to see with you...alone.* It was the goddamn truth, but I couldn't say it. It was too provocative—she might run away.

Instead, I looked around the room and saw it was empty. The snow fell harder outside, which must've sent some people home. I pointed over to the bench. "Let's sit down."

"It's such a beautiful room," she said, taking a seat.

"My mum would love it. The next time they visit, I should bring them here." A sick feeling came over me when I realized what I'd said. In the pleasure of Nicki's company, for a moment I had actually forgotten how unlikely it was that both of my parents would come to the States again—indeed, that Dad would ever leave Cambridge.

"Are they coming soon?"

"Nothing is planned." Taking a deep breath, I tried to find some grounding. For the second time that we'd seen each other, I became uneasy talking to her about Dad's cancer. Normally I could speak freely on the topic, but with Nicki, everything felt differently. I exhaled and said, "Actually, I don't know why I said that. They won't be coming again. There won't be any more plans. My dad is so ill that it's not possible."

"Oh, Adam. I'm sorry. How often are you able to see them?"

"I usually go home once a month. Sylvia does as well. I haven't been back in six weeks, though, so I'm taking time off after Berlin to see him."

"That must be very difficult."

I moved my head just enough to agree, then looked down.

She seized upon my silence and added, "It's still nice that you can visit often—that you can see him even though you live in another country. I bet he really appreciates it."

"Well, my mum does." I tried to find some humor in it. "I guess he likes having us around. Sylvia talks his ear off. He and I don't talk much, so we end up watching a lot of football."

"But isn't that what men do?" She smiled. "Instead of talking about important things, they just talk about sports."

In an instant, she changed my mood. I gave her a teasing glare. "Excuse me. Are you saying my father and I are insensitive?"

"Absolutely."

I searched for a way to change the subject. I needed to because what I really wanted to do was put my arm around her and tuck her into my side for support. "And do you see your family often?"

"Some. They were both here for the inauguration. I usually see my dad a fair amount. President Logan's home is still in Chicago. And when I'm in California for work, I visit my mom. Last year with the campaign, my life was crazy and I was never home, so she didn't visit me, but she'll come to DC now that I'm here."

"What about Houston? Do you ever go back there?"

"Occasionally, to see friends and…" Her faltering voice stopped altogether. It was a moment before she declared, "When I'm there, I stop by my sister's grave."

I was slow to respond as I got the feeling Nicki was disclosing something she normally didn't talk about. The last thing I wanted her to feel was uncomfortable, so I lightly said, "That's understandable. I would do the same thing. Besides, you grew up with her in Houston. It's home."

"But it's not home anymore." Her lips trembled, with tears soon rolling down her cheeks. "I feel bad that we've all moved away."

"Nicki." I never forgave myself for causing her more pain than she had already borne when we'd been young, and I hated myself for making her cry once again. Without a thought of our jobs or Juan Carlos, I wrapped my arm around her. "I'm sorry. I didn't mean to pry or make you sad."

"It's like we've left her behind," she gasped, burying her head into my chest, right where she belonged.

I pulled her in tighter; it was no time to be subtle. If I had to, I'd capitalize on her tears for her to consider me.

She must've sensed the intimacy, because she soon leaned away, drying her tears. "I know it's silly, but if I have to fly through Houston, I'll even schedule a long layover just to go to the cemetery."

"That's nice, but your sister isn't there," I said, rubbing her back. "Not really. She's with you. In your heart. Right?"

"I know it makes no sense. Intellectually, I get it. Her soul is gone and elsewhere, but I hate that her remains are still there in that cemetery when none of us live near her." She let out a throaty laugh. "I always said we should have scattered her ashes in the Gulf. Then she'd be everywhere."

"It does appear to have its benefits." I was glad she found some humor and let my hand wander down her back. I didn't want to let go just yet. "Do you talk with your parents about it?"

"My dad brings Lauren up occasionally, but my mother…it's not really a welcome topic."

"Still?"

"Time has passed, and I may be older, but my mom still doesn't talk about the death of her little girl."

"And probably never will." I sighed. Nothing seemed to have changed with her family.

"Nope."

Neither of us spoke, and I began to wonder if she was as aware as I was that I was touching her body. I decided to play it safe, withdrawing my hand and changing the topic. "Tell me about where you've been to—like China. I've always wanted to go there, but I haven't yet had opportunity."

"China is an amazing country, but we were there talking trade. It's odd that they're Communists because they're such ardent capitalists."

"I know. They're Communists only when it comes to their authoritarian government. They couldn't care less about redistribution of wealth."

"Exactly, but it's still fascinating to be there, seeing modern China contrasted against its ancient history. The people were so friendly, and we were able to do some sightseeing. The Forbidden City is amazing, and I also went to the Great Wall."

"That's something I'd like to see."

"Yeah," she said in an absentminded voice. "I wanted to go there because it was something Lauren always wanted to do."

Lauren. The name floated in the air. I wasn't sure how to reply, and I didn't want to cause any more tears. But I didn't have to ponder long, as suddenly she stood and said, "I need to find a ladies' room. I'll meet you back here."

Nicki evidently met up with Sylvia outside the Peacock Room, so they walked in together. Sylvia suggested moving on to the National Gallery, but Nicki's eyes were wide as she indicated her mobile. "My conference call this evening was canceled because people are stuck in airports. It's dumping snow outside. If I'm going to get a cab home, I should go find one now."

Before I could offer Nicki a ride, Sylvia chimed in. "A taxi? Don't be silly." She even took things a step farther than I'd planned. It was times like this when I loved my sister. "Adam can give you a lift, but really you should stay for dinner tonight if you're free. I'm cooking."

"Oh, that's nice of you to offer." Nicki looked befuddled as to what she should do.

"Please do," I said. "David's not there, so the place is actually clean for once."

"Oh…okay." She snickered, but she clutched her bag as if she wasn't altogether sure she'd made the right decision.

Nicki hadn't exaggerated that the snow was dumping onto Washington. When we arrived at my car, it was no longer black but white. I told them that they should sit in it and warm up while I cleaned off the windscreen.

"I'll sit in the back," said Sylvia happily. "I don't mind."

Avoiding Nicki's eyes, I hid my smile. Other than the erotic art fiasco, Sylvia was being helpful. We all got in the car, and I revved the engine, which wasn't affected by the cold. I glanced at Nicki sitting as compactly as she could in her seat, with her arms across her chest. She was chilled, but probably also feeling awkward to be in the front seat with me.

I felt the same. Wanting to both figuratively and literally break the ice, I said, "Sorry about the cold leather. The seat warmer switch is on your left if you want it. The control for your side of the heat is on the dashboard."

"Thanks," she said with a small smile.

The strangeness that had come between Nicki and me from the moment we reached my car continued throughout the drive and as we walked the steps to my flat. Sylvia kept the conversation going, but she might as well have been talking to herself. Nicki was quiet, and I certainly wasn't listening. I was trying to get my mind around Nicki Johnson being in my home.

Flicking on the lights as we entered the flat, I scanned the room to make sure nothing embarrassing was out. Everything looked fine, and I took their coats while they kicked off their wet boots. Nicki seemed more at ease as she surveyed the large open space that was my kitchen, dining, and living rooms all flowing into one another. Her eyes drifted approvingly. "Your place is so nice."

All it took was a small compliment like that to bring out the competition between Sylvia and me.

"That's because I designed it," Sylvia said.

"*You* picked out the art," I retorted as I hung their coats to dry. "*I* chose the furniture." And the squabble ensued until I feared she was making me sound petty. She was such a bossy bitch sometimes, but I let it go.

While I quickly fetched the wine, Sylvia led Nicki over to the fireplace. Above the mantle was a large painting Sylvia had done in school. It was really quite good, and she spent some time telling Nicki just why it was so great. After handing them their wine, I set to work on the fire as Sylvia droned on about the piece.

Just when I thought that was the end of the tour, Sylvia announced, "Let me take you through the rest of the flat."

Jesus fucking Christ. You'd think she owned the place.

Before I could stop them, Sylvia had led Nicki into the spare bedroom and showed her the attached bath she was especially proud of—something about the Italian tile that I couldn't, for the life of me, see why it was special. Nicki must've been underwhelmed, too, because they soon walked out. Sylvia turned to me and asked, "We can go in your room, right, Adam?"

What the fuck? I had never imagined that if I ever got Nicki back in my bedroom, Sylvia would be the one to lead her there. But what else could I say? "Sure."

I tagged along behind—I wasn't having Nicki near my bed without me. When we walked in, I watched her thoroughly appraise everything.

Sylvia interrupted the quiet assessment as she pulled Nicki over to my bed and pointed to the art above it. "This is a very special print. I worked on it for months…"

As Sylvia went into details about her own damn work again, I caught Nicki looking down. She was checking out my bed. Her face was blank, but before she raised her head back to the print, I could swear she pressed her lips to stop a smile from creeping out. Oh, how I wished I knew what she was thinking.

After she finished explaining her art, Sylvia turned to the rest of the room. Waving her hand over to the drafting table that served as my desk, she said, "That alcove is a work area I designed. I like a more open space rather than a separate office. Now let's go back to the living room, and I'll cook."

Nicki looked up at me and smiled. She'd been so quiet since we had left the museum, I was surprised to hear her voice. "You still draw?"

"Yeah." I'd pinned some of my caricatures and sketches on the walls of the alcove. No one ever saw them but me.

"That's wonderful."

"I don't know. It's only a hobby."

"Can I see?"

Without waiting for an answer, she walked over to the table. Sylvia shot me a knowing look and said, "I'll be in the kitchen."

As I went over to Nicki, she held a sketch in her hand and grinned. "So you're doing caricatures of President Logan?"

"I'm trying."

"Can I see some more?"

Nicki's eyes were bright; she seemed genuinely eager to see my work, so I was happy to show her. I pulled the stool out from the table for her. "Of course. Take a seat."

As I grabbed another stool and sat beside her, Nicki was already thumbing through the drawings on my table. She fussed over them. "These are so good, Adam. Why aren't you publishing them?"

"I don't think they're really good enough." I slouched in my seat. "Plus, it's a hard profession to break into."

"But you're already a journalist. I would think it would be a leg-up. People know you. It should be easier to get them seen."

"I'm a television journalist. You know we're looked down upon by print. It probably hurts me more than helps me that I'm already in the field."

Nicki frowned. I did sound a little defeatist, but those were the facts. She shook her head. "I still think you should try. You'll never know if you don't, and wouldn't you rather be drawing than your current job?"

"Well, yes, but it seems like a futile endeavor. Not even worth the effort."

Pursing her lips, she gave me a look as if she disagreed but dropped it. She turned her attention instead to the Logan drawings and commented, "You've really captured him well, but you could add something here. You're right that he's got a really long neck, but in this drawing—where he's angry—you should make some veins bulge out. They always do when he's pissed, though that's rare."

"Are you giving me secrets about your boss, Nicole Johnson?"

"Hardly." She smiled. "He'd think these were hilarious. Now, he may not like the captions you put with them, but he'd like the drawings themselves and wouldn't mind them being accurate. He's got a really good sense of humor."

"Thanks. That's good to know."

"I like that one, too," she said, pointing to a cartoon of Gordon Brown. "He's probably a fun one to draw."

"Definitely. He's got a million different expressions, and he looks uncomfortable in every one of them." Feeling a little bold, I pulled out my sketchpad. "This is what I'm working on right now. I thought I'd practice Angela Merkel since we're going to Berlin."

"Oh, let me see," she said, taking the pad. "This is really good. I've met her before. I'd give her a short necklace. She wears them all the time, even though they're not very flattering."

"What do you mean?"

"They show off her jowls."

"Let me add a necklace, then."

So I began drawing, with Nicki giving me direction. We talked and laughed with no awkwardness or tension. We were having fun—just like old times.

Everything was great until I noticed how her hair smelled and how closely she sat next to me. The stool was too short for her, so she was sitting on her knees with her arms resting on the table to look at the sketches. Her cute arse was up in the air, as if waiting to be pinched or perhaps given a little swat. I was tempted to run my hand over it.

I looked up and saw she had watched me ogle her. When our eyes met, she smiled shyly, but I didn't. All I could think of was grabbing that arse of hers and snogging just like we used to. I remembered I was supposed to be a good chap and a friend, but my body wanted to fuck her. We were in my bedroom, after all. I'd even caught her looking at my bed. Maybe it was on her mind as well. As my mind wandered, my dick got harder, and I tried to communicate with my eyes just how much I wanted to touch her. Her lips opened, telling me she knew exactly what I was thinking.

In a flash, though, she jerked back. Looking down, she mumbled, "I should go see what Sylvia is up to."

As I followed her back into the kitchen, I had to do some shifting to hide my erection. Hating myself for scaring her off, I pretended nothing had occurred between us, and she seemed to play along.

Our conversation with Sylvia during the meal was lively, but I noticed Nicki occasionally scan my bookcases from where she sat at the dinner table. They were expansive and went from the floor to the ceiling across the wall. Scattered among the books were a few framed photos and prints as well.

I'd forgotten about one special print. It was something that I might spend months never really seeing. Any casual observer wouldn't think it any different than the other pictures of family and places on the shelves, but Nicki would know it was significant. She'd given it to me for our first and last Valentine's Day together, on the beach. Luckily, she wouldn't know what was in the copy of Wordsworth behind it.

I held my breath, wondering if she saw the print, but if she did notice, she offered no reaction.

After dinner, she checked her watch. "I really should get home."

"When do you get to the office in the morning?" Sylvia asked. "Maybe we could meet for coffee."

"I don't think so. Unless you want to meet me at six. I'm at my desk by seven."

"Perhaps not, then." Sylvia giggled. She looked over at the mess in the kitchen. "I hope you don't mind, but I'll let Adam take you home while I tidy up."

If Nicki thought it might be uncomfortable being in a car with me alone, she didn't show it. She smiled at Sylvia. "Well, if Adam takes me home, then I have to say goodbye to you now."

After they exchanged their hugs and goodbyes, Nicki and I walked back to my car, which was covered in snow again. Everything was normal between us as I dusted it off and we drove up Connecticut Avenue to her flat. Maybe it was because the conversation was so mundane about the road conditions and the weather.

When we pulled into the driveway of her building, I wondered if I should walk her up, but that might have been too much like a date. Then I considered giving her a quick hug before she got out. It seemed like a friendly, unassuming gesture. I didn't have to choose, though, because she spoke first.

"Thanks so much for letting me crash your day with Sylvia, and thank you for dinner and the ride home."

"Well, you have to thank Sylvia for dinner, but the rest has been fun. I'm happy we got to spend some time together."

"I am, too," she whispered.

As the words left her lips, it was as if all the maturity and sophistication she'd developed over the years escaped from her. There was my shy girl again. Before we'd got together, I may have been dating Meredith, but I'd spent many a night wanking to my Nicki fantasies and many a day staring at her like a love-struck prat. She'd been too shy and humble to recognize any of it happening.

Yet now it was happening all over again. I wanted to lean over and kiss her and then do a lot more, and by the way she gazed at me, I was sure her mind was right there with me. Should I have kissed her? Maybe so, because I was certain she'd have kissed me back. I worried, though, she might freak out and that would be the last one. The safer route was to let her go — at least this time.

I smiled. "Now go on up. We've got a big week ahead, you especially."

"The president's first international trip," she said with a nod.

"Indeed."

Chapter Six

After our day together at the museum, everything changed between Nicki and me. The tension between us seemed to have passed. In the White House briefing room every morning, she treated me like every other reporter, but our one-on-one conversations were different from those of my colleagues. We smiled more, we laughed more, and we could pick up on what each of us was going to say next. Yet to the outward eye, anyone would think we were nothing more than reporter and source.

Unfortunately, that arsehole Dan Roark observed Nicki like a hawk. It was obvious he wanted to fuck her and was making a plan of attack. One morning, Nicki sought me out to clarify a question her boss had answered. It was something she often did with reporters if she worried he'd gone slightly off-point. As she and I chatted, maybe I gave her too big a grin or she finished one too many of my sentences. Regardless of the clue, Dan picked up on it.

When Nicki walked out of the room, Dan strode up to me with a suspicious smirk. "You two seem to get on well. What's your secret?"

Because Dan and I were both reporters, we were unusually good liars. We had to be to avoid betraying a confidential source or to keep a leak exclusive. Lying came easily to me, and I used it when necessary. This was one of those times that I needed to cover my arse—but only so far. There was a competitive part of me that wanted to confirm for Dan that Nicki did indeed have something for me that she didn't for him.

"Oh, I don't know. Probably my accent." *Take that, you fucking nosy arsewipe.*

"Humpf." He was definitely curious now that I'd confirmed something was up between Nicki and me—even if it was just flirting. "Maybe she likes accents. Her boyfriend has one."

"Yes, he does."

"Do you know him?"

"I've met him." I snickered. "He's short."

"I know." Dan snorted—he was tall, too. "I don't see the appeal."

I thought about saying, *"Well, we actually agree on something."* Instead, I stated what was often written about Juan Carlos Jimenez. "Well, he's a brilliant strategist, and he's very charismatic."

"There's gotta be something else," he said, eyeing Nicki across the room. "I don't know what. Maybe he's hung like a horse."

Juan Carlos's knob—now there was something I really didn't want to think about. But Dan's comment was something David would say, and it was pretty funny. I laughed and shook my head, dispelling the thought.

Dan's attention returned to me, and his eyes narrowed one more time. "But you have an accent. Lucky for you," he said and walked away.

Traveling to Berlin, the White House Press Corps felt a sense of pomp and circumstance flying on Air Force One for the first time. The interior was stately, and members of the US Air Force formed the plane's crew. Yet despite the immense space and multiple floors, the president's plane also gave us the feeling of being on a school bus. The press was relegated to the back like a bunch of noisy, annoying kids. Though we had a cabin of our own, Air Force One steerage was like any commercial flight with dodgy food and uncomfortable seats. The big difference was the freedom. Unless there was turbulence, you didn't have to stay in your seat and could move about as you wished.

That evening there was an air of excitement as it was the president's first international trip. Reporters were grouped in clusters, gossiping and chatting. Some played cards; others read or tried to catch some sleep. I wasn't really interested in socializing, so I put on my headphones and canceled out all the noise as I read *The Economist*.

I gradually became aware of a group that had gathered to my left, sharing wine and laughing loudly. It wasn't long before I felt a tap on my shoulder from Lydia Mixon, an ever so cheery but mousy reporter for CBS News. Pulling off my headphones, I asked, "Pardon?"

"Oh, we're playing a game. I think it should be your turn."

"What's that?"

She looked at the group around her for support before she flirtatiously announced, "We're talking about when we lost our virginity. Everyone's telling the name of the person and where they did it."

I laughed because wine and excitement over a big international trip with the president had made the press corps punchy. Dan Roark was in the rowdy circle and called out, "C'mon, Kincaid. I just did it. Her name was Charlotte Clark, and we were in the backseat of my car. I was sixteen."

I didn't need to know that about Dan, and I certainly didn't want to hear anything more. But everyone was staring at me. I had to say something, so I quickly released limited information. "Kate — in my childhood bed."

The group responded with a few *oohs* and *ahs* and questions about her last name and my age. I didn't want to answer any questions about Kate, though. I didn't like remembering my time with her because it was too entwined with splitting up with Nicki.

Placing my headphones again on my ears, I went back to my magazine until I saw Nicki walking down the aisle. She'd been on another floor of the plane with the rest of the White House staff, and she must've come down to our economy class to give us a message. Lydia began speaking with her, so I took off my headphones to hear the conversation.

As Nicki looked around the rowdy cabin, she laughed and asked, "What's going on?"

No doubt realizing she might get some major dirt on the deputy White House press secretary, Lydia smiled. "Just a little impromptu party." She gestured to the arsehole Roark. "Dan has us playing games that are making us laugh."

"Drinking games?" Nicki asked Dan.

"Nah. More like truth or dare, but without the dare," he answered.

"Oh dear." Nicki grinned.

"Well, it's a little silly," said Lydia. "But we're having fun."

"Dare I ask what 'truth' everyone is revealing?" Nicki asked.

As Lydia explained the game, I cringed as Nicki's smile went from genuine to forced.

Leaning over the back of a seat, Dan moved toward Nicki and seductively asked, "Wanna play, Nicole?"

I stopped breathing for a moment, wondering how on earth she would respond. Her expression gave nothing away. "Nah, I don't think so."

"I'll tell you mine," Dan said. "My high school girlfriend, Charlotte Clark, in my Mustang. How's that? Now your turn."

"Uh-uh." Nicki shook her head.

Dan didn't give up, though, and the cocksucker dragged me into it. "C'mon. Even Kincaid played. Right, Kincaid?"

Nicki turned to see my response. For the first time in weeks, her eyes were fearful as she looked into mine. I tried to downplay my part in the game by waving my hand as if to brush it all aside.

"So now he won't play. Whatever, Kincaid." Dan rolled his eyes and became a persistent bastard. "Kincaid's girl was named Kate. They did it in his childhood bed. Now you tell us, Nicole."

I couldn't have hated Dan Roark more than at that moment. All my work to build up some goodwill was about to disappear in front of me. Of all the ways Kate's name could have come up in front of Nicki, that was the worst.

Kate was my first and also the one I'd betrayed Nicki with. There. You've heard it. Despite my love for Nicki, I had cheated on her. I told you that you might not forgive me.

In my defense, it had been a complicated situation, but the complications hadn't changed the consequences. I studied Nicki now, waiting for some kind of reaction, but her face was impassive, and she was quiet. Did anyone else pick up on her silence?

Sixteen years earlier, I'd given Nicki variations on all the excuses a man says to a woman when he cheats on her: "I was drunk." "I was depressed." "You pushed me away." "We didn't actually have sex." And the kicker, "It didn't mean anything." And every single justification had been lost on Nicki. They may have had some truth, but they still sounded like pathetic lies.

In those few moments that she was quiet, vivid details of the last time Nicki and I had talked about Kate came back to me. She'd skipped school that day, and I was sure it was because she hadn't wanted to see me. Before my match that afternoon, I had stood on her front porch in my football kit, begging again for forgiveness. The night before, Nicki had been overcome with tears. A day later, she'd already hardened.

"You've been fine with us breaking up all along. You just don't want to be the asshole," she spat.

"Yeah, you're absolutely right. I am an arsehole. But, Jesus Christ, you're wrong that I want to split up. I've never wanted that. Not today… not ever."

She didn't even speak to what I'd said. She only shook her head, rejecting me outright.

That scared the shit out of me so much I got mad. "Goddamn it. I love you. I'm never going to forget you. I—"

"You're never going to forget about me?"

"No, of course not. I—"

"Well, you already did forget me…when you were with her. You forgot about me then, and you'll do it again."

That was where she'd been wrong. I would never do it again, but she hadn't known that then.

Whether it was pity or a bit of forgiveness, a month later Nicki had reached out to me. We'd only had two weeks left before I had to go back to the UK. Our last weeks together had been wonderful; we'd even had sex our final night. It was great, but it had made our goodbye that much worse.

To me, Nicki's silence was excruciating, whilst the rest of the reporters just found it annoying. Lydia finally begged, "Please, Nicole. It's not like we know the guy. It's just for fun."

Nicki turned away and faked a smile for Dan before calmly declaring, "At the beach."

Lydia and others approved with their coos, but it wasn't enough information for Dan. He was like a dog with a bone as he banged on at Nicki. "So how was it? Were you in high school? Was it any good?"

My stomach clenched. *Oh God. What is she going to say?* When I thought back to that day at the beach, I remembered being a boy consumed with love and lust and not executing either one very well. I'd given her some corny piece of heart-shaped jewelry and then took her virginity as I came in record time — even for a seventeen-year-old boy. It was embarrassing to think about, especially with Kate's name in the air, reminding both of us of the eventual demise of our relationship.

"No more information," Nicki said.

"Come on, Johnson," Dan said. "'At the beach' tells us almost nothing. We're reporters. You know you've got to give us something more than that."

I braced myself for whatever terrible thing I might hear from Nicki, but she was quiet. Without acknowledging me at all, she said, "Fine," and crossed her arms. "I was seventeen. It was Valentine's Day. That's all — "

"Were you in love?" asked Lydia.

"Yes," Nicki said decisively.

Her expression was placid, but her one word made a grin erupt on my face so wide that I probably looked like a complete idiot. I couldn't help it. Hearing Nicki loved me always made me happy. She didn't dwell on it, though. She immediately brought the subject back to work.

"Now that I've disclosed that bit of personal information, maybe you won't be too upset when I tell you the president won't take formal questions from the media until the joint press conference tomorrow."

I was still a happy fool, but the rest of the press corps complained about being shut out.

"Don't worry," Nicki said, giving everyone a reassuring nod. "You'll have more opportunities. Thanks, y'all." Her eyes then darted over to me but communicated nothing before she walked up the aisle and out of our cabin.

For the next few days, Nicki and I had no interaction, but that didn't stop me from thinking about her. I wondered if the incident on the plane had dredged up memories for her as well — good or bad. Regardless, I was sure I wouldn't know until we got back to the States.

The final afternoon of our time in Berlin, we'd just finished a short photo opportunity at the Bundestag's rooftop garden for President Logan and other European leaders at the summit. It was an impressive setting with the modern dome behind the leaders. Private meetings were to be held for the rest of the day before the president flew on to Nigeria. I planned on finishing my reporting on the summit and taking the next flight to London to see my dad.

Before I headed over to the BBC's Berlin bureau, I took a minute to enjoy the nice view when I felt my phone vibrate at the arrival of a text message. There was no name attached to the message, only a number I didn't recognize. *Who is it?* At once, I tapped the keys to get to the message.

> *Hi. It's Nicki. Any interest in catching a museum with me?*
> *I'll be at the Museum Berggruen at 3. It's across from the*
> *Charlottenberg Palace. I understand if you can't.*

I searched the large group of people mingling on the roof but didn't see Nicki. Rereading her text, I chuckled. *She understands if I can't make it.* She thought I might not want to come. Such a capable and accomplished woman was still unsure of herself and of me. I pondered on that. *Am I going too slowly? Do I need to open up more to her? She invited me, after all. What does that mean?* I didn't have time to think. I checked my watch and saw I only had two hours to file a story, book the last flight of the night to London, and catch a cab across the city. I replied that I'd be there.

When I walked up to the museum at three, Nicki stood outside the front door, typing away on her phone. She was surprised when I greeted her.

"Hello, Nicki."

"What? Oh. Sorry. I was just sending something." A flustered smile grew on her face. "Thanks for coming. I know it's out of the way, but Sylvia told me it's a great collection. Not many people come out here."

"Thanks for inviting me." I couldn't have cared less that it was a great collection. It could've been a museum of bad cartoons. I just wanted to be with her.

We spent the next half-hour strolling through a wonderfully intimate museum with an expansive spiral staircase and works of Picasso, Klee, and Matisse in room after room. Nicki was right that there were few people around, and I wondered if she'd chosen the museum for that reason. We weren't likely to run into any of our coworkers there.

Ironically, we didn't discuss anything personal the entire time. We spoke only of the art and work, and the work conversation was as dry as could be. Any of my colleagues would've killed to have that much access to someone so close to the president, but really all I got was background that could be used for color. Still, all the work talk did make things easy between us, which kept away any awkwardness. It also stopped me from continually thinking about touching her arse, which looked nice in her striped trousers.

We were done too soon for my liking, so when we got outside again, I asked if she wanted to sit in the park. She agreed, and I thanked God for my luck. Before we found a spot in front of the stately palace, I grabbed a couple of drinks from a street seller.

Nicki thanked me for the drinks, and I wanted to thank her as well — with a kiss. She was clearly tired from all the travel and the long days, yet the dark circles under her eyes only made her look more sincere and sweet. I stopped myself, however, and told her, "It's the least I can do. Thank *you* for inviting me today. It was very interesting. I haven't seen that many Picassos, except in the museum in Paris."

"Same with me."

"When were you in Paris last? With Logan?"

Nicki gave me a quick smile and shrugged. "No. New Year's." She took a sip of her Orangina then waited a beat before adding, "With Juan Carlos."

"New Year's in Paris. Nice." *Fuck him. Why does he get to go to Paris with her?* I bitterly said under my breath, "Why him?"

The words were out of my mouth before I'd even decided to say them. My subconscious was at work. Had Dan's questioning made me wonder, too? Was my curiosity finally getting the best of me? Or was I realizing that the more information I had, the better?

She didn't seem to have heard me, so I acted nonchalant by stretching my legs out. More casually, I said, "So tell me about Juan Carlos."

"You really want to talk about him?" Her brow furrowed.

"Sure. He's important to you, right?"

"Of course."

"Then get on with it." My patience began to fray, fearing she might be toying with me.

"Well…you probably know a lot. His family was part of the Mariel Boatlift from Cuba when he was a boy. They came here with nothing and became prosperous. He's been in politics for forever. He—"

"No. Tell me about him." I sounded frustrated, so when she hesitantly asked what I wanted to know, I played the friends card. "We're friends. You can tell me. What do you like about *him?*"

"What do I like about *him?*" She gave me a quizzical glare, likely wondering if I really wanted to hear everything.

"Yes." *Why are you with that short bastard and not me?*

When I didn't back down from her gaze, she continued, "Well…he's very charismatic, very personable. People just want to be around him."

"That's often said."

"It's true, though. He's not a very big guy, but he's got a giant personality. He's very endearing."

So far he sounded like he had the same qualities as a puppy. I smiled at my private joke and asked, "What else?"

"Well, we care about the same things. You know, have the same politics."

Check. I'd spent enough time with Nicki in the last couple of months to know we also had similar politics; she had to have noticed that, too. I prompted her. "And?"

She again gave me a wary look. "And he's a very passionate person. He couldn't be as dedicated to his work without that drive. It's one of the things that we have most in common."

"What do you mean?"

"Well, I work long hours. I miss a lot of personal stuff in life. Most guys don't understand that—even some political types don't get it."

But I got it. Nicki's commitment to her job—to her ideals—was one of the things that I found so compelling about her now. I also understood it because I worked hard, too.

I was quiet for a moment, wondering how I could show her that I was all of those things that she liked. I commented, "You do need someone understanding of that."

"I love his family, too," she said, her voice more energized. "It's big and friendly. Even though I'm not Cuban, they've been incredibly welcoming to me. I suppose knowing Spanish helped with that. His mom is great, and his father kind of dotes on me. He calls me *Blanquita*—like I'm Snow White because I'm so pale. It's really sweet."

My heart sank. Juan Carlos's dad had taken to her, but what had my father fucking done? When he'd known her, Dad had spent his time trying to tell me she was nothing special. Because he had always been cordial with her, though, she didn't know exactly what he'd said—but maybe she'd guessed it. Not really thinking, I mumbled, "A big family is nice."

"It is." She played with the cap on her drink and added, "Sometimes I feel very alone. It feels good to be around them."

"Do you want a big family?" I wanted to hit myself on the head for asking such a question, but Nicki didn't seem to find it intrusive.

"Yeah. Actually, I do. Not too big, but I'd like to have three kids." She took a long breath. "After Lauren died, I was by myself. I was the only child, and my sister—my friend—was gone, and I felt a lot of responsibility for my parents. I think with three kids, if something happens to one of them, you still have someone."

I smiled, wanting her to feel comfortable. "I feel lucky to have David. He's like a brother to me and Sylvia."

"I don't know, though," she said with a sigh. "I turn thirty-four this year, and I don't see kids on the horizon anytime soon."

Normally, when a woman over the age of twenty-seven mentioned her biological clock, it was time to run. It felt like entrapment. Yet when Nicki remarked on her age and kids in the same breath, I wanted to grab her and say, *"Well, let's get on with it."*

My biology was at work, too. Hormones and instinct told me she was perfect to bear my children. I wanted to fuck her on the grass and pass on my genetic code right then and there. I turned to her, thinking maybe now was the time to snatch that kiss…to let her know what I felt, but she leaned back and crossed her arms.

"What about you?" she asked. "Do you want to have kids?"

Never having really thought about it much until that moment, I was baffled at first. I'd always taken it for granted. Yet thinking about children with Nicki made me happy. "Well, of course. I'd love a family."

She remained quiet and lost in her own thoughts until she spoke as if thinking aloud. "Yeah, Juan Carlos is a really, really good guy, and he's good to me. And he's incredibly loyal. I mean…he works in politics…he's got pretty interns flirting with him all the time, but I trust him completely."

I froze. In a roundabout way, she'd brought it up—that I had cheated on her. And that she'd mentioned it in relation to how her new boyfriend would never hurt her made it all the more painful. She could trust him, but long ago she'd decided she couldn't be with me. She didn't trust me.

Panic struck her face as her whole body tensed. She became even more horrified when she saw the look on my face. "Oh, Adam. I wasn't bringing that up…I didn't mean anything by it."

She might've been thirty-three at that moment, with sixteen years behind her since we'd last talked about it, but I wasn't. I was seventeen again, begging for forgiveness. "Nicki, you have to know how sorry I was…how sorry I am. I've carried guilt and regret with me for the last—"

"No. Don't say that. I have my own guilt…my own regrets—so many." Shaking her head, she said, "God. Please, let's not talk about it. It was years ago. It's not a big deal."

Her speech was rushed, almost frantic, but I caught every word. She had her own regrets. She probably regretted ever being with me, and it didn't matter that it was a long time ago, because it clearly still was a big deal. Otherwise, a man's loyalty wouldn't be such a priority for her. I'd really done a number on her. I was an arse.

"Nicki, I want to talk, even if we're just going to be—"

"No. It's not necessary. We don't have to go there. I'm so sorry." She shrugged. "Let's let the past be the past and focus on the present."

"Okay."

What a chump I was. I couldn't even tell her how I really felt. Neither of us spoke, and things felt so tense that I checked my watch just for something to do. Unfortunately, the time told me we were going to leave each other that day on a sad note. "I'm sorry, Nicki, but I've got to run. I've got a plane to catch."

"Oh. That's right. You're going to see your dad."

"Just for a few days."

"Will you tell your mom hello for me?" She smiled. "And your dad."

"Certainly. I know they'll be happy to hear from you. They watch you on the news."

"That's nice of them. Yet so…odd. Do you know what I mean?"

"I know exactly what you mean."

She sighed, looking at her own watch. "I suppose I need to leave, too. We're off to Nigeria tomorrow."

"I'll be back in DC by the time you arrive in the States on Sunday."

Biting her lip, she timidly said, "Maybe we can talk again then."

"I'd like that," I said with a smile. "I'd like that very much."

Chapter Seven

Ever since Dad had become really ill, my family home hadn't been the same. It was still the home I grew up in, but the smell — the smell was awful. It smelled like a nursing home or hospital, and the scent only worsened the more he declined. With every new medical device or walking apparatus or nurse's visit, the odor intensified.

When I finally made it to Cambridge late that night, the smell was overpowering. Dad was sleeping, but Mum was waiting for me. Normally, she picked me up at the railway station, but my flight had been so late that I'd taken a taxi. Despite the late hour, Mum had a meal sitting on the table for me when I walked in.

After our greetings, she eagerly asked, "So tell me all about your trip with the president."

"It's been tiring. Frankly, I'm happy to have a break, though the trip to Nigeria would have been interesting."

"Why is he going to Nigeria?"

"Logan is just doing things differently. He needed to meet with European leaders first to show his allegiance to longtime allies and then go to Africa to show his interest in the developing world." I sniggered after saying it.

"What's so funny?"

"Nothing. It's just something Nicki said."

"Nicki?" Mum's voice lilted with interest. "She's been on the trip with you, hasn't she?"

"Yes, she has, and we've talked. She'd made a joke about Americans calling countries 'developing nations' when their cultures have been around thousands of years longer than that of the United States."

"Oh, she's a sharp one. It's obvious when she speaks on the telly, but there's also something sweet about her that comes through."

A deep conversation about Nicki with my shrink mum was not what I wanted so late at night. I fiddled with my fork, signaling I was bored, but Mum pressed on. "So do you two talk often? Sylvia told me about the day you three spent together. It sounded like you had a lovely time."

"We did. She says hello to you and dad."

I could've also told her a little about my afternoon with Nicki earlier that day, but I didn't want to. I was trying to sort it out. Nicki was confusing. Over the course of the conversation, I'd been heartbrokenly depressed, yet at times still sensed the same promise I'd felt since our snowy day together. Her asking to talk with me again gave me a great bit of hope. She wouldn't do so if some part of her wasn't interested.

Mum beamed. "Oh, it's so nice of her to remember me — such a pleasant girl. It's wonderful that you get to spend time with her again."

That was a warning that I needed to retreat. Changing the subject, I asked, "So how's Dad?"

"All right. He's chipper, but…we'll see if his mood changes when we get the test results tomorrow."

"Do you have any idea what the results might be?"

"He's been in a lot of pain, so that might mean something bad." Mum shook her head. "It's better for me if I don't try to guess."

"I can understand that." I didn't want to guess the worst either. Pushing back my empty plate, I announced, "I'm tired, Mum. You must be as well. Let's get to bed."

The following morning, I let Dad hold my arm as we made our way into his oncologist's office. The pain and exhaustion had crippled him so much that he normally used a walker. I think he wanted to use a walking stick to put up a front for me, but he still gladly took my arm.

The news from the oncologist was grim. The cancer had spread past the pancreas and lymph nodes into his stomach. It was only a touch, but the cancer had become more aggressive. "So we will be more aggressive with our treatment," the doctor responded in kind. Mum and Dad found that reassuring, but I kept my mouth shut. It sounded like a bunch of medical spin to me.

In the house, it was a surreal dynamic. Everyone spoke matter-of-factly about the cancer like it wasn't going to eventually lead to Dad's demise. We all talked about his illness as if he had a nasty sinus infection, which the doctors were working their hardest to control but couldn't quite pinpoint the allergen. Even when Dad was down for a nap and not listening, Mum kept a stiff upper lip, always being resolute and upbeat as she made her round of calls to Sylvia and the rest of the family. The house was a living, modern example of the propaganda "Keep Calm and Carry On."

Dad and I fell into our normal routine of watching football together when I was at home. During the highlights of the match between Spurs and Arsenal, he announced, "I see Nicki Johnson on the TV almost every day. She's a clever girl—quite lovely looking, too. She's very accomplished to be working in the White House."

My conversation with Nicki the day before came back to me. *Blanquita.* I wondered if Juan Carlos's father gave a toss if Nicki worked in the White House. He probably liked her simply because she was pleasant and loved his son.

I turned from the TV to see Dad staring at me, awaiting my response. I kept it short. "She is."

"Whatever was it that happened between you two?"

No doubt the cancer and the drugs had muddled his mind. Had he really forgotten? Or did he want to forget?

An old jumper that had fit him well his entire life was now baggy on his shoulders. He seemed so gaunt and fragile. Who was I, then, to question the motives of a dying man? I muttered, "We were too young. We lived too far apart."

"Well, neither of those is true anymore." He turned his attention back to the match.

Late that night, I was reading in bed in my old room, which Mum had partially converted into a storage room. There wasn't much left in it that was mine, but the space still felt like home.

Long past the workday, even in DC, I was surprised when my phone rang. Then I saw the name that I'd entered into my contacts just the day before. My heart leapt. I had to control the excitement in my voice as I answered, "Well, hello, Nicki."

"Hi, Adam. I hope I'm not calling too late."

"Not at all. It's good to hear from you."

"I'm sorry it's so late. It was a long day, but I wanted to see how you're doing."

"I'm fine. How are you?"

"Oh, you know." She laughed. "You've probably read what I was working on today."

"Indeed, I have. Logan has received great press."

"It's been an amazing day. Nigeria is fascinating, and the visit has gone really smoothly so far. There's a great American grad student helping us with logistics. She's here doing research for her dissertation on the Nigerian government. Her name is Funmbi. She's a big fan of yours, by the way. She asked me if you were traveling with us."

"Is that why you're calling me?" I chuckled.

"If I spent my time informing you about all your legions of female fans, I wouldn't be able to get my work done."

"Rubbish."

Then all the sarcasm left her voice. "I just wanted to make sure you were okay."

"Why wouldn't I be okay?" Worried that I sounded like an arse, I added, "Don't misunderstand me. I'm happy that you called."

"I know what it's like to be with someone who's really sick. You may not know this, but I went and lived with my grandmother when she had cancer…before she died. So when you told me you were seeing your dad, I was worried about you."

She garbled the last part so badly that I could barely understand it. But when I did, I smiled and ran my hand through my hair, absorbing the moment. Nicki had called me because she was worried about me. I was elated but also melancholy. It was incredibly kind that she was concerned how I was doing around my dying father, but it also brought home the seriousness of Dad's condition—not to mention I wanted her to call because of me, not my dad.

"That's nice of you," I said. "It's been a rough day."

"I'm so sorry. Is Felicity there?"

"Er. No." I looked over at an old Liverpool poster behind where Dad's walker now stood. I'd never thought to ask Felicity to come to Cambridge. This was a part of me where she was not invited. "Why do you ask?"

"I was just wondering. I thought she might be able to help."

Was Nicki jealous? I hoped she was. I'd talk up Felicity in that event. At the very least, Felicity could shield my pride against Juan Carlos.

"No," I said. "She's in London working. I'll see her before I leave." Usually when I was in London, I did more with Felicity than just *see* her—I wasn't a monk for Christ's sake—but this was a short trip, and I owed Felicity a call…or two. The truth was, I'd become even less interested in her since Nicki had come back on the scene.

Nicki seemed to perk up, however, as she said, "So tell me what's going on."

For the next hour, we talked about Dad. Until that conversation, I hadn't told anyone outside my family as much as I told her. I ended up giving Nicki more information than I'd even told David. I gave her the details that were the hardest for me to utter aloud—like how Dad was so riddled with pain that his hand shook while he popped another pill to quell it or how he was literally shrinking before my eyes as his body deteriorated. She listened to everything and was both helpful and understanding of all I was going through.

And somewhere along the way, the conversation shifted to everyday life and became lighter. She teased me, saying I didn't curse like I used to, which had the effect of me then saying "fuck" about ten times. I was so engrossed in our discussion that I looked at the clock twice when I noticed it was two in the morning.

Reluctantly, I said, "Nicki, I'm so sorry. I've been talking your ear off, and I didn't notice the time." I then remembered my place. "You probably want to call Juan Carlos."

"No. I already talked to him earlier today. He's on a cross-country flight tonight."

I smiled to myself, thinking that Nicki spoke with me last before going to bed. Had she saved the conversation? Did she know it would run late?

She continued, "But I should go to sleep. I'm not getting much of it these days."

"Well, thank you for calling…and listening. I really appreciate it."

"Don't thank me. I wanted to."

A warm feeling came over me. I didn't want it to end, but I knew it had to. "I suppose I'll talk to you in a few days when we're back in DC."

"No, I'll check in with you tomorrow. Night, Adam."

Before I could even comprehend what she had said, she hung up. I spent the next day wondering what it might mean that she'd reached out to me like she had. I also watched the clock, waiting for nightfall and hoping that she would phone again.

She rang me that night and then the next two nights. I dutifully updated her on Dad's health, during which she was a great emotional support, but that was only a fraction of the time on the calls. Most of our conversation concerned our lives, our work, and what was going on in the world. We avoided uncomfortable topics from our past and instead stayed in the present, where we could tease each other and laugh.

My last night in Cambridge, it was in the wee hours of the morning when I realized this was most likely the last long talk I'd have with her. We'd both be back in DC the following night. With Juan Carlos around, there was no way she'd be calling me before bed. Seeing the clock, I begrudgingly said, "It's quite late, Nicki. You need to get to bed."

"It's okay. I'm in bed."

An image of Nicki under the covers popped in my mind. "Are you now?"

"Of course. It's after three."

"You're in bed." A wisp of a memory floated through my mind. There was Nicki lying on her mattress, wearing cotton knickers with little flowers. I spoke my thoughts aloud. "Now, that's something I'd like to see…again."

"Uh…it's not very exciting. I'm staying at the Lagos Sheraton. I might as well be in Phoenix."

"What are you wearing?"

"A T-shirt."

I felt David channeling through me. "Anything else?"

"Adam…" she playfully admonished me.

"You can't blame me for trying."

When she was quiet on the line, I seized the moment to finally say what I felt. "Nicki…you must know by now how much you mean to me. I adore you. I always have."

The line remained silent, and I braced for the worst. After a moment, she softly declared, "And you mean…the world to me, Adam, but I don't know if…and then there's…" She sighed. "We should probably have this conversation in person."

"Probably so."

"I want you to know our talks have been the highlight of my trip."

"Mine, too."

Our declarations hung in the air. Eventually, she sighed again. "I should go now. Good night. Have a safe trip back home."

"I'd tell you to have a safe trip, but I think Air Force One is pretty secure."

"That's true. It's the only time I'm not scared at all to be on a plane."

"Well, go get some sleep…in your T-shirt and what little else you're wearing."

"Adam…" She giggled.

"Oh, don't mind me." I snickered. "Good night. We can talk next week."

After placing the phone back on the bedside table, I put my arms underneath my head on the pillow. Staring at the ceiling, I smiled.

I believe I've made some progress.

The next morning, I headed into BBC TV Centre in London for a few quick meetings before my flight that afternoon. As I was walking down the hall to visit one of the higher-ups, I heard a call from behind.

"Oh, Adam!"

I turned to the voice. There was Felicity—statuesque, stunning with her green eyes and fair skin, and always conniving.

"Hello, Felicity," I said.

Her tone lowered as she sauntered over. "Why haven't you called me?"

"Busy. Sorry about that."

"So Mr. White House Correspondent is too busy. Is it the glamour of it all that's kept you away?"

Felicity really could be a pain in the arse, but usually her looks and other talents made up for it. That day, though, I saw nothing redeeming about her. "I've been in Cambridge with my father. Not really the glamorous life."

"Oh, I'm so sorry." Her expression became sympathetic, and she touched my arm. "Do you ever want me to drop by and help?"

"Thank you, but sadly there's not much to do."

"Come, come," she said, waving me toward her office down the hall. "We should talk."

Good God. Whenever a woman said, "We should talk," a bloke was in for it. Yet I couldn't say no. I'd kept her in the dark for weeks now.

"All right," I said. "Though I don't have much time."

She sauntered ahead of me, saying, "We've done amazing things before in a short period of time."

Flashes of late-night sex in a dark closet—or on my desk or in her car—came to mind. We hadn't exactly had a deep relationship since I'd left England, but I followed her along all the same. When we arrived in her exquisitely decorated office, I sat down on her sofa. If only I could have sunk further into the throw pillows to cushion the beating I was sure to get.

After she shut the door and, with a flick of her wrist, closed her blinds, she took her seat opposite me on the sofa. Crossing her long legs, she patted my knee. "There, now. It's been too long."

"Not so long," I said, racking my brain trying to remember the last time we'd shagged. *November?*

"Long enough," she said with a toss of her hair.

"Sorry about that," I mumbled.

"Have you been giving me the silent treatment?" She eyed me like I was a junior government official standing in between her and an interview with the prime minister.

"Of course not." It was the truth. My silence hadn't been intentional, just a byproduct of my lack of interest in her now that Nicki was around.

The corners of her mouth set into a prim line. She must've had more to say on the subject, but she stopped herself. We'd had a long-standing agreement not to delve into each other's private lives so as not to spoil our time together. I prayed she would continue to honor our pact.

Slowly, she conjured up a superficial smile, which was, no doubt, more comfortable for both of us. "So tell me all about Washington with a new president. It must be so exciting."

I scratched my head. "I don't know if I'd call it exciting. It's certainly interesting."

"And are you enjoying being at the White House?"

"It's nice to be in the middle of it all. Getting to know the new administration from the inside. I like that."

"But I heard that you actually know one of Logan's staffers. What's her name? Nicole Johnson? The mousy one."

I blinked once—the only discernible sign that Felicity had hit upon something. "Yes, we were school chums."

"How is it that you were school chums with an American?"

"I told you I spent time in the States when I was a teenager. My father worked there for a bit."

"I know, but I always imagined you at a posh private school, not in class with the *hoi polloi*." She tipped her head, remembering. "You'd mentioned you'd had a girlfriend."

"I dated a few girls."

"One wasn't Nicole Johnson, was it?" Her expression became aghast. "I wouldn't think you'd have been friends with someone like *her*."

Ignoring her actual question, I actually welcomed Felicity's hostility because it was so plainly rooted in her snobbery, which was a continuing row of ours. We'd had plenty of conversations where I had taken her down a notch. Even though Nicki was at the center of this one, there was nothing out of the ordinary about it, so I could speak freely. "What do you mean 'like her'? She's quite clever, you know."

"Oh, I'm sure she's bright in her own way."

"Felicity…really. Nicole Johnson is very well-respected and a close aid of the president of the United States."

She looked down at the lapel of her jacket and smoothed the worsted wool as if she were speaking absentmindedly, which she clearly was not. "I know I'm a bit harsh. She's just so different. I think there's something manly about her, and her accent is just so jarring. What sort of people does she come from?"

"Her father is a barrister, and I believe her mother is a lawyer of some sort as well. There was nothing odd about them at all." I checked my watch, sensing an opportunity. "I really should run."

"No, not yet," she said, resting her hand on my thigh.

"Fel…"

"Just a moment. I have an idea."

"What's that?"

"I'll be in Washington in a few weeks, doing some research on a story."

"Really?"

"I'll be there for the White House Correspondents' Dinner, then." She raised her eyebrows expectantly. "You should take me as your plus-one."

Fuck. She was the last person I wanted to take on a date. "I'm not sure if I'm going."

"Rubbish. Of course you are. Why would you miss it?"

I scowled. I'd already thought of the dinner, and I knew I didn't want to attend. I didn't want to see Nicki on Juan Carlos's arm.

"I may have plans. It's not my sort of thing, really." Just in case Felicity planned on crashing at my place while she was in town, I added, "My cousin David will probably be visiting regardless."

"What does he have to do with this dinner? You go every year." She then tugged at my tie suggestively. "And this year, I'm in town, so you'll take me."

When I shook my head, she switched her tune. Now smoothing my tie, which she'd ruffled, she had an equally soothing voice, "Don't worry. I'll let you and David have your lad time together, and you and I can be friends. Just as you are with all your female friends."

"Goodbye, Felicity," I said, quickly standing up. "We can talk about it later."

"See you soon, Adam," she said with a sly smile. She opened the door with one hand while still lounging on the sofa.

I fled her office, saying under my breath, "Yes, soon."

After that, I was in a terrible mood, yet I had a big meeting. One of my bosses, George Kent, who'd always been helpful to me in my career, called me into his office. I wasn't sure what he wanted, so I started with another friendly thank-you.

"Kent, I want to thank you again for agreeing to let me work the White House post. It's been very rewarding."

Kent was a shrewd, seasoned man who held his cards close to his chest. When he did speak, his words were chosen so carefully, you knew he meant them. And I never knew him to be wrong. He fiddled with his tie and said, "Well, you know I was reluctant. Whilst I admit we miss your supervision of the Washington office, your reporting has been stellar. There's something to your stories—they have a very nice narrative to them."

"Thank you. Thank you very much."

"Your school friend whom you mentioned—Nicole Johnson—are you finding that contact helpful? Surely you've talked." He looked at me accusatorily. "Your reporting has a lot of insight into Logan. I don't see it in other people's stories."

How honest would I be? If I said too much, I could ruin everything. So I downplayed it, hoping that Kent wouldn't catch it. "Of course we have. We're friendly."

Immediately, I knew Kent suspected I wasn't fully disclosing what was going on. He blinked twice before standing and signaling the end of the conversation. I walked with him toward the door, unsure as to what to say. Gesturing the way out, he smiled and said, "Keep it friendly."

I nodded, and we said goodbye. Making my way to my next meeting, I mulled over his words, which could be taken many ways. What exactly had he meant?

The next morning when I was back in DC, I got a call from David as I walked to the office.

"What's up?" I said.

"I'm calling to let you know we have a date on Saturday night."

"Absolutely not. You know I hate it when you do this to me. I'm not interested." Inevitably, I got stuck with the boring and/or less attractive best friend of David's conquest.

"Oh, you will be this time, mate."

"Unlikely."

"We're having dinner with Nicki and Lisa—at Lisa's. I'm cooking."

"What?"

"You heard me."

"How on earth…" David was truly a miracle worker when it came to women.

"I've been working on Dr. Lisa Roberts since that night in the restaurant."

"I didn't think she gave you her number."

"Yeah, I figured it was too complicated to have you get it from Nicki. That would take bloody ages. So I just called her at her work."

I imagined David reaching Lisa at the National Institutes of Health. She'd be cloaked in a white lab coat, studying mutated cells, only to pick up the phone and have a Cockney bastard trying to chat her up. It made me laugh. "How did you break her down?"

"Persistence. We've talked a few times."

"I can't believe it. She seemed unimpressed."

"I finally got her attention last week when I sent her a dozen roses."

"And you asked her for a date in the card?"

"No. I told her I want to play doctors and nurses."

"You're kidding me." I shook my head. *How does he get away with this shit?* "So how did she respond?"

"She rang me up and told me to knock it the fuck off. I apologized profusely and asked if I could make it up to her by cooking her dinner."

"But you can't cook."

"Minor point. Anyhow, she said she'd accept my apology with dinner, but only if Nicki and you were there as well. I've got a suspicion she's been talking to Nicki about you."

"Why do you say that?"

"Because she avoids the subject when either of you come up in conversation."

"Well, I'm more than game, but does Nicki know?"

"Not sure. Ask her yourself. Cheers. I'll see you Saturday afternoon."

The prospect of dinner with Nicki played through my mind—even if it would be slightly bizarre with David and Lisa joining us. Was it a date? What did Nicki think? It was a good thing it was a slow day at the White House press briefing later that morning, because I caught little of what was said. Afterward, I strolled up to the middle of the room, hoping Nicki would meet me. I wanted to see if we would resume where we'd left things on the phone Saturday night.

I was pleased when she walked up and greeted me with a smile. "Morning, Adam."

"Hello. It sounds like you've got your work cut out for you on the health care legislation."

"Yeah…well, any reform we do will be compared to the British system. That's both good and bad, as I understand it."

"Anything free at the point of access has to be good."

"Excellent point. I'll remember that."

"Did I just give you a talking point?"

"Maybe." Her eyes darted around her before she asked in a low voice, "So, dinner with David and Lisa?"

"Yes." I smiled. "It's a bit odd…but I'm looking forward to it."

"I agree." She smiled back and motioned toward the door. "I've got a meeting. I'll see you tomorrow."

"Wait. Please. I've got a question." I couldn't let her go without some insight into why she'd agreed to the date.

"What's that?"

With my cold reporter's stare, I asked, "Are you going to tell Juan Carlos?"

"No." Her smile hardened. "There's nothing to tell. We're having dinner with friends. Have you told Felicity?"

"No, nor do I plan to." *Tell Felicity I was having dinner with Nicki in her home? Fuck no.* After my last conversation with Felicity in London, it would be bloody stupid to even off-handedly mention it to her.

"Because?"

"That could unnecessarily cock up everything."

"It could." She checked her watch and sputtered, "I'm late. We can talk this weekend."

"Yes, we can." I beamed. I loved it when I flustered her.

I let her run out of the room while I looked down at my reporter's notepad to hide my happiness. There were still so many complicating factors for us, and nothing was certain, but I was more confident than ever.

"There's nothing to tell," Nicki had said. As I saw it, there was nothing to tell *yet*.

Chapter Eight

As David knocked on Lisa's door, I looked in the shopping bag. "What did you buy?"

"You'll see." He patted the bag. "I told you, I got it under control."

The door opened, and standing before us was Lisa wearing slippers, tight jeans, and a man's shirt halfway buttoned with a lacy vest peeking out. If her casual attire was a signal that she didn't care about David, he ignored it. His smile grew wider as he focused on the bit of lace over her cleavage.

She noticed where his eyes had settled and smirked. "Evening, you two. Thanks for coming over."

"Thanks for inviting us." I extended my hand to her, but the knowing expression didn't leave her face as she shook it.

"Not a problem." Under her breath, she added, "Happy to be of service. Welcome."

David walked in first. "Lisa, you look as lovely as a flower of the Nile."

"I told you to drop the African crap, okay?" she said.

"Well, that's good, then, because I don't have any lotus flowers." He handed her the elaborate bouquet he'd been hiding behind his back.

"This is very thoughtful. Thanks," she said in a softer voice. She touched one of the exotic branches. "What's this?"

"Pussy willow," he said triumphantly.

"Hmpf." She put a hand on her hip and declared, "I'm sure you asked for it just so you could say the word. Was the florist pretty?"

"Not as pretty as you," he crooned.

She laughed and playfully swatted him with the bouquet. "C'mon. Nicki's in the kitchen." As we followed behind her, she said, "I'll put the *pussy* willow in a vase."

"Yes, *pussy* really should be kept wet," David said.

Lisa peered over her shoulder in feigned dismay. "Oh God. Are you going to be like this all night?"

"I'll be like this as long as it takes, princess."

"I'm not royalty either, okay? This is America."

Tired of listening to David's routine, I interrupted, "Your place is very nice."

"Thanks," she said. "It's not mine, though. I'm just subletting. The owner is a doctor at NIH who's over in Paris at the Pasteur Institute for the next year or so."

David surveyed the large room and the French doors that must've led to a balcony. "It's bloody huge."

Lisa called back, "He's loaded. I lucked out. He picked me because I'm quiet."

"Little does he know…" David sniggered.

Lisa didn't even respond. She just shook her head as she opened up the swinging door to the kitchen. Nicki stood in front of the work surface, slicing tomatoes. Her dark eyes were warm as she smiled at me, and she looked so cozy in a bright blue jumper that I wanted to grab her waist from behind and hug her.

"What a beautiful bouquet," she said, reaching over to the flowers.

"Not as pretty as the ladies tonight," said David. The bastard gave her a peck on the cheek. "How are you, Nicki dear?"

"Great," she said, giving him a big grin. "Thanks for coming."

I frowned at David. How was I supposed to follow that? I tried for the sympathy approach. "Evening, Nicki. You do know you didn't have to cook."

"Oh, we just thought a salad might be nice." She shrugged.

"Just in case dinner was crap?" I asked with a wink.

"Maybe…" She smiled. "No, I'm sure David is a great cook."

David took the bag from me. "Let me show you what's for dinner." He began displaying the contents on the worktop. "I'm making a traditional British meal—bangers and mash and spotted dick."

Oh God. I should've found out what David was up to before we'd come. I looked over at Nicki, who giggled and nodded, confirming that she remembered when Mum had served spotted dick to her long ago. I held up my hands in surrender. "I've had nothing to do with the planning of this meal."

"You're a reporter," she said, pointing to my chest accusatorily. "You know ignorance isn't a very good defense."

Lisa picked up the pack of sausages and the tin of spotted dick. "I detect a theme here."

"That's nice to hear, treacle," David said, putting his arm around her. "I was worried you might not pick up on it."

Rolling her eyes, Lisa snuck out from under his arm and handed him the bag of potatoes. "You should start peeling if we're going to eat before midnight. I'll get the water on."

As the four of us drank wine and shared the cooking chores, we talked mainly of Lisa's work at NIH. She was doing something none of us had any experience in, so it was interesting to listen to her.

David leaned over to her and said in that voice I'd heard him use on women far too many times, "Such a big brain in such a pretty little head. We could have beautiful children."

"Yeah, right," Lisa said, and she quickly changed the subject.

David actually managed to produce a decent meal, except for the pudding. Lisa pushed her plate toward him. "I'm not very hungry anymore. You can have mine."

"You don't like spotted dick from a tin?" David asked.

Nicki took a bite, and she pursed her lips. "Um, Adam, I think I remember your mother's being better."

"My mum's is much better," I said, pushing the pudding around my plate.

I looked across the dinner table to Nicki. She smiled, acknowledging again our time together years ago. I gazed back at her, but it must've been too intense. Her head quickly dropped, and she went back to studying the nasty dessert.

It was only after dinner that the evening took on the air of a date. Prior to that, I had thought Nicki could plausibly argue she didn't have anything to disclose to Juan Carlos. It could be described as a dinner among old friends.

After the plates had been cleared, though, Lisa forced the issue. She needed little pretense to push Nicki and me out of the kitchen and off to a place where we could be alone. "I can't clean with everyone in here. Nicki, you and Adam go out on the balcony. It's a nice night."

Seeming a little unsure how to act on the cue, Nicki nodded. "Yeah. I guess so. Let's get another glass of wine."

The balcony was spacious with a beautiful view of the city. In the distance, the Washington Monument rose through the darkness. I sat down on a chair and placed our wine glasses on the side table, but Nicki remained standing. She leaned her forearms on the rail, and we were both quiet.

When she finally spoke, she didn't turn to me; she simply revealed into the night, "I was sick the morning of that first press briefing, when we first saw each other again."

"You were ill? I'm sorry."

"Not that kind of sick. I was nauseated because I was nervous."

"It was an important day — the start of a new presidency." That seemed like the right thing to say, but I hoped there was more to the story than just her work.

"It wasn't just that, though it certainly was a big day. But I've had big days in the past. I don't mind the spotlight." She turned around and, leaning against the railing, stared at the floor. "It was you. I couldn't believe you were going to be there."

The way she'd said it sounded almost accusatory. How was I to respond? At the time, I couldn't believe I would be there either. It was as if I'd been directed by an internal compass, unconsciously making life-changing decisions. It still felt that way sometimes.

"When did you hear?" I asked.

She raised her head and looked at me as she spoke this time. "Juan Carlos and I had just gotten back from our vacation in Paris when I heard that you'd taken a White House correspondent job. I got nervous immediately. Then, as it sunk in that I'd be seeing you every day, I was…well, Juan Carlos said I'd become 'distracted.' That's what he called it. I blamed it on my job."

"Distracted?" I smiled. "I'd say I've been distracted myself."

"I suppose it's good to know I'm not the only one." She chuckled, but the smile soon left her face. "But that morning was bad."

"You didn't seem nervous at all."

"Oh, of course not. Over the years, I've become pretty good at putting up a front."

"I certainly can't argue with that. I'd say you're an expert."

I'd meant it as a joke or even a compliment, but she didn't seem to find any humor in it. She stiffened and said, "Yeah, well… Anyway, when you came up to me to talk that day, I just couldn't do it. I didn't know why you were there—what you wanted. It was a shock just seeing you, and I needed to focus on work. That's why I walked away."

"I doubt I would've had very many good answers to your questions. It wasn't a rational move for me to have taken the job."

"Right," she said grimly. "They're probably done cleaning. Let's go back inside."

I couldn't let our talk end so poorly. I walked over to the railing next to her and hurriedly declared, "No, Nicki. Let me explain. I *was* happy to see you that day. I'd been curious about you for years. And you looked the same…exactly the same. Just as beautiful as ever, but now you were this brilliant adult woman. After seeing you that morning, I knew I'd done the right thing. It was nice just to be near you again."

As it all burst out of me, her frown morphed into a beaming smile. "I felt the same way."

The time was ripe for a kiss. But just as I was about to lean in to her, she turned away.

"It just made things worse, though," she said.

"Why?"

After a quick breath, she exhaled and looked me squarely in the eye. "Juan Carlos has asked me to marry him."

Marry him?

It felt like I'd been told I was losing a race I didn't even know I was in.

I didn't respond; I couldn't.

Nicki was engaged?

When she saw I wasn't going to talk, she went on. "It was last year. We'd only been together a few months, but he's a stereotypical

Latin romantic. He said he knew from the beginning. Unfortunately, I was the opposite. I'm never sure about things like that. I'm always waiting for the other shoe to drop. I told him I needed time."

"What about the living together? Are you still going to do that?" Could she detect the panic in my voice? They were simple questions, but really I was begging for time.

"That was the compromise I made late last year. I mean…" She glanced wistfully beyond the balcony. "I do love him. He's a wonderful man, and he's been very persistent. Any woman would be crazy not to be with him."

"So why haven't you found a place?" I took a drink, wishing it was single malt whisky instead of wine. I needed something strong to reinforce my weakening heart.

"That's Juan Carlos's question. And he's right to ask it. It's been my fault. I could've picked an apartment—there are many—but I haven't."

"He's going to live there, too. Why didn't he find it?" I *knew* he was a tosspot. "I'd say you have the more important job by far."

"Yeah, well…there may be a little machismo there. I think the bigger issue is that the more I see you at work, the more distracted I've been with him."

She seemed so uncomfortable as she spoke with me, furtively looking off into the darkness or staring at her shoes as she shifted her stance. I wanted to say something to put us both at ease, so I came up with a most convenient lie. "I've had the same experience with Felicity."

She exhaled with exasperation. "I don't know what to do. Even if you're waltzing back into my life just to waltz right back out again, the fact is, I don't feel for Juan Carlos like I should."

"Even if you're waltzing back into my life just to waltz right back out again." That's what she thought I'd done to her in school—I'd come into her life, wrecked it, and run back out. No wonder she was so cautious around me. That I could not tolerate.

"I don't really waltz," I replied.

"I'm sorry. You get what I mean, though, right?"

Then there were her final words: *"I don't feel for Juan Carlos like I should."* I'd thought the same thing about Muff. I cocked my head.

"Sort of. What do you mean 'like you should'? How *should* you feel about Juan Carlos?"

"Well, I've been with people…I've had relationships, but they've never felt like what we had together all those years ago. It could just be because we were so young and it was such an intense, short period of time, and maybe I'm romanticizing it. But I'd like it if some part of that feeling—that intensity—was there in a relationship with someone else."

I knew exactly how she felt. After five years of a relatively happy relationship with Muff, I had broken it off. I couldn't handle the pressure to get married—to have the life that was expected of me. Mum had supported my decision. She'd said if it didn't feel right, then going our separate ways was for the best. Dad, on the other hand, had told me that he was disappointed in me—that I wasn't acting rationally.

I couldn't contest that. It hadn't been rational to break things off with Muff. She was nice, we had mutual friends, the sex had been good, and I'd loved her in a way. Of course, I hadn't felt for her like I had for Nicki, but I didn't expect that.

It was only over time that I'd realized Muff was someone I could live without. We'd never been apart where I couldn't wait to see her again; I had never spent my days or nights wondering what she was doing. Not once. That's what told me I didn't love her like you were supposed to love someone who you might marry.

Whilst our break-up had been privately ugly, as with most upper-class British relationships, its end was publicly civil. I had even attended her wedding to Liam Hendrix. David called him Lord Stick Up His Arse, which he was, in addition to being one of the most boring blokes I'd ever met. They seemed well matched.

My time with Muff had taught me that I needed something more—someone like Nicki. Juan Carlos may have already proposed, but now I finally had my chance again. I had to snatch it while I could. Leaning down to kiss her, I said, "Nicki, you still feel right to me."

"Oh God, no." She spun away, only to turn back to me again. "I'm sorry. I shouldn't…I don't mean…"

"I…uh…" Why was she doing this? I'd thought we were making progress.

"No, I need to finish. Please, I need to tell you more."

Her tone was so business-like, I pulled myself together. "Right. Okay." I took a moment to cross my arms to signal I could be as distant about all of this as she. "It's all right. I'm listening. So you and Juan Carlos—what's your 'status,' so to speak?"

"We're still seeing each other. He's my date for the White House Correspondents' Dinner. What about you and Felicity?"

"The same," I lied.

"I don't want to do anything drastic, but I hate this hellish limbo."

"Why are you in limbo? And why is it hellish?"

"Why?" She practically laughed at me. "Why? Because *you're* here! Because I've got a loving boyfriend I *was* thinking of marrying, and now that you're here I don't know what to think. I've got a job that I love, but if I were acting ethically, I wouldn't be standing here with you right now. I can hardly resign, though, because I've no idea what's going to happen with you. I don't want to throw this all away just to relive some good times for a couple of months."

She was dismayed but still smiling—as if she'd thought about her situation so much it had become funny. She went over to the table and took a drink of wine. Easing herself into a chair, she said, "I could go to Logan tomorrow and say, 'Mr. President, you've known me a long time. You know I wouldn't do this lightly, but I've got a little problem. You're busy fighting terrorism and fixing the American economy, but I need to be reassigned somewhere in the bowels of government so I can hook up with my high school boyfriend, Adam Kincaid of the BBC.'"

"Well now, you wouldn't actually be talking to the president about this, would you?" I took the seat beside her. "You'd talk with Matthew. He's your boss, right? What would he say?"

"Oh yes, I would talk to Logan. I'd tell Matthew, too, but I'd go directly to Logan first. I owe him that. He's like my dad—not to mention friends with him. Logan would ask a lot of questions, and I'm not sure how it would go from there. I'd be a little political liability that needed to be fixed. They'd probably tell me to quit, or they'd reassign me to some crap job. But then, say, six months later, things end between you and me…for whatever reason. I can't go back to my old job—not to mention it would be a while before I get another decent one as a press secretary. I'd have a reputation for sleeping with the press. That would be horrible."

I had to lighten the mood. If she continued to over-think what was going on, I'd never have a chance. "Sleeping with the press — like me? That would definitely be *horrible*."

The charm I'd mustered up worked. She even giggled. "Horrible. It would be *absolutely* horrible." She gave me a playful slap to the head. "You know what I meant."

"I know what you meant." I considered the scene for a moment: me teasing her, her returning the favor, us laughing — the same old connection was there. With all seriousness, I asked, "But what if we lasted more than six months? What if we lasted…years?"

I expected her to weigh the consequences, but she didn't flinch. "It would be worth losing everything…it would be more than worth it."

"It would be. You know, Nicki, I don't have to stay in my job. I don't really even have to bloody work."

She outright rejected the idea I hadn't even yet proposed. "I would never ask you to do that. Besides, your quitting really doesn't fix the appearances issue. I don't want to be a distraction in any way for Logan."

Rubbing my forehead, I pondered the conundrum she'd created in her mind. Certainly, the majority of it was true, but some of it seemed like unnecessary walls she'd built to protect herself. Then I remembered Juan Carlos. *Him. Short-Arse.* Couldn't she just dump him? I sighed. "So what do you want to do?"

"Be your friend. See how that goes." She winced after she said it.

"I can play that game, but…"

"But what?"

"Well, you said yourself we were never just friends."

"Yeah, but you were the one who said that we should try. Shouldn't we see if there's something lasting between us first — before we make a mess of things?"

"I get the logic, but I now see that it's harder than I thought."

"What do you mean?"

"For one thing, I feel like a seventeen-year-old boy again around you."

"Well, I certainly don't feel my age around you. I'm not an anxious person normally. I'm fairly self-confident. I don't wander around in a state of confusion, but now that you're here, it's like I'm a day-dreaming teenager with a hopeless crush on the most popular boy." Arching her eyebrow at me, she said, "And it's really fucking annoying—especially at work."

"It's harder for me."

"How so?"

"Seeing you…every day…looking so lovely, I just want to touch you all the time."

Nicki gave me a half-hearted smile, and I worried that I'd sent the wrong message. Slowly, I moved my hand over her cheekbone. Her skin was as soft as ever, and I ran my thumb lightly over the small wrinkle on her forehead—the one I was sure I'd had a hand in making. I expected her to pull away, but her eyes remained fixed on mine.

"I loved you, Nicki," I said. "And to my eyes, you're still the fairest of them all."

"Adam…"

A sheepish smile overtook me, and I sighed. "But now you're also this fascinating woman. I want to touch you, but I want more. I want to hear your stories. I want to listen to your opinions on things. I want to get to know you again."

She smiled and took my hand in hers. "I loved you, too." Like me, she'd declared her love in past tense; it would be foolish to presume anything different. Yet it was nice just to hear about what once was. Then she added, "I also want to get to know you again."

"Actually, that's not my preference."

"Really?"

Running my hand down her soft skin to her shoulder, I said, "My preference would be to take you to my bed, shut the fucking door, and let no one see us for days. The rest of the world be damned."

"That sounds…fun." She giggled for a second, but then that damn seriousness took over again. "But the world is still out there, Adam. We can't do that."

Just then, Lisa called from inside, "Nicki? Adam? We're gonna watch a movie. Do you want to come inside?"

"I think we should go in," Nicki said. "Is that okay?"

It really wasn't okay. Yet I felt like I'd made some headway with her, so I said, "That's fine. Though I hope she didn't let David choose the film. He has terrible taste."

His pick of films was always designed to get a woman away from the television and into another room. That proved to be the case again when Lisa objected to tonight's choice.

David said, "We don't have to pay attention, love."

"Ha," she retorted with an annoyed look.

The room was set up with a couple of sofas and chairs. Lisa and David sat on one sofa, respectably apart from one another. Nicki and I did the same, but as the lousy film started, she settled in. She kicked off her shoes, curled up on the sofa, and sank down deep into the cushions. I wanted to maneuver my way closer to her, but I thought it would be too much.

After only a few minutes, David's maneuvering had worked once again. Lisa deemed the movie "unwatchable." I could hear him try to get an invitation to her bedroom, but she only allowed the balcony. I caught Nicki watching them, too.

With David gone, I thought I might offer to switch channels, but Nicki gave me a little smile and sank further into the sofa. After a short time, I realized she'd fallen asleep. I smiled. *That's right. I remember now.* Nicki used to always fall asleep during films.

She looked peaceful, if uncomfortable with her head flopped to the side. I had an idea. First changing the channels to find something better, I settled on the replay of Tottenham versus bloody Chelsea. Then I situated myself comfortably into the corner of the sofa before gently moving Nicki's head so it rested on my shoulder. When Nicki started to move on her own, I froze. *Shit. I woke her up.*

But her eyes didn't open; instead, she surprised me and nestled her head onto my chest and clutched onto my sleeve. Then she sighed. I smiled. Feeling her against me made me want to sigh, too.

Only nominally paying attention to the football match, I thought back to when we were young and found ourselves alone. We'd quietly talk and laugh and fuck—a lot. We'd also sleep, though. Living in the memories, I wrapped my arm around her, and Nicki responded by curling her body against mine. I studied her to make sure I hadn't woken her up, but she was still asleep.

She was so beautiful in my arms. She felt light and warm, and her mouth looked ready to be kissed. I wanted to do it, but I knew she should be awake for something like that. Then, just as I was raising my eyes to the television, I heard her say my name.

My eyes went back to her. She still appeared to sleep. Then she whispered my name again. I watched her eyes, but she didn't stir. I quietly laughed to myself. *I forgot. Nicki talks in her sleep.*

I used to love listening to her talk. I'd stay awake sometimes just so I could hear her. Most often she mumbled random things, or she'd be in a dream with her mum and let out a whining, "Mom, please!" She'd also say her sister's name, which was heartbreaking to hear. I'd hug her tightly when I heard that. At times she'd say my name, and at others she'd say she loved me. Those were the best times.

She was quiet for a minute until she whispered, "I missed you."

She seemed sad, yet I considered her words and decided it didn't sound like I was headed for rejection. She then said something that gave me hope: "Please don't go."

What was she dreaming? Not caring if I woke her up, I answered aloud, "I won't go anywhere without you, Nicki."

Her nose crinkled as if I'd interrupted a private conversation, but soon her expression softened when she snuggled her head against me. She slept again, and I went back to watching the football match. Occasionally, I'd touch her hair, reminding myself she was really there.

I must've sat for an hour like that until she started to stir. After flinching a few times at the light and the sound of the TV, her eyes blinked open. I smiled down at her. "Did you have a nice nap?"

My voice put her whole body on red alert. She jerked up and out of my arms. Looking around for her bearings, she apologized. "I can't believe I did that. I'm sorry."

"Don't worry about it. You were tired."

"No, really. I shouldn't have." She stopped speaking and stared at a wet spot on the throw pillow. "Oh God. I drooled."

"Don't worry about it."

"I'm so embarrassed. I—"

"Nicki, it's okay." I touched her hair and stated the obvious. "It's just me."

The obvious seemed to be less so for Nicki. She gazed at me as though comprehending something for the first time—like something had just clicked. Then faster than I myself could understand, her mouth was on mine.

It began as a brief kiss, followed by a hesitation. Just when I thought she would pull away, in seemingly one motion she was on her knees and straddling me, her hands cupping my cheeks. Her touch made me want to smile, but as my mouth opened a bit, I felt her tongue on my lips. My whole body felt the invitation.

So, for the first time — once again — we really kissed. I met her tongue with mine as my hands found her back and pulled her closer to me. For some reason, I had to tell myself, *It's Nicki.*

For the next few minutes, hands were in hair, bodies were pressing together, and our mouths couldn't get enough. A faint voice in the back of my mind said maybe I should pull away so we could acknowledge what was happening between us. But my body quickly dispelled that notion; it just wanted more Nicki, and she was all over me. She may have been petite and soft, but her mouth and hands were aggressive and demanding. The only thought that occurred to me was to do exactly what I wanted to do: take her to her bedroom, slam the door, and damn the world.

Of course, my dick got me in trouble. Acting on instinct, I grabbed her bum and pulled her toward me. She eagerly pressed herself against my erection, but when I rubbed it against her, she froze. Then she broke the kiss.

I cringed, not wanting it to end. I feared she would pull away, but she didn't. Placing her forehead on mine, she sounded a bit out of breath. "I…I'm sorry, Adam. I shouldn't have let this happen. It's not right."

That hurt — it had felt very right to me. Had she not been there with me? "Not right? Are you sure?"

"No…I'm not sure about anything." She did pull back then and looked at me squarely. "Wait. That's not true. I'm sure about one thing."

I must've looked like a sad, petulant child. I sourly asked, "And what's that?"

"That I want to spend more time with you. *That* I know for sure."

I remembered what she'd said in her sleep…what we'd talked about outside. She'd come a long way in one night. There wasn't any reason to push it.

"Well, get some control, woman," I said, deciding to joke. "Get off me before you kiss me again."

She bit her lip but soon became radiant. Giggling, she tousled my hair one more time before she sat next to me. It wasn't close enough for my liking, but it would most definitely piss off Juan Carlos. I liked that idea.

We talked football as we watched the end of the match. She informed me she'd dated some bloke at university who'd spent a term in London and become a Chelsea fan. I sneered, "I hate him."

"Why?"

"Because he dated you when I couldn't and he's a fan of the most God-awful annoying team in the Premier League."

"Juan Carlos likes soccer, too. I can't remember who he likes in the UK. I get the names confused. Maybe Arsenal?"

"Even worse! Why did you tell me that? Now I really hate the short-arse!"

"Short? Come on. Not every guy towers over the world like you."

"Why are we talking about him?"

"I don't know."

"Let's change the subject."

"Yes, let's." She poked my arm. "You know, I still have that Liverpool scarf you gave me."

"You do? I'd forgotten about that." What a lie. Of course I remembered, and learning that she'd kept such a silly gift pleased me to no end.

David and Lisa soon walked back in the room. When David saw the TV, he said, "Football? Why didn't you tell me?"

"I should've. Nicki's a Liverpool fan."

Nicki elbowed me in the ribs, and as David praised her, he eyed both of us, looking for signs of what had happened while they were out. I glanced at Lisa, who shifted awkwardly as she patted her hair. It appeared David might've convinced Dr. Roberts to play doctor with him.

Everyone agreed that it was time to call it a night. David gave me a look indicating he wanted a minute alone with Lisa, so I let him walk into the foyer with her while I turned to Nicki. I thought I might swoop in for a peck, but she pointed in our friends' direction and whispered, "I want to listen."

From the foyer, we could hear Lisa say, "We have absolutely nothing in common."

"After that kiss, I'm pretty sure we'll have the most important thing in common," David said.

"Whatever. You can't base a relationship on that."

David was relentless. "Are you kidding, princess? It's the key to any successful relationship."

"Well, he's right," I said to Nicki.

"I suppose so." She giggled softly.

"I should leave before you attack me again." I hoped to get a rise out of her.

"I think I can control myself." Then her dark eyes twinkled. She leaned in and kissed my cheek. "Now get outta here."

As David and I walked back to my car, he said cockily, "Well, cuz, I'd say we made some progress."

Still high from being with Nicki, I had a spring in my step, and I slapped him on the back. "Indeed."

Chapter Nine

Over the following few weeks in the White House briefing room, Nicki was a little cooler to me, but it didn't feel cold. I'd stare at her, and she'd glance over at me and twitch her mouth. We both knew she wanted to smile.

One Friday, I cornered her. "Good morning, Nicki."

"Good morning," she said cheerily.

"So your big date is tomorrow?"

"You mean the Correspondents' Dinner?"

"Yes. Are you still going with Juan Carlos?" I hated even saying the guy's name.

She frowned, looking annoyed. "Of course. I told you I was."

"What makes him so special that he has to have two names?"

"What about Felicity? What kind of name is that anyway? It's not a name. Happiness is a state of being. Are *you* still taking her to the dinner?"

So my little Nicki was jealous. Very jealous. That was a good sign. It made the stupid date with Felicity worthwhile.

"Yes," I said, trying not to laugh. "I'll see you tomorrow."

The next night, Felicity was a pain in the arse from the moment I met her before the dinner. Her hotel lobby was bustling with black ties, gowns, and plenty of American tourists, so at least it was so busy she didn't cause a scene.

She walked out of the lift, pulling at the evening gloves extending high on her arms. She practically spat at me, "Why did you make me come down here? Why didn't you meet me in my room?"

"I told you I didn't want to be late."

"You know, you could be timely and a decent date by picking me up properly." She looked around the busy lobby. "Having me meet you down here is so…platonic." Taking a deep breath, she thrust out her already-protruding tits. "Well, if you're lucky, you might be able to see my room later on."

Though I could've easily made excuses otherwise, I'd decided to escort Felicity to the White House Correspondents' Dinner after all to keep the peace between us at work. I also sure as hell wasn't going to that damn dinner alone if Nicki would be there with Short-Arse. But the possibility of seeing the inside of Felicity's hotel room wasn't part of the equation for me at all. I stole a glance at her tits and gave her a false apology. "Sorry, Felicity. I'm all out of luck."

"What is going on with you?" she asked, throwing a hand on her hip.

"Felicity…we've been through this before." I was losing my patience.

"Yes, we have." She took a step closer to me and became stern. "And you also still occasionally end up in my bed, or at least you used to."

There was no getting out of it. I was being a jerk. If Nicki weren't in the picture, things would have been different. I'd have kept in better touch with Felicity, I'd have slept with her when in London, and I would've considered her a real date for this damn dinner. I may not have wanted to be with her, but she did deserve an apology and a bit of explanation. "I'm sorry. I don't think it's wise anymore."

"Are you seeing someone else?"

"No."

"Liar."

The woman had become venomous and far too perceptive, so I tried to ratchet the situation down. "You're my colleague. Meeting you in the lobby of your hotel is appropriate." I pointed to the hotel entrance. "And the damn dinner is across the road."

"Then let's go so I can get a drink," she huffed. "I don't know what's going on with you, Kincaid, but I will find out."

Either Nicki was hiding from me or she arrived late. I had looked for her throughout the cocktail hour and couldn't find her until I spotted Juan Carlos guiding her to their seats just as dinner started. My table was painfully dull, except for listening to Felicity make her moves on a Greek shipping tycoon, Gus Papadopoulos. He had to be at least twenty years her senior, but Felicity didn't seem to mind. By dessert, I was pretty confident she had her hand on his thigh.

President Logan was a hit that evening, so after the dinner Nicki was happily shaking hands and passing out hugs. It took a bit before she saw me staring at her. She then patted the arm of a congress-woman and made her way toward me.

She was stunning in an elegant silver gown. She looked svelte and confident and very, very sexy. I greeted her. "Good evening. You look ravishing."

Her hand went to the silky material that respectably covered yet clung to her breasts. All her confidence was gone, and she was awkward Nicki again. "Thanks." She nodded. "You look dashing…as ever."

"Thanks. Think you can control yourself this time?"

"You're such fucking arse," she said and swatted me.

I held my hands up to protect myself. "I always loved it when you cursed."

"What's this?" I heard Felicity's most posh voice say. "Attacking the press?"

"Hello, Felicity." She'd placed her hand on my shoulder like somehow she had a claim to me. I couldn't very well shrug her off, though, so I hardened my voice for what was sure to be a difficult conversation. "This is Nicole Johnson." I then looked at Nicki, no doubt like a guilty schoolboy. "Nicole, this is Felicity Chambers." I felt Felicity's glare at my lack of propriety. "Lady Felicity Chambers, I should say."

"I normally don't use the title." She smiled with perfect insincerity.

Nicki should've been a politician herself, she was so smooth as she extended her hand. "It's nice to meet you. I've seen some of your work on TV."

"Yes. As I've seen you," said Felicity, shaking her hand. "Of course, Adam has mentioned you before."

"We've known each other for a while," Nicki said, dryly.

"So he's said." Felicity finally took her hands off me, thank God, but then she only made matters worse when she said, "He told me of your upbringing. I think it's such an endearing story about how you came from nothing, and now look at you. You're at the height of government. Truly amazing."

"Fel, I never said that." I was sharp in my retort. I couldn't have Nicki thinking I ever considered her in such a way. "Nicki's family is highly educated and somewhat well-to-do."

"Oh, you know what I mean," Felicity said.

"I suppose our notions of class are different in the US," Nicki said, clearly miffed. "We're a meritocracy and don't look down on the middle class."

"Oh, I'm not looking down on you. I think it's a rather heartwarming story."

"I actually think it's pretty boring." Nicki looked away as if she really did find the conversation dull. "But maybe it's similar to how Americans admire British royalty though we would never want any ourselves."

"Wouldn't you now? I think Americans are obsessed with the monarchy."

"Obsessed? Only in a celebrity-gossip way." She focused her attention on Felicity and slayed her with logic. "You have to admit picking the firstborn kid of the firstborn kid of the firstborn kid of an inbred family is a lousy way to choose a head of state."

"Now, Nicole," Felicity said. "You're smart enough to know we have a constitutional monarchy."

Nicki glared at me for a moment before turning back to Felicity. "Actually, I'm even smart enough to know that despite your constitutional monarchy, the Queen is still the head of state."

"I suppose you are trained in protocol in your position," said Felicity.

That was it. I could allow Felicity to make a fool of herself socially; I was certain Nicki found it mildly amusing. But belittling Nicki for her work in the Logan administration—that was a bridge too far. I clapped my hands. "Felicity, pardon me. I need to speak to Nicole alone for a moment about a story I'm working on."

"But of course." She smiled at Nicki. "It was a pleasure to meet you."

"And you," said Nicki.

I waited until Felicity sauntered over to Gus the Greek before speaking, but Nicki spoke first. "That was interesting."

"I'm so sorry," I said.

"Did you think you had a cat fight on your hands?"

"More like the start of an international incident." I wiped my brow in relief. "She must feel incredibly threatened by you to speak that way."

"And she's otherwise charming?"

"Maybe not charming." I snickered because Nicki had always been onto me about women. "But she's a smart reporter. She knows you don't piss off someone who has the ear of the president of the United States."

"You have horrible taste in women, you know. Always have."

The indignant pout on her face was adorable. If the entire Washington establishment wasn't around us, I would've stolen a kiss. Instead, I could only spar with her. "Only when I'm biding my time, waiting for you to come around."

"Clearly, I was an anomaly."

"In the best way."

"Her breasts are certainly on display for you and everyone else in the room."

I whispered, "Are you jealous, Nicki Johnson?"

"No!" She looked annoyed. "Maybe."

"Good. Now you know how I feel about fucking Juan Carlos." It didn't sound quite as playful as I'd intended it.

"Remember I spent a good part of my junior year of high school jealous as hell because you were with Meredith Daniels."

"Was that her name? I'd forgotten."

It had been a stupid joke on my part. Nicki looked like she was going to blow a gasket, her eyes roaming the room as if she wanted to get away from me. "If we weren't under the surveillance of stupid Dan Roark right now, I'd punch you in the arm for that."

"Sorry. I'd deserve it if you did." I leaned down as near to her as I could without raising any eyebrows. It was so close, but so far away. God, how I wanted to kiss her neck. "You know, you're the one I've remembered."

She didn't reply, only breathed a little roughly.

After a moment, I asked, "Are you going home with him?"

"Juan Carlos?"

"*Si, Juan Carlos,*" I said, imitating the bastard. "Who else?"

"There's no one else. You know that."

"So then, Juan Carlos, or JC. Are you taking him home?" I gave her a fierce stare whilst my wobbly insides prayed she would answer no.

"He usually stays with me, but I don't know. He's not too happy with me right now. We could very well end up in another fight." It was her turn to stare me down. "Are you going home with her?"

I debated what to say. Maintaining the air that Felicity and I were together was going to require me to lie to Nicki, which I really didn't want to do. Yet what if Nicki did end up in bed with Short-Arse whilst I was alone in mine? I decided to save a little face and say a half-truth. "She usually stays with me. After her little run-in with you, I'd say we're guaranteed to have a fight."

"Good." She threw her hand over her mouth like she'd let the cat out of the bag, but I could still see her smile.

I looked Nicki up and down. She was so gorgeous in that dress. I wanted to offer my arm, take her out for drinks at the Hay-Adams, talk to her until they kicked us out of the bar, and then take her back to my place and slam the door shut.

"I feel the same way," I said happily, and she walked away.

An hour later, my patience had abandoned me. I'd dutifully chitchatted and made merry with colleagues and foes alike, just as the evening had called for. I had also kept tabs on Nicki as she did the same. Occasionally, she'd speak to old JC, who was cordial but not affectionate toward her. She seemed equally chilly to him. It was a relationship demise I enjoyed watching, though in the end I just wanted the night over.

When Gus finally left Felicity's side to speak to the head of the US Chamber of Commerce, I went over to her and said, "I'm heading out."

"You are?" she asked with some indignation.

"Of course. I believe you're otherwise occupied." I nodded to Gus, who was still with the Chamber guy but also staring at Felicity and me.

"So you care not if I spend my evening with Gus Papadopolous?"

"You two seem to be enjoying yourselves." I could just hear what David would say at that moment: *"Let's hope he doesn't have a heart attack when he bangs you tonight."*

Luckily, David wasn't around, and I was too polite, so Felicity had her moment to shine and make me feel like shit.

"He's fascinating. We get on quite well," she said, arching her neck defiantly. She then searched the room, and at that moment, Nicki and JC were together talking with two major Democratic Party donors. Felicity smiled. "Are you leaving because your little friend is off with her Latin lover? Juan Carlos Jimenez is quite a catch, you know."

"So I hear." I shook my head with a bitter taste in my mouth. "What happened to your manners, not to mention your professionalism, with Nicole?"

"I was perfectly polite and professional toward her."

"Not if you ever want to cover the White House."

"Now, why would I need to do that when the BBC has you and your 'special relationship' with her? Maybe you've never got over your schoolboy crush."

Damn women's intuition. "Good night, Fel," I said with a roll of my eyes before walking away. My only consolation was that she'd soon be back in London. The less time she spent around Nicki the better.

Hoping to clear my head, I took a roundabout way home from the White House Correspondents' Dinner. Driving along the bends of Rock Creek Parkway with music blaring in the background was always a good way for me to work through something. In this case, the something was how to get closer to Nicki.

The night we'd kissed, she'd said she wanted to spend more time with me, yet neither of us had followed up. I suppose I understood her reservations, but what was holding me back? I had always regretted moving so slowly and acting so foolishly with Nicki at school. What was my excuse for not pursuing her now?

Since January, I'd let her take the lead; I didn't want to push her, given all the years and other issues standing between us. There was also the fact that I didn't really know her anymore. I only knew how I used to feel about her. That had been enough to take a job I didn't want, but I couldn't let the past dictate every step thereafter.

What I'd learned of Nicki since January taught me that I did still want her by my side. And now that we'd at least cleared some of the air between us, I was aware that she thought a future was possible. She just wasn't sure if I'd stick around for her.

Well, I was certain I would. I wondered if I should take more control of the situation. Perhaps it was time to step things up.

Chapter Ten

When we left for Ohio on Wednesday morning, it was a beautiful spring day, but we were heading into the rainy American heartland. Owing his election to the voters in many of the electorally important Rustbelt states, President Logan planned his first American tour through Ohio, Michigan, Wisconsin, and Pennsylvania.

The weather was horrible, which threw our entire schedule up in the air. That first day, Nicki was already so harried from the turmoil that I didn't bother her. Occasionally, she'd smile pleadingly at me like she needed a break, but she couldn't get one. Midway through Thursday afternoon, though, I knew the president was in a meeting with the governor of Michigan, so I hoped she had a free moment. I texted her as she talked with another staffer.

You look tired. Can you get away at all?

I watched as she noticed my text and typed back.

Not today. Probably not tomorrow. I'll call you tonight.

I cocked my head at that. I couldn't see her, but I'd get to talk to her. We hadn't had a real conversation in a while—not since the dinner with David and Lisa.

I answered at once.

Great.

It was after nine that night when I checked my phone for the tenth time. Still no call from Nicki. Stretching out on my bed, I'd begun to search the movies on pay-per-view when the hotel phone rang next to me. It was a surprise; those phones never rang anymore unless there was a problem.

I answered hesitantly, "Hello."

"Hi, Adam. It's Nicki."

"Well, hello. Why are you calling me on the hotel phone?"

"For kicks. Did I surprise you?"

"A little bit." I thought about it a moment. "Actually, it reminds me that we're in the same building."

"We are."

"Which floor are you on?"

"The twenty-second. And you?"

"I'm on the twentieth. We're neighbors."

"Not really. My neighbors are Secret Service snipers on either side of me."

"Snipers? I never really thought about the president traveling with snipers."

"Well, he does — in case they need to easily kill someone trying to kill him. You're not supposed to see them, though."

"That is the job of a sniper. So should I be looking at the rooftops and belfries to find them?"

"Yeah, during the day when the president is outside, that's a good place to start. Right now, you could just wander along the twenty-second floor. Both of those guys have the TV blaring in their rooms. They'd be easy to locate."

"And so I could figure out that your room is the quiet one in between theirs?"

"Yeah…"

"I'm coming up, then."

"What?"

"Scared you, didn't I?" I laughed.

"Maybe."

"You have to admit it's a bit frustrating we're finally talking and even in the same building, but we're not in the same room."

"Yeah, but…" Nicki giggled. "I don't think being in a hotel room alone together is a good idea."

"Now, why would that be? We would just talk…well, I would just talk. Considering your behavior the other night, I'd have to fend you off."

"You're never going to let me live that down, are you?"

"No, I won't." I flipped the remote control in my hand as I brought up a nagging curiosity. "So you never told me what happened with old Juan Carlos."

"We're taking a little break. What about Felicity? I mean Lady Felicity."

A little break! I grinned and sat up in bed. A break usually ended with a break-up. *Brilliant!* I needed to answer her question about Felicity, though, and decided to sidestep the issue—for different reasons now entirely. It would be a disaster if Nicki knew Fel was on to something. "Now, be nice…" I said playfully.

"You've got to be kidding me after the crap she said to me."

"You don't need to be angry with her. I'm angry enough for both of us, and I gave her a right bollocking." A worthy lie, given I didn't want Nicki antagonizing her.

"So did you kiss and make up?" she asked pointedly.

"Not really." I had to clear my throat to hide my laughter. "Do you actually want to talk about this?"

"Not really."

"Seriously, Nicki, I want to see you again. When can we spend some time together? Next weekend?"

"Um, I'd like that, but my dad visits next weekend."

"That's nice." I had never met her father when I'd lived in Bellaire, given that he lived in Chicago and had been a bit removed from her life.

"Yeah, he's coming for a visit. He arrives on Friday morning and leaves Sunday afternoon."

Before I could catch myself, I blurted out what was at the top of my mind. "Will you two be going out with Juan Carlos?" I pinched the bridge of my nose, wincing at my own words. *Fuck! Why did I ask that? I sound like a jealous bastard.*

"No." Her voice was low and serious. "Given what's going on with Juan Carlos and me right now, I don't think it's appropriate to go out with my dad together. There'd just be too much expectation around it."

"Ah. Okay," I said as my grin returned. It appeared that old JC was almost out of the picture. Things were looking up.

By the end of the hotel room call, Nicki had agreed to come to see David and me play football, even bringing Lisa along. Over the week that followed, Nicki and I would exchange a few texts or have a short call, but I didn't push her. Since I already had a date on the books and we were both busy, I didn't see a reason to. That changed on the following Friday.

At the daily press briefing that morning in the White House, I noticed a gray-haired, stern-looking man off to one side of the room. I didn't recognize him, and at first thought he was a new member of the press—maybe an older reporter filling in for someone. When I asked Matthew my question that day, I noticed the older gentleman give me a curious look.

It was only after the briefing when I saw Nicki introducing him to everyone that I realized who he was; they shared a resemblance. I knew what to do. If there was ever a sign I could give her that I was serious, reaching out to her father had to be near the top.

When I started walking toward the two of them, she gave me a pensive glance. Seconds later, she hurriedly ushered her father out of the room. I frowned. *What happened there?*

I needed to do some follow-up work at the White House that morning, so I put it out of my mind as I interviewed one of President Logan's advisors. Then, my cameraman shot the introductory footage for my report from the White House lawn. When I finished the shoot, I spotted Nicki walking with her father. No longer caring what her odd look toward me might've meant, I strode toward them.

Nicki didn't see me come from behind, so she startled when I greeted her. "Good morning, Nicki."

The two turned around to face me. Her father's brow furrowed, and she fumbled. "Oh…uh. Morning, Adam."

Setting her mouth in a determined smile, she introduced us. "Adam, this is my father, Kevin Johnson. Dad, this is Adam Kincaid… with the BBC."

At once, I extended my hand to him. "It's a pleasure to meet you, sir." I would've called the man "sir" even if he weren't Nicki's father. He was older, serious, and dressed so conservatively that he deserved nothing less.

Shaking my hand, he composed his features, but the suspicion didn't entirely leave his face as he obviously mulled something over. "Good morning, Adam. Your name. It sounds familiar. Why is that?"

I glanced at Nicki, who seemed more nervous and grieved than I'd ever seen her. I was going to comment on my being on TV, but her expression hardened, and she answered him first. "Dad, Adam lived in Bellaire for a while when I was in high school."

For a brief moment, the man withdrew his cold stare from me. He eyed Nicki and then turned back to me, the bastard who'd broken his little girl's heart. There was no way to change the facts, but I told him something he most likely didn't know. "Meeting Nicki was the best part of my year in the States."

Nicki pursed her lips and faked a glance at her watch. "Yeah, that was a fun year. Dad, we need to get going if you're going to get to your lunch in Alexandria."

He nodded quietly at me. "Nice to meet you, Adam." His eyes darted over to Nicki as he added, "After all these years."

"Yes, you too, sir. Enjoy your holiday. Bye, Nicki."

"So long," she said as she maneuvered her father in the opposite direction.

Knowing that Nicki was spending the weekend with her dad, I didn't contact her on Saturday. The encounter with her father had been strained enough. I didn't want to make things worse for her.

When I'd told David about Nicki bringing Lisa along on Sunday, he was pleased. "Just the extra nudge I need for that one. She's been toying with me, but I like it."

"I think this is the first time you've ever needed any help."

"True, but I'm confident. Besides, I like the anticipation. I think she does, too. We can play her little game for as long as she feels like it."

"That might be a long time."

"Pfft. Don't care. It's fun—like I'm fifteen again. I kiss her. She turns the other cheek. I cop a little feel. She swipes my hand away. Then she's a tease and accidentally rubs against me."

"Sounds like a fun game."

"It is. And it's only a matter of time, cuz. Just a matter of time…"

But as our match on Sunday neared the end, I began to wonder if Nicki and Lisa would show up. Dribbling down the pitch, I tried to concentrate on the ball rather than on Nicki as I passed it toward David. We were playing a bunch of complacent French and lazy Americans, who were no match for the disciplined, fierce style of play of the Germans, Brazilians, and David on our makeshift team. David seized my pass and connected with his left, kicking the ball straight past the blond head of the French goalie.

In true dramatic David fashion, he fell on his knees and stripped off his shirt. Then he jumped up, hugging anyone and everyone he could. I ran over and gave him a high-five followed by a slap on his back. With so little time left on the clock, we quickly got back to work and finished off the match in a few minutes.

As we walked back to the sidelines, I pulled the sweaty shirt off my back before I noticed Nicki and Lisa standing not far from where we'd dumped our gear. They appeared to be joking around—probably taking the piss out of us. David saw them, too, and called out, "Did you see my goal, princess?"

"I did," Lisa said flatly.

Then I saw what David meant by Lisa being a tease despite her words. When he stood before her, she slowly ran a finger down his chest. "You need a shower."

"Only if you'll join me," he said as he grabbed her for a celebratory dance.

"Gross! Don't touch me." She swatted him back. "You stink."

"You're a doctor. You're not supposed to mind the human body."

"I don't, but I prefer them clean."

I turned to Nicki, who was laughing at her friend. While David and Lisa continued to spar, I said, "Thanks for coming out here."

"Thanks for the invitation."

We made small talk about the match and the day. I didn't bring up her dad. In fact, I was trying to work out where Nicki was look-ing—or, more notably, where she wasn't. She was a good deal shorter than me, even more so when she wasn't wearing heels, so she now stood eye level with my chest but seemed to focus either over my head or into the distance. Then I understood.

"I hate to be presumptuous like my incorrigible cousin, but I do get the feeling you're averting your eyes."

She acted annoyed, but a smile betrayed her. "No. Why would you say that?"

"So it's not because I'm standing here half-naked?"

"Can you not say that word?" She smirked and looked away.

"Oh, forgive me. I know how difficult this must be for you."

"Will you please just put on a shirt?"

"Sure. Give me a second." I grabbed a towel out of my bag to dry myself off. As I rubbed away the sweat, I nodded across the pitch and said, "You can look over there if this gets to be too much."

"Whatever."

I pulled on a clean shirt, then turned to her. She was dressed in shorts, trainers, and a University of Chicago sweatshirt and had her hair pulled back in an elastic band. I tousled her ponytail. "When your hair is tied up like this, you look seventeen again."

She grinned. "I don't think so."

"You're prettier now, though."

Her mouth twitched like she was debating whether to say some-thing. Tentatively touching her hair, she said, "Well, you don't look seventeen anymore either."

"Are you saying I look old?"

"No." She twitched her mouth again. "You've just…changed since then."

"Ah! Not how you remember me? Not a skinny lad anymore?" My healthy male ego thoroughly enjoyed the fact that Nicki had spent some time evaluating my body. "And you like that, do you now?"

Nicki shifted her weight and pretended to whistle. "Doo-dee-doo. I'm not answering that."

"I'm sorry. It was cruel of me to bring it up, given your inability to keep your hands to yourself."

"That joke only has so much life in it," she said, shaking her head.

"Not if you pounce on me again."

"Believe me, I can control myself."

I winked at her. "It's good that one of us can."

After David and I got our gear together, we all followed our teammates in our respective cars up to a dive Mexican joint on the outskirts of Adams-Morgan. In his irrational exuberance, David invited the other team, too, who happily joined us. We were a giant, loud table, which grew as the other players' girlfriends and friends arrived. The scene seemed to put Nicki at ease. The two of us were out in public together, but it was with a big, boisterous group. No one could tell where she fit in the picture.

On the other hand, I was certain both Nicki and I were aware of what was going on between us. We mainly kept our conversation to ourselves, only joining in the laughter occasionally. When David began to teach everyone how to do tequila shots, I cheered him on, but he soon crashed and burned. He tried to get Lisa to let him do a body shot on her, to which she reacted with an insulted sneer. Dr. Roberts wasn't about to be one of his playthings.

Even he must've feared that he'd crossed a line, because he immediately went from provocative flirt to ardent pursuer. I watched him whisper God knows what sort of smarmy bullshit in her ear. Whatever he said didn't work, however; she appeared resolutely unimpressed.

Nicki laughed. "David needs to go back to spending time with Lisa alone. He might've done some permanent damage trying to show her off."

"I'm sure she'll forgive him." I arched an eyebrow. "Maybe we could do a body shot?"

"Ha!"

"Well, say we were at a beach in Mexico and you were in a bikini..."

Nicki took a sip of her margarita and said, "I don't wear bikinis, for starters."

"Why ever not?" I gave her an admiring look. "You've got a great body."

The line between her eyes deepened as she gazed at me. Then she glanced down and gave the signal that didn't need any words. Crossing her arms over her stomach, she mumbled, "My scars."

I wanted to kill myself right then and there. Of course I remembered her scars from the accident. I wouldn't forget that about her. She'd been too embarrassed by them to wear a bikini back then as well. *She must think I'm a total shit. Fuck! I'm such an arsehole!*

"Nicki, I'm so sorry. I'm such a bloody idiot. I swear I haven't forgotten. It just came out because you're so pretty and—"

"Don't worry about it. I wouldn't expect you to remember." She shrugged. "It's not a big deal."

Not expect me to remember? How could she think that? "How could I forget? I didn't, I promise. I—"

"Please, let's just drop it. It really doesn't matter."

I couldn't just drop it, though. Putting my arm around her shoulders, I pulled her to me and kissed the top of her head. Then, murmuring into her hair, I reminded her, "I told you many times I didn't care about a few silly scars. I still don't."

For a moment, I worried I would be rebuffed as badly as David had been, but Nicki reacted just the opposite of Lisa. She nuzzled into my chest. "I know," I could faintly hear her say.

In reality, we stayed like that for maybe thirty seconds, yet to me it felt wonderfully long. And a memory came back that I hadn't thought of in at least a decade. It was the moment I'd realized Nicki would no longer be mine.

"Why are you still wearing this?" I asked, tugging on her T-shirt as we stood before the Gulf of Mexico. The warm Gulf water was too hot for my English and Scottish blood.

Nicki touched her shirt hem like it wasn't long enough. "I don't have a one-piece. My scars look pretty bad in a swimsuit."

She could be ridiculously self-conscious sometimes, so I frowned and pulled the shirt over her head. She covered her torso with her arms and said, "See? I told you."

When she'd said, "See," I did as I was told and gave her an objective look, and all I saw was the wonderful girl I was losing. My throat tightened, knowing this would be the last time we'd ever be at a beach together. I felt the need to give her some advice.

"Any tosser who can't see past a few silly marks isn't worth your time. I hope you know that."

Certain I was on the brink of tears, I closed my eyes and dove into the safety of the waves.

But now, here she was, back in my arms, and I wasn't going to let go. The embrace was long enough that I saw both David and Lisa give us an enquiring eye. Nicki didn't seem to notice, though. She still looked down as she pulled away, then straightened up and gave me an appreciative smile. "Thanks."

We talked more, and eventually I found the right time to ask, "You don't have to tell me if you don't want to, but what was that with your father on Friday? It seemed like an odd conversation."

"It was."

"What happened?"

She scrunched her face up as she thought. After the pause, she declared, "I don't want to talk about it right now."

"Why not?"

"It's about after you left and…"

I waited a moment, but she never finished her sentence. "Nicki, I don't want to talk about when I left either." It was true. I was dismayed, and the more time I spent with her, the less I wanted to talk about how we'd ended things between us. Yet the past kept coming up. There was no way around it, so I pleaded, "But if we're going to move forward, I think we need to…at least once."

She was quiet as her eyes searched the room, seemingly focused on nothing. Eventually she said, "Okay, but not tonight. Not here."

"When?"

"Next weekend. Come over on Saturday." She smiled toward David. "And bring him. He'll probably still be in the doghouse."

"You've got a date, then."

"It's not a date," she said, waving her finger at me.

"Okay. It's not a date. It's dinner at an old friend's."

"Exactly."

The following weekend, David and I were once again at Nicki's door. Lisa answered it, dressed just as casually as last time but now in a tight white T-shirt and jeans.

David nodded approvingly at her shape. "Evening, Lisa. You look absolutely lovely."

"You called me by name. That's a surprise."

"I know your name." He gave her a sly smile. "You're my angel."

His angel ignored him. "Hi, Adam. Come on in."

"Evening, Lisa. Where's Nicki?"

"In the kitchen, cooking."

"She didn't have to cook. She worked all day. I told her just to order takeaway."

"I said the same thing, but she wanted to cook," said Lisa, holding up her hands helplessly. "Pasta or something. She kicked me out of the kitchen."

Pointing to the paper bag he carried, David said, "We brought a few bottles of wine."

"A few?" Lisa eyed him.

He smiled and pulled out a bottle of champagne. "Well, one is a special bottle for you." He held it out to her, saying, "Congratulations."

I had no idea what he was up to, but I was impressed. Her entire demeanor changed as she cooed, "Aw, thanks, David. That's really sweet."

Proud of himself, David informed me, "She just got a paper published in a big journal."

She looked up at him warily. "It's thoughtful of you to remember."

Before David could make another pass, I said, "That's wonderful news. Then we have something to celebrate tonight."

Lisa led us into the kitchen, where Nicki was stirring a pot at the stove. She looked cute, wearing a little dress and apron and her hair pulled up. We'd talked a few times that week, but I'd missed her. This time I went in for the kiss on the cheek.

"Evening."

"Hi." She smiled. "It's good to see you."

I peered into the simmering pot. "Hmm. Tomato sauce for pasta?"

"Hence the apron. It's a little messy."

"You look lovely tonight," I said, touching her arm.

"Thanks." She tilted her head shyly away before handing me the spoon. "You stir. I need to get the pasta going."

Like our last dinner together, the four of us had a great time. When the meal finally ended, Lisa even sent Nicki and me away again so she and David could clean—and whatever else they did when alone. I suggested to Nicki we go outside.

She answered, "Sure," then grabbed a full bottle of wine.

"The whole bottle?" I smiled.

She flashed me a look. "If we have to talk, I might need it."

I put my arm around her shoulder and laughed. "I might need it, too." When we got out on the balcony, I realized it wasn't the location I'd really like to have a tough conversation. We needed to be in a safe place—somewhere we could be close. I had a vision of being on her bed, but I knew that was out of the question. Then I spotted the large chaise lounge in the corner. Once I'd placed our glasses and bottle of wine on the side table, I pulled her toward the chair. "Over here this time."

She saw where I was headed and balked, but I tugged on her arm. "Oh…okay," she said.

I lay down, taking her with me. She willingly curled up next to me, and I kept an arm around her. "Now this is more like it."

"It's nice."

"It's more than nice."

"You're right," she said with a sigh. "I'm sorry we didn't talk much this week."

"We were both busy." After a brief hesitation, I ventured, "What's going on with Juan Carlos?"

"We're in touch, though not like before. And Felicity?"

In touch? She's "in touch" with the sorry arse? A pathetic phrase like that was music to my ears. For all intents and purposes, they'd broken up, though, for whatever reason, she wasn't quite willing to recognize it. I wanted to break out another bottle of champagne and tell her that hopefully Felicity was on a yacht in the Aegean bonking a Greek senior citizen, but I had to be more tactical than that. I couldn't let Felicity completely drop out of the picture just yet.

In measuring my response, I faintly remembered seeing her name on a list of international correspondents. "She's been sent on assignment to Indonesia. We haven't been talking much because of that."

"Only because of that?"

"No, of course not." I squeezed Nicki's arm. "I think the fact we're together tonight is a sign there are other reasons." I left it at that, giving her an opening to say more.

She didn't. Instead, she was quiet, and I knew I'd have to push the conversation along. "So what about your dad? What does he know of me?"

Without looking at me, she spoke softly, "It seems so long ago. Well, after you were gone, I hated being in Bellaire. I didn't spend much time with my friends when I was there, and I ended up at Dad's in Chicago a lot."

"So that's how he knows me? You talked?"

"No, not really. He must've gotten your name from Mom. That's why your name rang a bell with him. He never forgets anything."

"He must not. He wasn't overly friendly."

She finally looked at me and smiled. "Oh, don't worry about him. He was surprised to see you, but I was the one he interrogated."

"What did you say about us...now?"

"That we're friends." Her eyes landed on my arm around her, and she chuckled. "Close friends."

My reporter's instinct took over. I had to ask, "And did he believe you?"

"At first...but when I told him Juan Carlos and I were taking a break, he became suspicious. He warned me up, down, and sideways about what might happen to me professionally and also to Logan."

"So he probably doesn't think much of me."

"Dad doesn't think much of anyone. He's innately suspicious."

"So why did you spend so much time with him in high school?"

"Because he left me alone."

Her words weren't directed at me, but they were damning. I felt like a complete arse. I wanted to explain myself to her — tell her what had happened. I had never rehearsed how the conversation would go or even what I might say — other than that I'd apologize for being a bloody idiot. I didn't want to begin there, though. Instead, I started at the beginning.

"Yeah, for a while all I wanted to do was be alone — from the moment I left your house. I remember I went home, where my family was waiting for me beside the hired car we took to the airport. I must've looked like utter shit from crying." I patted her bum and waggled my eyebrows appreciatively. "And from rolling around in bed with you all night."

"Yeah, we did some of that, didn't we?" Nicki giggled.

"My God. We did a lot of that. Every damn day."

"I know, all the time. Now that I'm older and look back...well..." She shook her head. "We had a lot of hormones then."

"I'd say I'm struggling with my hormones right now." I was laughing, but it was too much having Nicki cling to me now while remembering all the ways we'd fucked back then. My hand desperately wanted to inch up her skirt and feel her thigh. I took a breath and discreetly adjusted my dick. I wasn't sure if she noticed.

"Yeah, I know the feeling."

"Maybe I should get back to my story."

"Good idea."

Trying to get my thoughts back on track, I exhaled. "So…when my family saw me, they didn't say anything about me being out all night or even my appearance. They let me sleep, so I slept in the car and for most of the flight back to England." There was no way I could go through a blow-by-blow account of those painful days. I cut to the chase. "When I got home, I was still sad. I missed you terribly."

I held my breath a second before telling her the truth I needed her to believe. "Just so you know, I never got back together with Kate—at all—ever. In fact, I didn't have a relationship with anyone for a long time."

Nicki's sad brown eyes looked up at me. When she nodded, I thanked God that she believed me and continued. "Even when I did start seeing people again, I tried to keep up with you from the bits of information I got from Sylvia."

"And then?" She sounded hopeful.

"Then when Logan was running for president, I occasionally saw you in the press. And when he was elected and appointed you a press secretary, I asked for the White House job. You know the rest."

Nicki was silent. I began to worry I'd said something horribly wrong. Then she slowly sat upright and, after taking a deep breath, said, "I'm sorry I put both of us through that. I just couldn't handle any more pain. I was confident that if I saw you, we'd just break up again. I knew I couldn't take it." She looked so ashamed. "I'm sorry. It was mean of me…I was selfish…I was all those things you called me before you left for your grandfather's funeral."

"I won't have you apologizing to me, Nicki. I was an immature boy and cruel to you."

"But I've wanted to apologize. I don't think things would've changed between us, but it was awful of me to ignore you. I've felt so guilty."

"Please don't. Looking back, I now know you were right. I was foolish and more than a little selfish myself. You'd just lost your sister.

Your whole family was grieving. Yet I asked you to leave them." Then I rued the rest of it all. Everything I'd wanted to say to her during our years of enforced silence spewed out of me. "And you were right. We would've broken up. We were too young. We lived too far away. Even if we were just friends, things probably would've fizzled out—maybe badly. And my dad…well…he had his own ideas about my future."

"I thought so."

"Really?"

"Well, you'd mentioned it, and frankly, I got a similar talking-to from my parents, especially after you left." Her voice trailed off, and she all but whispered her last sentence. "After you left, I missed you so much."

Tilting her face up to mine, I said, "Nicki, like I told you, I missed you, too."

"But now…"

"No buts. If we dwell on all the obstacles between us, we'll never get anywhere." I tucked her hair behind her ear, and at that moment, it felt like fate that she was back in my arms. "Maybe we had to be apart all those years so we could be together now."

"Adam…" Her voice broke at the end.

Seeing the tears well in her eyes made me choke on my own. I used my thumb to wipe away the sadness. "I can't have you crying, Nicki. You're going to make me start, and blokes aren't supposed to."

She tried to smile but seemed overwhelmed. Her tears spilled over, and I couldn't bear to see them. Taking her face in my hands, I kissed her wet cheeks and tasted their tart salt. After my lips found hers, I felt her hand caress the nape of my neck. She kissed me softly but so intently that it felt like she was trying to tell me something. I wasn't sure what, though, because I could still feel her sobbing.

If she hadn't been bawling, I would've been all over her, but the tears confused me. Boys were taught at a young age to be gentle when a girl started to cry. It was often incredibly frustrating if you were angry or annoyed, but it was a rule.

So there I was, passionately kissing Nicki through her tears, sensing that both of us were making up for lost time. It was then that I realized she was the love of my life. A love I'd found and lost and then, remarkably, found again. I relished each and every kiss because of that.

Eventually, she broke away and snuggled beside me, with her leg and arm crossed over me. She seemed worn out, so I stroked her hair, trying to calm her. After a few minutes, I discovered that she'd fallen asleep on me once again, so I closed my eyes and soon peacefully followed right behind her.

We only woke when David knocked on the glass door. "Adam? It's late. We should get going."

Disoriented, I shook the sleep out of my mind. "Right. Yeah. Be there soon."

Propping up on her arm, Nicki blinked at the brightness coming from indoors. "We must've slept for a while."

I checked my watch. "It's past three."

"Sorry." She giggled.

"Don't be. It was nice." I touched her cheek that was red and wrinkled from sleeping on my shirt. "You probably have to work tomorrow."

"I do."

"I do, too."

"You don't usually work that much on the weekends."

"I know. I try not to, but I'm leaving on Wednesday to see my dad."

"How's he doing?" she asked, her brow furrowed.

"My mum won't say much. I don't think he's responding to the treatment as well as we hoped he would, so I'm going to see for myself."

"I'm sorry. I'll call you when you're there." She kissed my cheek. "I'll try not to call too late."

"I'll stay up for a phone call from you." Something hit my gut then. I really wanted to ask her to come with me. It felt like the right thing to do, but it also felt forward. We weren't exactly back together — not yet. Until then, I decided to focus on how close we were. I squeezed her tightly to me. "Maybe we can get together when I get back."

The smile on her face grew bigger. "Well, I'd like to see you again. Tonight was…good."

"It was very good." And I kissed her one more time, trying my best to show her just how good I thought it had been.

Chapter Eleven

The strong morning sun woke me up the following day. Squinting in the harsh light, I saw that it was gone ten. That was late for me, but then I remembered why I'd slept in — I'd been up late with Nicki the night before. As I smiled, the blinking light on my phone caught my eye.

I picked it up and saw the screen displaying a text from Nicki that had arrived over an hour before.

> *Morning. I had a good time last night.*
> *Hope you have a nice Sunday!*

Quickly, I typed back.

> **I didn't have a good time.**

I checked my email because I didn't expect her to immediately respond, but she soon replied with the question I wanted.

> *Why not?*

I wanted her to ask so I could emphasize how I felt about what was going on between us and get a better read from her. It worked; the conversation flowed.

> **Because I had a GREAT time.**

> *:) I did, too.*

Are you at work already?

Yes.

I need to head into the office myself.
I just woke up, though. I'm still in bed.

You're in bed? Now why did you tell me that?

I think you know why.

Er, yeah. On that note, I'll say goodbye.
Talk to you later. Bye for now.

Thus began the series of flirty texts and short calls between Nicki and me for the next few days before I left for my journey back to Cambridge. Sometimes she'd text me right before the morning briefing, and I'd answer as soon as the briefing concluded. Unfortunately, she slipped up at one point, texting me about an official matter on her personal phone. My eyes widened when I read the message.

Neidermeyer's staff say they can't control what the
Congressman will say about Logan if the bailout bill doesn't
go after the bank CEO's compensation packages.
Neidermeyer will go ballistic on us.

I typed a quick response.

I'm guessing this wasn't intended for me.

Shit. No.

No worries. It's not a state secret Neidermeyer would do that,
and he's never scripted.

Despite my reassurance, I knew she was still spooked by the mistake. Her next message clinched it.

Yeah. Damn. I'll call you tomorrow night
when you're at your parents, okay?

Sure. Travel safe.

I will. Take care of yourself.

Frowning, I placed my phone back in my pocket. A mistake like that was bound to happen between us. *But Goddamn it. That may be the last text I get from Nicki.*

As I tried to sleep on the flight to London, I tossed and turned with worry about Dad. Despite our daily calls, Mum was less than forthcoming when it came to his health. It was only when I saw him that I realized why she'd been so evasive. He was a changed man.

As soon as I could slip away, I called Sylvia. When she picked up, I didn't even bother with any pleasantries. "Sylvia, why didn't you tell me? You were only just here!"

"Well, hell-bloody-o to you, too, Adam."

"What the fuck, Sylvia? He looks horrible. I swear he's yellow."

"I know." Then her voice softened. "I thought so, too."

Running a hand through my hair, I winced. As much as I wanted to have a go at her, there was no reason to berate her anymore for leaving me in the dark about Dad's condition. It obviously had affected her just as much as it did me, so I asked, "What did Mum say about it? I haven't had a moment alone with her yet to ask what's going on."

"Mum said the increased dosage wasn't having any effect. The cancer has spread from his stomach to his liver."

"So that's why he's so jaundiced—it's in his liver?"

"He was only a little yellowish when I was there last week. It must be spreading really rapidly."

"Shit!" I was exasperated by her. She sounded so detached—almost nonchalant. "If you knew all this, why aren't you here?"

"I asked him if I should stay, and he said no. He seemed happy. I could see he didn't want me there."

"What do you mean you 'could see' that?" I knew Sylvia loved Dad, and she wasn't daft, but what was she doing? "Of course he's going to say no if you ask him if you *should* stay!"

Sylvia sighed, and it sounded as if I was frustrating her just as much. "Adam, calm down. We've all known this was coming for a while now. Well, at least I've known; maybe you haven't processed it yet."

"I haven't processed it yet? Jesus Christ, Sylvia. You've lived in America for too long. Don't give me that therapy bullshit."

"Do you want to talk to me or not, arsehole? Stop being so hostile if you do."

She was right that I was losing it. I took a deep breath, then exhaled. "I do want to talk to you. I know he's dying. I've *known* he's dying. I'm just shocked at how much he's physically deteriorated. It's been over a month since I've been here, but even so, I can't believe it."

"It is shocking, but I think that's why he told me I should go home. He didn't want me to see him like this. And you know how close he and Mum are. Maybe he wants to be alone with her."

I swallowed and asked the hard question. "Did you ask her about how long he might—"

"No. And I'm not going to. I'm just keeping my calendar open enough so I can leave when I need to."

"Huh. Okay." I thought I should leave it at that. I knew when I wasn't going to get more information out of a source, and as one, Sylvia had clearly dried up.

"Listen," she said. "Why don't we catch up when you get back? I'll come down for a visit, and we can compare notes on Dad. Maybe I can see Nicki as well."

My day suddenly brightened hearing an easy way to spend some time with Nicki. "That would be nice. Come on Saturday."

"Will do. Now go and talk to Mum."

I wished her well and went off to find Mum. She was in the kitchen, making dinner while Dad took an evening nap. The fact that he needed to rest before dinner left me the perfect opening for broaching the subject. Sitting down on a kitchen chair, I said, "So, Dad seems to be sleeping more than the last time I was here."

"Mmm. Yes. I suppose he is." She paused from trussing her chicken and smiled. "It's good for him. He needs it, and the morphine makes him sleepy."

"Mum, he doesn't look very well."

"No, he doesn't." Her attention was back on the puckered bird in front of her. "His mind is still sharp, though. You've seen that, haven't you?"

"Sure." I tried a roundabout question. "But are you worried?"

She didn't turn around at first. She simply answered, "No, Adam, I'm not."

I was silent as I "processed" yet another non-emotional response to my father's death. I was a reporter, a profession that required distance and calm, but I wanted some recognition from my family that Dad wasn't going to be around much longer. Lost in my own thoughts, I didn't notice Mum quickly washing her hands and sitting beside me.

"Adam, I realize this is hard for you—not having seen him in a while. He has changed and will continue to. It's difficult to see, but dwelling on it right now doesn't help anyone. When you're here, just be with him like you normally would. If he wants to talk about it, he will. If he doesn't, let him be. Enjoy your time with him." Giving my hand a motherly squeeze, she smiled wistfully. "That's what I try to do."

I nodded, deciding there was only one person I wanted to talk to at that moment, only one person who could help me make sense of all of it.

She didn't fail me. Exhausted from travel and the time difference, I settled in bed just as Nicki rang me. "Just the person I want to talk to right now," I said.

"Aw, thanks. I know you're probably seriously jetlagged. I called as early as I could."

"I told you I'd wait up for a call from you." I took a breath and added, "I've missed you."

"I've missed you, too. How are things?"

"Not so good."

I told her everything I'd witnessed since arriving home. She listened patiently, only commenting enough to prod me into telling her more.

When I finished, she asked, "Is your dad still eating?"

"Yes. Why?"

"Well, I just remember with my grandmother that she was doing okay until she stopped eating. I think both she and her body decided they couldn't fight the cancer any longer. I don't know if that's true for everyone, but maybe it's something you could look out for."

"Oh. Okay." I thought about Dad's condition for a moment and regretted being such a git to Sylvia. Just as we all grew by milestones like walking or talking, Dad was dying by milestones whether we noticed them or not. I needed to start paying attention. "So do you think I can go back to DC? Or should I stay here in case he gets worse?"

"I don't know, and I really don't know your family very well. But if Sylvia thought she should leave, you might want to do the same."

"But why wouldn't he want his children here? We're a close family. It still doesn't make sense to me that Dad only wants us to visit — not stay."

"Like I said, I don't know about your dad. But I'm pretty sure one of the reasons my grandmother liked having me around was that it spared my dad from having to see her so sick."

I took everything Nicki said to heart, and it was our talks each night that made the trip bearable. She gave me just the right balance of lending an ear but also getting my mind off things. Despite the heavy conversation, I always teased her; sometimes it was laced with sexual innuendo, which got me a reprimand. Her giggles told me she loved it, though, so I kept it up.

During the day, I did my best to do as I was told by all the women in my life — Mum, Sylvia, and Nicki; I just let Dad be. We watched football and talked casually about politics, but he slept so much that we didn't have that much time together. The last night of my stay, I couldn't help but ask what he wanted me to do.

We'd finished watching *Match of the Day* and turned over to the BBC News Channel for the headlines when I said, "You know, I'm going to be back here in a fortnight for Logan's visit to London. Maybe I should just stay here until then."

I promptly received a stern, baffled look. "What on earth for?"

"Maybe to help Mum."

"No need. We're doing fine."

"Are you sure? I could —"

"You should carry on, Adam," he said with an intense stare.

My father and I rarely had heart-to-heart talks. The few that we did have were horrible — like my battles with him over Nicki or Muff or even when I had announced I wanted to go into journalism. Yet when he simply told me to "carry on," everything about the way he said it sounded like it came from his heart. Sylvia was right. You could tell what he meant.

So I nodded, acknowledging what would be one of his last directions to me as my father. I would carry on. As I turned back to the television, he pointed to the screen and exclaimed, "Now, there's that Nicki Johnson again. How is she?"

They showed a shot of Nicki on the BBC, giving some details about President Logan's upcoming trip to London. I smiled. "She's good."

"I get such a kick out of it whenever I see you two spar."

"I wouldn't say we 'spar.' I just ask the appropriate follow-up questions."

"Oh no, you spar. There's a repartee. Your mother thinks so as well. Perhaps you don't notice it, but others do."

His comment caught me off-guard, as I wondered if my friendship—or whatever it was—with Nicki was noticeable to those who didn't know us. I quickly dispelled the thought, though, when I saw how chipper he'd become. Physically, he was a shell of the man he used to be, but at that moment, he seemed bright and sharp.

I told him something I thought would make him happy. "Nicki's asked about you."

"Really? She was such a nice girl." He briefly shook his head as if his mind had wandered. Then he looked at me once more and ended the heartfelt conversation with a mindless question. "So, do you still go to the embassy to watch football?"

That night, I kept my conversation with Nicki short. I had to leave early in the morning to catch my flight back to the States. When it came time for us to say goodbye, I suddenly felt awkward. I fumbled for the right words but only found the uninspiring. "Thank you for calling every evening."

"What? Don't thank me. I love talking with you."

My mouth opened and immediately shut when her words registered with me. She'd said "love," in regards to me, in present tense. I had no idea if it meant anything to her, but it meant something to me—so much so that I almost reflexively replied, *And I love you.*

My feelings for her had been creeping up for weeks, and since our night together the weekend before, they'd only solidified. I did love her. Again.

Yet, I didn't want to tell her on the phone. I needed her to hear it from me in person or else I worried she wouldn't believe it. While I mulled everything over, my stupid silence must've made her uncomfortable. She quickly sputtered, "Well, I gotta run. Catch up with you when you get back. Night."

The line went dead. I wanted to kick myself. *Goddamn it. You're a fucking idiot. Now she's hurt.*

At once, I tapped a desperate text to her.

> You didn't let me say goodbye. Goodnight, sweetheart.

I wasn't sure if she'd like it, but it made me happy to write it. Then I got her response.

> :) Goodnight.

Throughout my travels the next day, I racked my brain, thinking of how I could get Nicki alone — really alone — to tell her how I felt. It was time. I was tired of the game. Of course, I would wait as long as it took for her to come around, but I wanted to speed it up.

I still hadn't decided how to best approach her when I got a phone call from David the following morning. "Hey, cuz. You can thank me again."

"For what?"

"I booked a date with our two little birds for this weekend."

"David, I really don't think they qualify as our birds yet."

"Speak for yourself. I've got Lisa right where I want her."

"Are you sure? Knowing Lisa, I bet she wouldn't even like being called a bird."

"Fine. Then, she's my swan."

Tired of his routine, I cut him off. "What did you plan? You know Sylvia is coming down on Saturday."

"That's fine. She can join us. We're going boating on the Potomac."

"Boating?" I was more of a rower than David, but that wasn't saying much.

"Yep. It was Lisa's idea. I bet if I row her along, it will melt my ice queen's heart. Sylvia can be in your boat."

Sylvia's presence would make Nicki comfortable, but she was also going to be really fucking annoying. I grumbled, "Great. Thanks. You're always thinking of me."

"Not really, but I'm happy to be of help when I can."

"Are you sure you can row a boat?" I ask.

"Not at all, but I'm already planning on capsizing."

"Why on earth would you plan that? She'll be irate."

"Maybe, but she'll definitely end up half-naked."

I could envision a soggy Lisa ridding herself of a wet T-shirt. "It might work."

"And you know what comes after half-naked?"

"What?"

"Fully naked," he said with supreme confidence.

That week, Nicki and I occasionally chatted but kept it light—until the end. I always called her "sweetheart" when we said goodbye. Late one night after I'd said it, though, she was quiet and then replied, "You used to call me that. No one else ever has."

Why *was* I saying it? Was it only a meaningless term of endearment, the kind David threw around? Or did it mean something more? Had I ever said it to anyone else? I couldn't be sure, but I remembered calling Muff "honey." Felicity had been one of the women I'd called "babe."

In fact, there'd been a number of "babes" in my life, but I didn't want another, so I told Nicki what I wanted. "Well, I hope that one day you'll be my sweetheart again."

"That's very…sweet." Her speech was hesitant and soft. "I'm not sure what to say."

"You don't have to say anything. Just think about it and know I mean it."

"Okay."

"See you on Saturday. It should be fun."

I could hear the happiness in her voice as she said, "Yes, I think it will."

On Saturday, we all met up at the boat hire place on the Potomac, which was more of a dirty urban river than a clear mountain stream. Still, boating would be fun, and it would've felt like an official double-date had Sylvia not been in tow. David and Lisa were in one canoe, whilst Nicki and I shared ours with Sylvia, who I was sure would be an irritating combination of nosy little sister and backseat boatman.

When we got on the water, Sylvia lounged at one end of the boat in her resort wear, nattering away. Occasionally, she'd answer a phone call and completely ignore Nicki and me. Whilst it was rude of her, it was nice to talk with Nicki alone, but Sylvia would always quickly be off the phone and again babbling about everything and nothing.

Despite having to contend with the annoyance of Sylvia interrupting my time with Nicki, it was a pleasant day to be out on the water. Not far from us, we could hear Lisa and David bickering about how to row the damn boat.

After a while, David perfectly executed his planned capsizing. There they were, flailing about in the water, Lisa both angry and laughing. Soon after they pulled themselves back in the boat, both were down to only their swimming costumes. Lisa wore a hot little bikini that was definitely worth staring at. David didn't only ogle, though. He had a running flirty commentary about her body that got me thinking of how much I'd like to get Nicki half-naked.

I looked over at Nicki, who glanced back at me. It seemed David and Lisa's sexual tension was wearing on her, too. I stared at her with a sly smile so she could know exactly what I was thinking. Her cheeks reddened, and I said under my breath, "I really wish my sister wasn't on this ruddy boat."

Nicki's blush deepened, and she looked down, embarrassed, as Sylvia called out, "I heard that, Adam!"

After a few hours, we headed back to dry land. Putting herself to some use for the first time that day, Sylvia announced she would cook us dinner at my flat. As we rowed back, I watched David and Lisa quietly confer. Afterward, she told Nicki she'd be heading to their place to get some clothes. I shook my head. My cousin's plan was unfolding perfectly.

So Nicki and I went back to my flat with my third-wheel sister tagging along again. When we arrived, we all decided a shower was in order. I offered the guest bathroom to Nicki, who immediately went in while Sylvia started cooking in the kitchen.

Knowing that Nicki and Sylvia were occupied for a while, I had a leisurely shower, with a quality wank for good measure. I'd stared at Nicki enough on the boat and caught a glimpse up her shorts more than once. Green swimsuit. High cut. What lay beneath was what I thought about in the shower.

As I pulled out a pair of jeans from my chest of drawers, I saw the time. I'd been gone for half an hour. I panicked a little at the thought of Nicki sitting alone in my living room, and walking back in there, I saw my instincts were right. There was a freshly showered Nicki standing in front of my bookcase. She'd been looking at the print she'd given me so many years ago, and when she placed it back on the shelf, she pulled out the book of Wordsworth that sat behind it.

I swallowed hard. Of all the books on the shelf, why did she pick that one?

She looked up at me and said, "Hi. Sylvia is in the shower." She stroked the book's leather binding. "This is beautiful. It looks very old."

"It was my grandfather's."

"Really? That's wonderful." After opening it, she innocently touched the pages. My heart stopped when she noticed the small gap in the middle of the book and asked, "What do you keep in here?"

Without pausing for an answer, she opened the book to the marker. It was a blessing she hadn't waited for me to respond, really, because I wasn't sure what to say—it meant too much. So, in un-ceremonious silence, she pulled out a photo of herself that I'd taken our last day together sixteen years ago. Surrounded by sunlight, there sat my young Nicki, smiling at me.

Her eyes widened as she recognized the photo, and they soon darted down to the opened page. After reading for a moment, she whispered, "Splendour in the grass."

When she looked back up, she gaped at me in disbelief. I only nodded. How could I explain what had made me keep her photo there for years? It was silly and sentimental. I had nothing to say, so I let Wordsworth speak for me as I recited some of his poem:

> *"What though the radiance which was once so bright*
> *Be now for ever taken from my sight,*
> *Though nothing can bring back the hour*
> *Of splendour in the grass, of glory in the flower;*
> *We will grieve not, rather find*
> *Strength in what remains behind."*

When I stopped, Nicki looked stunned. Under her breath, she said, "Yeah, I know it. I was an English major." She looked back down at the photo. "That was a long time ago."

"Not so long ago."

Her doe eyes met mine, and I swiftly grabbed her into my arms and leaned down to kiss her while she placed the book back on the shelf with one hand. The first kiss was soft and quick, but when I went in for the second one, her mouth opened to mine, and our tongues met.

I tried to make the kiss as soulful and romantic as possible, and after a time, Nicki gasped, "Adam, what are you doing?"

In between kisses, I told her exactly what I was doing. "I'm falling in love with you again."

She didn't answer me aloud. Instead, she wrapped her fingers around the base of my neck and pressed her whole body against me. The feeling of warm romance between us soon rose to one of heated passion, so when my dick got hard, I made sure she felt it.

Sounding almost dizzy, she whimpered, "We can't."

My lips found her neck. "We can."

"But no…"

"But yes."

I pulled away and held her face in my hands. She seemed happy, but bewildered. It was time for me to tell her my intentions. She needed to hear me, and I needed to say it.

"I love you, Nicki, and it's not simply that you're an old flame. This is new." Her stunned expression came back, and I smiled to put her at ease. "I love you, and as long as you know it, I don't care who else does."

First wrapping her hands around both my wrists, she slowly pulled my hands off her face. That confused me. Maybe she wasn't ready for a declaration of love for me? Or God forbid, was she about to say that she now only loved me as a friend? I might need to fall to my knees and cry like a baby again if she told me that.

As if to answer my private questions, she stood on her tiptoes and beamed. "I love you. I think I always have."

My joy was overwhelming. I nodded toward the Wordsworth book back on the bookshelf. "Well, you can see a part of me never stopped."

Just then, Sylvia called from behind, "Adam, you left me no hot water. The shower was freezing."

I winced in sheer hatred of my sister and her God-awful timing. When I opened my eyes, Nicki giggled. I stroked her hair and grinned. "Obviously, this isn't the end of our conversation."

She grinned right back at me. "I hope not."

Sylvia must have understood something was up, because as soon as she walked toward us, she gushed, "I'm sorry. Pardon me. I didn't mean to interrupt."

"Well, you did."

Nicki squeezed my hand but then dropped it, saying, "Sylvia, let me help you cook."

While they busied themselves in the kitchen, I sat on a stool, drinking beer and chatting with them. Occasionally, Nicki and I would look at each other and smile. Each time, she'd give a slight shake of her head, marveling with me over what we'd begun—again.

Almost two hours later, David and Lisa arrived—their hair still very wet. Nicki spoke in a low voice as she took her change of clothes from Lisa, likely asking what had taken the two of them so long.

Lisa shrugged with a poker-faced response, which brought Nicki's volume back into earshot as she looked at her friend as if she were mad. "That's it? Who takes a shower together and doesn't have sex?"

I choked on my beer. Nicki had a point.

I looked over at David, who had just poured Lisa a glass of wine. Handing it over to her, there was a genuine smile on his face rather than his usual smirk. "Here you go, love."

Despite the earth shifting with Nicki telling me she loved me again and Lisa succumbing to David, dinner was light-hearted as Sylvia entertained us with her stories of singlehood in Manhattan. Afterward, we sat outside on my patio, talking and drinking late into the night. As usual, Nicki fell asleep on my shoulder, and when she finally woke up, everyone agreed it was time for the rest of us to sleep.

As the others walked back into the flat, I pulled Nicki into my arms and kissed her hair. "Stay here. With me."

She nuzzled into my chest but said, "I think Lisa wants to leave now. I should go inside."

I leaned my head down so I could look into her eyes. "No. I mean spend the night with me." It was an impulsive request, but I wanted it badly.

"I can't, Adam."

She sounded sorrowful, but clearly my declaration of love only had so much of an effect on her. I decided not to probe all the reasons that she couldn't be with me that night. I could handle the ones about our jobs or even Juan Carlos still hanging about, but I didn't want to hear that she was unsure of me.

Instead, I asked, "Tomorrow? Can I see you tomorrow, then?"

She kissed my cheek. "Yes, but it has to be late. I've got to work. You know…big trip this week."

"Of course." It was an important week as the president went to London at the end of it and onward to Istanbul for a NATO meeting. I planned on flying out a day earlier so I could spend time with Dad. I tousled her hair. "So I'll come over at nine in the evening, then."

"Great." She buried her head into my chest again and sighed.

I let myself just enjoy the moment, but she soon gave me little kisses all around my neck. That caught my attention. I lifted her chin to kiss her properly before I told her again, "I love you."

My heart leapt when she answered, "I love you, too."

Chapter Twelve

The following night, I arrived at Nicki's at nine on the dot. Just as she shut the door behind me, I wrapped my arms around her for a kiss. Whilst there was no holding back for me, she returned the kiss but with more reserve. "This is quite a hello," she said.

"I thought I'd try some nonverbal communication."

"Very funny."

"I think we're good at it," I said, kissing her again.

"We sort of learned together, didn't we?" she said demurely.

"We did." Any recognition of the best times of our past was a good sign for me. I nodded toward the living room. "Where's Lisa?"

"In her room. On the phone with David. I swear I might've heard her giggle, but I know she's still toying with him."

"She's playing him perfectly, as far as I can tell."

Nicki laughed and announced we should get some beer, and eventually at my suggestion, we ended up on the balcony again. I knew we were there to talk, but conversation wasn't on my mind. Sitting on the chaise lounge, I drew her into my arms, and when she objected, my kiss stopped her from saying anything else. In fact, nothing was spoken aloud by either of us for the next few minutes as we snogged away like teenagers. In my arms, she felt soft and warm and mine.

I thought she was right there with me, but she abruptly stopped, whispering, "I love you. But I need to slow down."

Not thinking, I said what my body felt. "I don't want to slow down."

"But I need time."

I'd always told myself that I'd wait for her — that I was fine taking things slowly to get her back. At that moment, though, I felt just the opposite. We'd wasted too much time already; I wanted her now. I decided my only shot was to tell her the lengths I would go to for her.

"You know I'll resign tomorrow if it will make you feel better."

"That's sweet," she said with a half-hearted smile. "But it doesn't change—"

"And I don't care if you have a reputation for sleeping with the press."

"Oh, that's fine for you to say."

Then I surprised both of us with the punch line. "In fact, I'd like for you to have a reputation for sleeping with me. As my wife." It was such an off-the-cuff quip that I instinctively second-guessed myself after hearing my own words. Yet in another flash, I knew it was true and the right thing to say. A marriage proposal really hadn't been on my agenda for the night, but with the way Nicki was acting, it felt necessary to get the idea out there.

"What?" Her eyes widened as she pulled away to assess my intentions. "Adam, I—"

"There. I've put my cards on the table. I love you."

"I...I love you, too." Her brow furrowed, and her voice was staccato. "But I don't know if I'm ready for this. I don't know if you're ready for it."

"Well, I am ready. I'm bloody sure of it."

Shrewd Nicki raised a brow at me. "Are you?"

She was testing me, and I grasped at something to show my commitment. Felicity seemed like a convenient example. "I rang Felicity this morning. Told her we needed to talk when I was in London this week. I'm going to break things off permanently."

While I tried to ignore the guilt of lying to her, Nicki softly said, "Oh..."

If she wanted to test me, I could just as easily put her on the spot. "What about Juan Carlos?"

She was quiet and held up her hands.

What the hell does that mean? A sneaking fear made me frown. "Well, seventeen years since we first met, I'm certain. But I think you're not certain about me."

"I'm certain I love you," she tenderly declared as she touched my face.

I was about to kiss her, but she looked away. Fidgeting with her watch, she said, "But we loved each other before, and look how that turned out."

"Aw fuck, Nicki. *That's* what's holding you back? Me messing around with Kate." It was a bit disingenuous for me to be surprised, but I needed to get us both past our past. I'd spent the last sixteen years in silent contrition, and that had got me nowhere. Maybe anger and impatience would work. "I'm sorry I broke your heart, but you'd broken mine. I was seventeen and a scared, hurt idiot. It's history, and that's not me anymore. I want to be with you and only you."

She stared at me before her face crumpled like I'd put the weight of the world on her shoulders. She whispered, "This is all new…I need time, and this is a bad week for me, and—"

I wasn't seventeen anymore, but I still carried the same temper. It flared, fueled by the same feeling of rejection she'd instigated all those years ago. Only this time, I wasn't going to let her get away with it.

"Well, I don't need time, and it's not all new. On one level or another, I've known this for half my bloody life. It sounds like you may have as well, otherwise you wouldn't have avoided me for a decade and a half."

"But right now isn't a good time—"

"Bollocks. It's never going to be a good time. We just have to make it happen. If you don't see that, you're not as clever as I thought you were."

Insulting Nicki's intelligence wasn't my best move. Her back straightened, and her lip curled. "Given the situation, I think I'm acting very intelligently."

I rolled my eyes. Even if I'd ticked her off, I wasn't going to give in. "Maybe acting intelligently, but not smart."

She pursed her lips, either thinking of what she should say next or stopping herself from saying something rude. I couldn't tell. We'd hit a stalemate.

I closed my eyes and grasped for straws. *How can I make this woman see?* Then it hit me. I blurted out, "Come with me to see my dad. Come home with me."

"What?"

"Just as I said. I want you to come to Cambridge with me. I'd like for you to see my dad before…well, before. It's important."

She was quiet as she digested what I'd proposed. Slowly, she answered, "Adam, I want to be there for you, but you know I can't do that."

"Well, why the fuck not?"

"Because."

"Because what?" I wasn't angry with her—she had her reasons. But my whole body raged with hurt and aggravation.

She looked lost and was quiet. I stared at her in silence, trying to squeeze a response from her. She grumbled softly, "Give me some time. I'm thinking it through…"

"Goddamn it, Nicki." I shook my head, then climbed around her and off the lounge. Yet I kept my eyes on hers and demanded, "Then think. Think about why you won't. What else is holding you back? Juan Carlos? You don't love him. If you did, you wouldn't be here with me. Is it your job? It's just a fucking job. I'll tell you, in the grand scheme of things, whatever it is, it's not important. You're what's most important to me. And from what you've said, I'm important to you. So let's stop pissing around and get the fuck on with our lives."

Nicki sat there stunned. Given her expression, I didn't expect an answer that night. She didn't even look like she could formulate a sentence.

After a swig of beer for the road, I informed her, "You know how to reach me. I'm leaving for the UK on Thursday." Walking away, I muttered, "Good night."

The moment I got home, I wanted to call her, but I wouldn't let myself. Nicki had to come to me.

I'd joked with David that he and Lisa were playing games, but in reality, the same was true for Nicki and me. For months now, we'd led each other to and fro. We'd made a great deal of progress, but it was time to get on with things. That's what I told myself, and that's what kept me going when she didn't call.

For the next few days, I worked hard at ignoring her every morning at the White House. I'd occasionally look over at her and wonder if she was doing the same to me; it felt that way. I'd always cross my arms, thinking, *Two can play at this game.* Unfortunately, my obstinacy hindered my job. I avoided talking with her, asking others questions instead and getting no information because Nicki was the one with the answer.

I slowly understood what my editor, Kent, had meant by saying I should keep things "friendly" with Nicki. As long as we were on good terms and friends, our past relationship didn't matter; in fact, it only helped. On the other hand, getting romantically involved led to bad terms ninety-nine percent of the time, and bad terms made it so that I couldn't do my job. I'd tell myself that we'd be the one percent that made it, but as the days wore on without hearing from Nicki, my confidence started to crack.

After I landed in London on Friday morning, I went directly to the BBC before heading to Cambridge. For the next few days, I'd be reporting on Logan's trip but staying at home. I thought that might make Dad happiest. I could see him, but also carry on.

As I walked the corridors, I bumped into Kent getting onto a lift. He waved to me as the doors shut. "Morning, Adam. Good to see you, and good reports you've been sending in."

I thanked him but all the while thinking he may have seen the last of the "good reports" if I didn't get things sorted with Nicki. I needed to focus on my job, so I put the dark thoughts in the back of my mind as I combed through old B-roll footage of past presidential visits. Unfortunately, I had my worries about Nicki thrown back in my face when I ran into Felicity.

In her heels, she stood as tall as me and used her height to her advantage. She always sidled up close so that our faces almost touched. Stroking my cheek down to my chin, she cooed, "What's with the scruff, Adam?"

"I just got off a plane from DC."

"Maybe you need a shower?"

"It can wait."

"You could go to my flat. It's not far away." She took on a sexy, smug air. "You know your way around my place."

I should've politely extracted myself from the conversation, but I was too irritated, so I let a flippant remark slip. "I'm sure someone else knows it better now."

She played with one of her earrings and straightened her shoulders. I'd hit a nerve, and not one I should've. "Maybe. How about you?"

I shrugged as a non-answer, but she took it as a confirmation.

"Oh really?" She was suspicious. "Who is it? Mousy Nicole Johnson?"

"I thought we were supposed to be above commenting on a woman's appearance in a professional setting."

"I'd say this is both a personal and professional conversation." She became coy. "So do you think she's attractive?"

I looked aside. If I didn't answer or said no, she'd be onto me. "Like many spokespeople, she's attractive. I don't think she's mousy at all. In fact, she's rather pretty."

"Is she now?"

Shit. I fucked up. "Don't be daft, Felicity. You've seen her for yourself." Then I lied without misstating anything. "I speak with her every day for work, so of course I know her well."

"And you've also known her in the past. Are you close?"

"Yes. I suppose."

Not the right thing to say. Her eyes narrowed in inquisition. "How close?"

"Felicity…" I sighed, hoping my understated dramatics would throw her off.

"Someone has kept your attention for the last few months, and you're mum on the topic. It has to be her."

"You're nutters." I shook my head, hoping my nightmare would end soon. "Nicole and I are old friends. What's missing in my relationship with you was already evident, with or without Nicole. I'm sure you've found me lacking as well. I'm a lousy long-distance boyfriend."

What I thought might clear the air between us, Felicity took as an insult. Given her status, wealth, and looks, she wasn't used to being slighted, and it only provoked her. She sneered at me, but after a moment, her face brightened with a menacing smile. I knew I was in for it as she patted my shoulder. "Ah, well then you'll be interested in the snippet I saw in *The Reliable Source* blog this morning."

"You read *The Reliable Source*?" It seemed strange that Felicity would read *The Washington Post's* gossip section.

"Of course, I like political tittle-tattle."

"So what was it?"

"There was just a photo of Juan Carlos Jimenez entering Tiffany's. The caption remarked that *The Reliable Source* was confident that his girlfriend Nicole Johnson knew what he was shopping for."

My stomach turned inside itself, but I kept a straight face and delivered the line that would let me escape the conversation. "I'm sure Nicki knows." I smiled and strode past her. "Good seeing you, Felicity."

Desperate in my thoughts, I pinched the bridge of my nose as I walked along.

Why the fuck is Short-Arse buying Nicki jewelry?

Impulsively, I took my mobile out of my pocket. When I saw it in my hand, though, I came back to earth.

What are you doing, you fool? Calling her to propose? Again? She hasn't even bothered to call you after the first time.

Granted that hadn't been a proper proposal and I'd stormed out on her, but if we were going to have a future, she needed to call me.

That afternoon, I trudged home with my luggage and a heavy heart. When the antiseptic scent of the house hit me, I felt even worse. Mum was so happy to see me that my spirits lifted a little, but they came down again when I asked after Dad.

Smiling with all her maternal warmth to reassure me, Mum said, "He's in bed."

"Already?"

"Well, he hasn't been getting out much lately."

With his shrunken frame, Dad looked almost boyish as he sat in his pajamas, watching the telly. They'd never had a television in their bedroom before, but all the time he spent in there must've made it a requirement. The scene was so pathetic to me, but when Dad saw me, he practically cheered. "Adam! I'm so happy you're home."

Before I closed my eyes in bed, I checked my mobile one last time. No word from Nicki. She always called me when I was home, but not that night. No call. No text. Nothing.

It was heartbreaking.

Thanks to my arrival the prior day, I was one of the first members of the media at Number Ten Downing Street the following morning. When President Logan arrived, Nicki hurried ahead of his entire entourage. She successfully warded off the aggressive tabloid photographers by promising an extra, exclusive photo-op with the First Lady later in the day. It was interesting watching Nicki work, and I did so most of the morning as I went about my reporting, but I doubted she saw me.

At one point, Matthew whispered something to her. She flinched and smoothed her hair back. She looked knackered.

Of course. They traveled last night. Maybe that's why she didn't call.

I didn't let my hopes get too high, though, because when she did finally look me in the eye, she didn't smile, so I didn't either. I just gave her the same blank, demanding stare that I'd had all week. Her response was different this time, though. Rather than ignoring me, her brow furrowed. She then walked out of my sight.

On the train back to Cambridge that evening, I berated myself over what to do next. I'd always considered myself a person with resolve and willpower, but I was no match for Nicki Johnson. If this was going to be a game of chicken between us, then she would surely win.

But I didn't want to give in. I still wanted her to come to me, and I especially wanted her to come to me if she was fucking engaged.

Dinner with Mum and Dad was pleasant, if a little depressing. Dad wasn't eating anywhere near as much as he used to. Nicki's warning about his appetite kept haunting me.

After dinner, I cleaned the kitchen while Mum helped Dad in the bath. It was then that I understood why he wanted to be alone with his wife. He needed so much intimate assistance that he wished for some privacy. Dad didn't want his children underfoot, even if we were adults.

It was after nine when I heard the doorbell ring. I was loading the dishwasher, and I heard Mum call from the living room, "I'll get it!"

"Fine with me," I said as I rinsed a plate. I didn't need to make small talk with the neighbors as they gave us another meat pie for Dad.

"Well, hello there!" Mum's voice rose in the distance.

I stopped what I was doing. It didn't sound like she was talking to a neighbor.

"Adam, stop with the dishes. Come here!"

Quickly drying my hands, I walked to the vestibule. As I entered from the hallway, I balked for a second when my heart jumped. There, talking with Mum, was Nicki.

Mum saw me and cried out, "Adam, you didn't tell me Nicki was coming."

Answering my mother but speaking directly to Nicki, I smiled. "I didn't know if she would."

Nicki still wore her suit from the workday, so she must've come straight from an official function. Her eyes were tired, but her skin was bright against the red of her blouse. She looked gorgeous and not the least bit mousy.

"I'm sorry I'm so late," she said.

Gazing warmly at her, I walked straight over and took both of her hands in mine. After I kissed her cheek, I said, "Better late than never. Thanks for coming, sweetheart."

Chapter Thirteen

My lips had barely left Nicki's cheek before she squeezed my hands. Whilst I took her gesture as a good sign, I didn't want to read too much into it. Even though she was standing in my parents' home, I didn't know why Nicki had come all the way to Cambridge.

After all, she could've been acting out of guilt and come only to maintain our friendship. Or worse, *The Washington Post's Reliable Source* was right, and Juan Carlos had given Nicki a ring. The very possibility made me sick.

With that uncertainty in the back of my mind, I gently released her hands. She gave me an anxious look and slipped her hand back into mine. *Why does she need reassurance*, I wondered, but I didn't linger long on the thought. I was too happy to be holding her hand again, which cured me of my panic. *Good. She's not engaged…yet.*

I glanced over to Mum, who was beaming at us, intently watching our actions. She startled when I caught her staring, and she sputtered, "Oh. Yes. I should tell Dad that Nicki is here. He's probably still awake, watching the telly."

As Mum hurried to their bedroom, I turned back to Nicki. "Thank you for coming."

"I wanted to."

She punctuated it with a sheepish shrug, which I took as encouraging. I brushed a stray hair from her forehead. "You look tired."

"It's been a hard week."

Knowing that my storming out on her had something to do with that, I wanted to frown as well. Instead, I squeezed her hand and murmured, "You and me both."

Then Mum called from the hallway, "Adam, your father is awake, and he'd love to talk to you, Nicki."

Holding Nicki's hand tightly, I led her down the dimly lit hall toward my parents' room. When I noticed that I had to pull her along, I looked back to see why she lagged. I thought she might be dreading going to see a dying man; instead she was examining the family photos on the walls. I chuckled. "If you really must see photos of me on my first day of nursery school wearing school shorts, I'm sure Mum can show them to you later."

"I'd like that." She laughed.

When we entered the bedroom, Dad was under the covers in his pajamas and dressing gown, though upright and alert. He greeted her at once. "Nicki! Good evening."

"Good evening, Professor Kincaid." Nicki walked straight over to him and extended her hand with a smile. "Thank you for seeing me this late."

"Not at all." He shook her hand and held it a bit longer than his usually reserved manners allowed. "It's so kind of you to come all the way out here. I'm sorry we couldn't visit you while you're in London."

"Oh, it was an easy trip for me." Pointing toward the hall, she added, "And this way I got to see some old photos of Adam."

"Ah, yes. I'm sure he loved that." Dad gave me an approving grin, but it wasn't for anything I'd done. It was for Nicki.

Finally.

Gesturing to the armchair by his bed, Dad said, "Nicki, please sit here with me for a while. I'd love to hear about your work."

Nicki dutifully sat next to him and answered all of his questions. I sat in another chair at the end of the bed, listening to the conversation between them. Mum stuck around for a few minutes but then left to finish cleaning the kitchen.

Nicki would occasionally glance over at me as they talked, but Dad never did. His attention remained squarely on her. Whilst he appeared as sickly as he had at dinner, his mood was happier — like he looked forward to something. It was odd for him to be so eager, given what lay ahead. Yet, at that moment, he was fully engaged as if he was still a part of this life.

Indeed, he was so enmeshed in their conversation that he started lobbying Nicki to tell President Logan to increase funding for geological research. Not wanting to put Nicki in an uncomfortable spot, I began to interrupt him, but Mum called for me.

Shit.

I stared at the scene before me. Given our history, Dad's failing mind, and Nicki's unpredictability, I wanted to monitor whatever they might talk about. Dad's lobbying was the least of my concerns about what topics they might cover.

What if he brings up the past?

Just as I was about to tell Mum to wait, Dad urged me, "Go on, Adam. See what your mum needs."

"But...er..."

"It's okay," Nicki assured. "I'll keep your father company."

There was nothing I could do, so I nodded and promised to be back straightaway. When I entered the kitchen, Mum had concocted the most ridiculous chore, asking me to switch two entire china dinner services from one cupboard to another. We never used that china. She obviously wanted Nicki and Dad to talk alone.

I glared at my mother's simpering smile. "Can't this wait until the morning?"

"No. You're leaving early tomorrow. I want it done now."

"All right..."

I worked as quickly as I could, but I had Mum haranguing me for every clink of a dish. After ten minutes or so, she declared, "Okay. I can do the rest."

Fleeing back to the bedroom, I walked in to see Dad's eyelids half-closed as he droned on, remembering different places around the States. Nicki sat listening patiently to him and answering his questions. I no longer cared about what they'd talked about while I was gone. All I could think about was how much I loved her.

Nicki glanced up at me and smiled before she said to Dad, "Oh. I'm sorry to interrupt, Professor Kincaid, but Adam is back. I should get going if I'm going to catch that last train."

Dad fought to raise his eyelids, a losing battle as he reached for her hand. "Yes. You should. Thank you for coming, dear. It's been nice to catch up with you."

"I feel the same way. Thanks for having me. This was the most fun I've had all day. Good night."

Then as if confirming his own thoughts, he said, "Such a pleasant girl." He focused on her for a second before adding, "Take good care of my boy."

My heart stopped at what Nicki might say, but she took his request in stride. She patted his hand. "Of course I will."

I cleared my throat, but not for effect. I needed to remove the lump that had lodged in the back. "Nicki, I'll take you to the railway station."

When our eyes met, the wondrous warmth in hers gave me enough encouragement to walk over and place my hand on her shoulder.

Dad smiled, withdrew his hand from hers, and closed his eyes. "Good night, you two."

As he rolled over onto his side, I escorted Nicki out of the room. Walking hand in hand with me down the hall, she said, "You know you don't have to drive me. I can take a cab."

"Ridiculous. I'll give you a lift."

I didn't want Nicki to leave, but the fact that she had to was the only thing that got her out of Mum's clutches. Before she left, Mum extracted a promise to see her again the next time she was in the UK, and Nicki happily said yes.

As we drove to the train station in Dad's old Benz, we didn't talk about him. Nicki asked questions about Cambridge — the different buildings, my neighborhood. She seemed genuinely interested, but also like she was directing the conversation.

When we pulled up to the station, I saw that she had some time to wait. "You have a few minutes," I said. "Don't leave yet."

"I won't."

Turning off the car, I noticed her staring at her hands. I felt guilty as hell. My blow-up at her the last weekend had made everything awkward between us again. I was about to beg her to forgive me for being such an arse — to tell her how much I missed her — to let her know she could take as much time as she wanted to decide about us.

But she broke the silence first. "I'm sorry about your dad. This is so hard for you."

My instinct was to react as I always did when someone told me that — I'd shrug and make a fatalistic comment, moving quickly to another subject. But this was Nicki, and she'd just seen everything. I stared at the steering wheel and whispered, "It is hard."

"Oh, Adam …"

I felt her hand at the nape of my neck, and I silently leaned into its comfort as I closed my eyes. Feeling my own pain, I updated her on Dad's condition. "He's declined. A lot. He's barely eating, and the jaundice is awful. It probably won't be too long."

"No, it probably won't."

I heard a rustle, and then Nicki leaned over and kissed my forehead.

That was it. I was tired of her ambiguity. I looked her straight in the eye. "Why did you come here, Nicki?"

"I came for you."

"That doesn't tell me much."

"Maybe you're not listening."

She smirked as she said it, and I sighed. When she was being cute like that, it was hard to press her. Plus, I knew I wasn't going to get anything more definitive from her that night. It was late, and we both needed to get going because the president left for Turkey the next day. Our next big talk would have to wait.

She surprised me, though, with a breathy kiss. "I love you, Adam."

"I love you." I smiled. "Thanks again for coming."

"Thanks for asking me." Her eyes darted to her watch. "I need to run. Istanbul in the morning, you know."

"Take care. I'll see you in the morning on the plane."

She leaned in once more for a peck, but I surprised her this time by sneaking my hand onto her hip and opening my mouth to hers. She responded at once with a deep kiss and gripped my shoulder tightly, so I slid my hand between her legs. Catching me being naughty, she let out a warning, "Adam…"

"The tease doesn't like being teased, does she?"

She let out an evil giggle and landed a swift kiss on my cheek before she was out the door. "See you tomorrow."

Chapter Fourteen

The following morning, Mum was cheery at the breakfast table. Dad was still sleeping, so we were alone. She only mentioned Nicki's name once, but it was enough.

"It was so nice of Nicki to trek out here last night."

"Yes, it was." I didn't look up from the *Financial Times*. "She didn't have to do that."

"No, she didn't."

"You've become very close again, haven't you?" Her voice was hopeful.

Looking up from my paper, I smiled at my mother's eagerness but decided to say as little as possible. "We're friends."

Mum's grin widened at my simple statement. Clearly, less meant more.

I noticed the time. I needed to leave the house early if I was going to fly on Air Force One with the rest of the press corps. Checking the kitchen clock again, I said, "I'm sorry. I need to leave soon. I don't want to wake Dad, but I'd like to say goodbye."

Mum waved her hand, brushing my thought aside. "Oh, don't worry. He won't mind, and he'll roll over and go back to sleep."

The bedroom door cracked as I opened it, but Dad didn't stir. I panicked that something might be wrong. Luckily, I could see him breathing, though his breaths were slow and shallow. Placing my hand on his shoulder, I said, "Dad, I need to leave, and I'll be gone for a week. But I'll be back soon."

His face twitched as he heard my voice. After a moment, he blearily blinked his eyes, saying, "You carry on, Adam."

There was his order again. I was supposed to go on with my life. "Sure. I will, Dad."

"Good. Give us a call later." Then his eyes shut tight again, and he mumbled, "That Nicki is such a pleasant girl."

"Yes, she is." I smiled down at my father. "Goodbye, Dad. I love you."

"I love you, too, son." With that, he pulled the blanket over his shoulder and went back to sleep.

We landed in Istanbul late that morning, and the NATO meeting started soon after our arrival. The long day of talks meant that I barely saw Nicki, so we only exchanged hellos and a few knowing looks during the main press event. It was a grueling schedule, and I had multiple interviews to do back-to-back. By the end of the day, I was exhausted. I planned on going straight back to the hotel and staying in for the rest of the night.

When I was leaving the loo, though, I ran into Matthew, Nicki's boss. The NATO talks had gone well for the US that day, and he was especially cheery.

"Adam! Good to see you! You doin' okay?"

"I'm good, thanks. You all right? You must be chuffed with the day."

"Yes, it's been a good day, and we get to go home tomorrow." He grinned. "Hey, we're going out with some of the press corps tonight. Come with us."

No matter how tired I was, "yes" was the appropriate answer to such an invitation from Matthew Foster. And another thought came to mind that made me really want to attend: *Nicki might be there.*

After I got to the restaurant, the party was already in full swing. Nicki wasn't there yet, so I sat between two German reporters I knew from my early days at the BBC when I used to cover Europe. We talked football, and as much I liked them, if Nicki wasn't going to show, I would rather be in my hotel room actually watching a match.

Unfortunately, when Nicki finally did arrive with Matthew, that arsewipe Dan Roark waved her over to him. As they sat and ate together, I kept an eye on Dan, who I could tell was looking down Nicki's blouse when he got a good vantage. *Bastard.* I decided to stay out that evening as long as Nicki did. There was no way I was leaving her with that leering wanker.

After dinner, Matthew and I spoke a bit, but a DJ had started playing music, and the place got too loud for comfortable conversation. Matthew soon tapped his watch, saying he needed to get back. He called to Nicki, who looked like she was going to follow him, but Dan, Lydia Mixon, and a few others begged her not to leave. Nicki's eyes darted over to me, and she quickly said, "Oh, I'll stay around here for a little longer."

A group of reporters left with Matthew, so I moved over to Nicki's table to better hear her. She still wasn't sitting beside me, but at least I could listen to what Dan said to her. The two weren't talking, though. The female journalists had taken control over the conversation at the table, gossiping about a recent wedding.

Talk of wedding flowers was mind numbingly boring. Weary of the subject, I looked around at others at the table. I soon noticed that Lydia kept staring at Nicki. I wondered if it was because of Dan, but despite my hatred of him, he didn't appear to do or say anything inappropriate. Then I clued in to what had to be on Lydia's mind—Juan Carlos. Always gossipy, she would be the one to inquire about the published photo of him walking into Tiffany's. She'd get the answer I'd been wanting.

As soon as there was a lull in the conversation, Lydia casually remarked, "So, Nicole, if we should believe *The Washington Post*, I think you've got some news for us."

Also bored by the wedding talk, Dan became as alert as I was when he heard the new topic. He leaned back in his chair and eyed Nicki. "Yeah, that's right. *The Reliable Source* mentioned Juan Carlos at Tiffany's. Should I offer you my congratulations?"

The questions were personal, but no one could say they weren't reasonable—especially Nicki. Even if the photograph and caption were located in a gossip section, it still constituted a report in a re-spected newspaper. Inquiries about it were appropriate.

Nicki's expression was bland like she was already bored with the topic, even if we weren't. She toyed with us. "How do you know what he was buying or who it was for?"

"Well, we don't," Lydia said, her eyes growing wide at the prize gossip she was about to obtain. "But you do. Please, Nicole. Are you engaged?"

"No." Nicki shrugged. "He hasn't asked me."

"Are you going to say yes?" asked Dan, leaning in even closer to her, the bastard.

"Why on earth would I tell you?" Nicki laughed a little nervously and looked at me. For once, I wish she'd actually answered a question from Dan.

"That's a good enough answer for me," he said, poised to rise from his chair. "You're still single at the moment. How about we dance?"

Nicki agreed and took his hand without looking at me. I glared at them as they moved onto the dance floor. A naff love song was playing, and Dan seized on the opportunity to take Nicki in his arms.

A few eyebrows at the table went up in curiosity, but no one said anything as they danced. Dan was a notorious ladies' man, so most dismissed his flirtation and nonsensically parsed every one of Nicki's words instead to see if she might actually be engaged. Their chatter was background noise to me. I was busily monitoring the scene, paying special attention to Dan's right hand and whether it would wander over Nicki's bum. I also studied Nicki, but she just smiled and talked to the arse.

My rational brain knew she was just being polite, but my jealous side wasn't so reasonable. As soon as the song came to an end, I was on the dance floor right beside them. Within seconds of their hands releasing, I asked Nicki, "May I?"

Her eyes disapproved, but she said, "Sure."

"I see I've got some competition," Dan said.

"No competition at all, mate," I replied, leaving him to wonder what I meant.

Nicki chuckled awkwardly and thanked him for the dance. Despite her reluctance, she still took my hand as the DJ switched to Frank Sinatra. She smiled for whoever might be watching us, but to me, her words were harsh. "What are you doing?"

"Dancing with you."

"Adam…"

"If you can dance with that arsehole in front of everyone, you can dance with me."

She settled down a bit, though still said, "But it means something when I dance with you."

I looked over at our table, and many of its members were staring at us, including Dan. "They can't tell," I reported back.

"But I can."

"I can, too." Drilling my eyes right back at hers, I said, "So old Juan Carlos has bought you a ring. We haven't talked about *that* yet."

"No, we haven't. Apparently he's purchased it, but it's true that he hasn't proposed. He's waiting until I get back."

"And does he have reason to believe you'll say yes?" I realized that I sounded a touch too demanding, so I joked, "Or *si* in this instance?"

"Don't be silly." She shook her head. "I had no knowledge he was doing this. It's some weird last-ditch, grandiose gesture to get us back on track."

"Latin tosser."

"Huh?" She looked at me quizzically. "Is that some British cricket term? What does this have to do with sports anyway?"

"Never mind." I laughed to myself because Nicki still didn't understand my language. "Start at the beginning, then. What's been going on with you?"

She was so quiet for a moment that I thought she might not talk, but she soon looked at me sadly. "Well, when you stormed out on me last Sunday night, I was angry. I'd been trying really hard to do the right thing and be fair to everyone—to you, to Juan Carlos, to my job—and you gave me no credit for it. I wasn't happy, though after thinking things through, I have to say you made some valid points."

"I suppose you're right. You've been quite fair in what is a very hard situation." Then I tried to lighten her mood by squeezing her waist and saying, "Except for when you haven't been able to control yourself around me. That's been a little unfair. You've been drinking tonight. I hope you can keep your hands to yourself."

"You're horrible," she said, fighting a smile.

"Only because I adore you."

"And I you."

"So you'll get rid of JC?"

"I can't just 'get rid' of him, Adam. This is a little more delicate than that."

"Shit, Nicki, when are you going to make a choice?"

She was defiant. "I've made my choice. It's you. Don't you see that?"

"Then when are you going to act on it, damn it?"

"Act on it? I am! I'm trying to do things in order. It's not like—"

"It's not that difficult. Don't you see that I'll do whatever it takes to make things work between us? Hell, I've already broken up with Felicity." Technically, that was true.

"I don't think your situation with *Lady Fucking Felicity* is the same."

"Oh, really? Given the row we had when I ended things, she might disagree." Technically, that *wasn't* true, but I didn't care because I somehow needed to get through to Nicki.

She was in a huff when the Sinatra song ended. "We should go back to the table. This isn't a good place to talk. Let's do it when we're back in DC."

I didn't want her to run away angry. I gripped her tightly as the DJ switched genres again, now to R&B. Leaning in, I whispered, "Don't go. I'm sorry. One more song."

She glanced around us. Was she looking for another dance partner to save her? Dan was back at the table. Like she was stuck with me, she took a step closer. I tried to be encouraging. "I promise not to complain."

"Oh, all right. There are worse things than dancing with you."

"Like what?"

"Dancing with Dan Roark."

"I swear, I hate that wanker. I don't like seeing him with you."

"You say I don't listen to you. Do you listen to me? There's no way I'd ever be with that guy—or any other guy, for that matter."

"Well, maybe we should both listen and not talk," I said, caressing her hand in mine.

"Okay."

I tried to be aware of people watching us, but in the end, I didn't care. She was in my arms once again. That's what mattered in life. As the soulful music droned on, I inched closer to her, and she did the same to me. It wasn't long before her thighs were brushing against me while her head rested on my chest.

Then, like she'd been electrocuted, she jolted away. "We can't do this here," she whispered. "We have to stop."

"It's okay, Nicki."

I didn't even believe myself after I'd said it, and Nicki gave me a look like I was mad.

"No, it's not," she insisted as she released my hand. "Let's talk tomorrow…when we're back in DC."

Heading straight back to the table, I saw Dan leading the group in a round of shots. "That was a long dance," he said, peering up at me over his shot glass.

I tried shrugging it off, but Nicki took care of things. She took a seat beside him. "I'll have a shot, Dan."

"Great," he said, as if she'd chosen him over me. "Here you go."

"No need to pour one for me." I placed some Turkish lira on the table. "I'm heading out."

Dan's brow furrowed, but I ignored him, saying goodbye to Nicki just like I did to every other woman at the table.

When I got back to my room, I was still wound up, so I had a shower and enjoyed a satisfying wank. A little more relaxed, I flopped on the bed naked and spent the next hour watching football. I'd texted Nicki to call me when she got back to her room, but my phone never rang.

Long after midnight, I was about to turn off the light when there was a knock from outside my room. I pulled on a pair of boxer shorts so that I was somewhat dressed. As I got near the door, I asked, "Who is it?"

No one answered.

I cracked the door ajar, then threw it wide open when I saw Nicki staring at me. Without speaking, she walked straight into my room.

As soon as she was inside, I shut the door and chuckled. "Well, good evening. This is a nice surprise."

When she didn't immediately respond, I asked, "What's all this about?"

She remained quiet, and then I figured it out. I knew the look in her eye, though I hadn't really seen it since high school. Nicki was drunk and horny. Her words and accompanying pungent breath confirmed it. "What did you say earlier? Why wasn't I acting on it? You said something like that, I think."

"I did."

"Well, I'm here to act on it."

With that, she stepped forward, and in a series of swift motions, she was most definitely acting on it. As our lips met, her tongue touched mine, and she simultaneously palmed my dick. I exhaled at once.

"Fuck…"

"Yes," she hissed.

We both abandoned any thoughts of going about our relationship in an orderly manner. The only thing Nicki seemed concerned about was how quickly she could get her hand inside my trousers. As I kissed her with all my love and lust, she slipped her fingers inside the flap. They were cool against my dick, but I still got hard.

My body raced ahead of my mind, maybe in fear that if I thought about the situation I might have an untimely bout of English gentlemanliness and stop her from drunkenly throwing herself at me. Instead, my hands were on her shoulders, and I gripped her tightly as my erection grew under her touch. When she tickled me around my foreskin, I grunted and groaned like the undersexed sod I was. Despite the fact I'd just jerked off, I hadn't been with a woman in forever. Now I was with one, and it wasn't just any girl — it was Nicki. If I didn't watch it, I'd blow my load within minutes.

"Let's go to your bed," she slurred.

"Gladly."

Leading her across the room, a thrill ran through me thinking about fucking Nicki once again. I turned toward her once we approached the bed, but she pushed me onto it. I landed with a laugh. "Assertive, aren't we?"

"A little," she said as she smiled and kicked off her heels.

Propped on my elbows, I lay on my back and watched her perform an impromptu strip show. Off came the blue trousers and knee-high stockings. And peeking out from the tails of her conservative white shirt was a black, lacy thong.

I stared at her crotch until, moving toward me, Nicki reached down and tugged my boxers down my legs. She first stared at my bobbing stiffy, then briefly kissed and licked it before removing her knickers and placing her knees astride my legs. I grinned up at the sight of her straddling me. Taking my dick in my hand, I rubbed the tip right against her, making her moan. With her long hair hanging down her arched back, she looked like a study in ecstasy.

"God, you're beautiful," I said.

A smile overtook her lips, full of warmth and lust. She wrapped her hand around mine so that we were both playing with each other's bodies. "Do you like watching me do this?" she asked a little cheekily.

"Fuck, yes."

"I love the feel of you against my pussy."

My mouth dropped open in disbelief. There was no doubt I was in the moment. I'd fantasized about banging her for years and years, and lately, I'd been wanking off wondering what it would be like when we were together again. But I never expected my old sweetheart, Nicki, to talk dirty. Was it the alcohol? Or was this the way she was now?

Whatever the answer, she continued rubbing herself on my dick. My hands reached down to her bum for leverage. Then a naughty, wasted Nicki mumbled, "I want to feel you inside of me. Now."

"Uh…" My cock heard her just as much as my ears did, but I questioned myself for a moment. *This is not how I imagined being with Nicki for the first time…*

My body didn't care, though, and Nicki appeared not to either. I did remember aloud that a condom might be a good idea, but Nicki dismissed it, saying she was on the pill.

I wanted to take off her shirt, but Nicki lifted the front tails so she could see as we maneuvered my dick beneath her. My eyes widened when the head of my penis first felt her wet warmth, and they instantly closed when she quickly lowered herself onto me. I was quite certain nothing would ever feel that good again unless it was with her.

Hearing her sigh, I raised my eyelids to see her giving me a small smile as I thrust my hips to hers. She simply declared, "At last."

"At last."

My main goal was to outlast my first time with her over sixteen years before. If I hadn't wanked earlier, I might not have done it. My second goal was to make sure Nicki came early and often. That wasn't too hard when she'd already taken control of things by being on top. I just provided the dick and played with her clit a bit.

When my goals were accomplished, I felt like I was the king of the world. Everything about being with Nicki was the same, only better. I hugged her closely, both to calm down and to make sure she knew I never wanted her to leave.

"I love you, Nicki," I said, pressing my nose into her hair.

"I love you."

She raised her head to smile, and I gave her a little kiss—only, my drunk Nicki took it the wrong way. Plunging her tongue into my mouth, she was ready to go again. Unfortunately, I needed a moment, so I bought some time by slowly unbuttoning her shirt. Underneath was a lacy bra that I popped off in short order. There were Nicki's pretty little tits, all for me again.

I went to work on her beauties—which she seemed to enjoy. Wanting to make it even better for her, I slowly started to move my head southward, thinking she might like a lick. When I reached her torso, though, I found her scars. They were still there—much lighter in color and with a slightly withered texture. Instinctively, I did just as I always had—I kissed them all, wishing they would go away so they couldn't hurt her anymore.

As I brushed her with kisses, I heard her whimper in what I thought was pleasure. When she continued to make noise, however, I realized she wasn't enjoying it at all. She was crying.

Blimey. What did I do wrong?

Raising my head, I saw Nicki's face showing an expression of devastated disbelief. She sobbed as she spoke. "I missed you…I missed you so much. For years, I missed you."

The time had come, and she needed to hear me loud and clear. I moved up so I could look her in the eyes when I gave her my pledge. With my hand on her cheek, I said, "Nicki, I will never leave you again. Never. But you have to stay with me. Okay?"

I held my breath, waiting for an answer. What if she said no again?

But she didn't fail me. Not this time. Her tears weren't finished, but she smiled. "I'll stay with you…always."

Chapter Fifteen

The early morning light woke me up before my alarm. Blinking a few times, I soon remembered what had happened with Nicki the night before. Instantly, I looked right, expecting her to be there. She wasn't.

I racked my brain for a moment, reconfirming that it hadn't been a dream. I remembered it all. She had, indeed, come to my room in the night; we had fucked like the horny teenagers we once were, and she had ended up crying in my arms as we pledged ourselves to one another. We were together again. Yet, despite my vivid recollections, there was no Nicki.

Sitting up in the bed, I examined the pillow next to me. There was the evidence of my memories—a slight indentation in the pillow from her head and a couple of strands of curly brown hair. Then I noticed the piece of hotel stationary sitting on the bedside table. It was a short note.

Adam,
I'm sorry I have to leave early.
I'll talk to you after I get everything lined up on my end.
I love you,
NICKI

I lay back on my pillow. *Huh. "Lined up on my end?" What does she mean?* I remembered further back into our evening and how we'd danced together in front of everyone. Knowing Nicki, she was probably out doing damage control with our colleagues.

Then I thought again about how we'd had sex—we'd crossed a line. She needed to fix it.

I bet she's going to tell the president about us.

After a morning press event in front of the Blue Mosque, we were scheduled to fly back to the States. As I flashed my credentials to security in order to get behind the ropes for the event, I saw Ned Dupree, a reporter for *The Washington Post*, standing near Lydia Mixon. Upon seeing me, he casually elbowed Lydia. First, she looked at him and then toward me. She gave me a little grin, but I knew better than to think it was a friendly gesture—it was calculating. I was under surveillance by my peers. They couldn't know the whole story about Nicki and me, but they knew something was amiss. I returned the smile as if nothing were wrong.

The rest of the morning confirmed my suspicions. Until we could be out in the open, I knew how Nicki was going to act. She ignored me assiduously, but her disregard didn't stop the stares and whispers.

In true arsehole form, Dan actually spoke to me directly about the gossip. "So, you got close to Nicki last night. That dance has caused a lot of talk."

I shrugged. "I think I left when you two started doing shots."

"Yeah, right," he said, sounding even more of an arsehole than usual.

Until I talked with Nicki again, further conversation about the night was a bad idea, so I walked away. The bastard didn't deserve more information anyway.

Before I boarded Air Force One for the flight back to DC, I checked on Dad one last time. He was always napping when I called, which was very frustrating—and it happened again. Mum assured me that Dad was okay, even if he had been sleeping more since I'd left. For a moment, I wondered if I should go back to Cambridge instead of to DC. I cringed at the thought, though, because I needed to talk to Nicki again. We'd set a lot in motion the night before, and she was already acting on it. I needed to do the same.

Still, I suggested to Mum that I skip the trip to DC and head straight back home. "I could be there when he's awake and help round the house."

"Adam, there's not much to be done at this point," she said.

"But—"

"I promise I will call you when I think you should come home." I ended the conversation with a feeling that I'd be getting that call sooner rather than later, so I boarded the plane. Protected from intrusion by my Bose headphones, I sat through the flight lost in thought, pretending to read or work. I told myself I was doing just as my father had wanted—getting on with my life.

So I made plans. I would resign the next day. I could plan on how I would do it, but I couldn't account for exactly what I would say. I needed to talk to Nicki before I did that.

Unfortunately, Nicki kept ignoring me. A public conversation between us would be unreasonable for me to expect. Yet when we got off the plane, I caught her eye as I held my phone, signaling that I would text her. She glared at me so hard that I stopped at once. I'd forgotten she didn't like texting me anymore. I glared back at her, *Well, then how the fuck am I supposed to talk with you?*

Then out of nowhere, her boss strode past me. He smiled in a most knowing way. "Evening, Adam."

"Good evening, Matthew. I bet you're glad to be home."

"Yes, I am." His voice lowered and he almost sniggered. "I'm sure you are, too."

He didn't wait for my response as he walked on. I glanced again at Nicki, who turned away. That was when I knew: she'd told her boss and she'd told the president.

With that information, I became incredibly impatient as I waited for her phone call. Back at my flat, I tried to keep busy. I sorted clothes and packed a bag of laundry to take to the cleaners. Then I ate dinner, watched TV, worked, played around on the computer—and kept checking my phone. No sign from her. *Why hasn't she called me? Where is she?*

Late that night, my doorbell rang. When I opened the door, Nicki leaned against the doorjamb with slumped shoulders and bedraggled hair. She smiled and sighed. "Hi."

There she was, in all her beauty before me, but I wasn't going to let her get off so easily. "So have you come to shag me senseless, tell me you love me, and then abandon me again? That seems to be your M.O."

"Very, very funny." She placed her hand on my chest and pushed me aside as she walked in.

After I closed the door, I wrapped my arms around her. "Well, that is what you did last night—especially the shagging."

"So I was a little forward."

"A little?"

"Okay. Maybe I jumped you. I'd say we both crossed a line."

"We crossed it a few times."

"We did, which is why I had to leave. I—"

My kiss stopped her from talking, and she didn't seem to mind because her body responded immediately. She pressed into me, and I wasn't about to let her go.

Eventually, I said between kisses, "So you admit you wantonly seduced me, but you claim you were forced to abandon me?"

"Pardon me," she said and pulled away, "if I had to go tell my boss, the leader of the free world, that I'm fooling around with a member of the press."

"We more than fooled around last night, but let's sit down, and you can tell me what happened." I grinned and kissed her forehead before offering her a drink.

After we were situated on my sofa with a beer for me and a glass of wine for her, I had her tell me everything that she'd done since she'd left me.

"Start at the beginning. What did you do this morning?"

"Well, I woke up—hung over. That sucked." Then she kissed me on the cheek. "But I was with you, so that was nice."

"But you left…" After finally getting back together, I really didn't like that.

"I didn't wake you because it was really early, and I had to get back to my hotel room without being seen in the same clothes that I wore out the night before. Luckily, I don't think anyone saw me."

"Ah…the Walk of Shame. I forgot about that."

"Yes. Something to be avoided in our situation."

"Indeed." I found her hand and squeezed it. "I should tell you that I got more than one look from my colleagues and also a nasty comment from Dan about our dancing."

"Yeah, I figured as much. I got a lot of comments, too. Oh well. We can't do much about that now."

"No, we can't, so tell me more about this morning."

"After I left you, I got cleaned up, packed, and did some work before I went to talk to Melba to get on Logan's schedule."

"You didn't want to talk to Matthew first? Or Juan Carlos?" I leaned back, evaluating her strategy. I was the last person who wanted Nicki to spend time with old JC, but it was odd that she wouldn't contact him. He had been her boyfriend for all appearances, regardless of their actual status. Some might think he deserved to hear things first since many people would assume she'd cheated on him though she really hadn't. No one knew how things had broken down between them.

"I thought about it, but after last night, I decided I needed to just go straight to Logan. He's been like a dad to me for so long. He deserved to hear things first."

"So when did you talk?"

"Not until we were on the plane. Logan thought I was going to resign so I could get married, so I first had to tell him I wasn't marrying Juan Carlos."

"What did he say to that?" God, I hoped Logan wasn't upset.

"He was surprised, and then when I hemmed and hawed, he asked that I just tell him everything." She sipped some wine like she needed a breather and then said, "So I told him our story, starting at the very beginning after Lauren died."

"You started back in high school? Really?"

"It seemed easier to tell him that way, and frankly, I think it was more compelling. I said after over fifteen years, we'd found each other again, and over the last few months, we've fallen back in love."

Nicki's synopsis made me feel like an eleven-year-old boy who has just been told the girl he really likes, likes him as well — and like a boy, I responded by teasing her. I tousled her hair to show my appreciation and asked, "Well, what did he say?"

"Professionally, he's disappointed in me. I've caused a headache for him. But he's still very fatherly and happy that you and I reconnected. Matthew, on the other hand, was a little pissed and taken aback when he did find out, but not totally surprised."

"I have to say I'm feeling a bit guilty you're taking all this heat."

"Don't feel guilty." She winced and took a breath. "But I do have to ask something huge of you. I understand if you don't want to do it. There are other ways out."

"What's that?"

"Logan, Matt, and I talked through our options. Of course, you and I can't be in our current roles together anymore. The fairest option is that you and I both quit our jobs. The problem with that one—and the reason Matt doesn't like it—is that it looks like there was some wrongdoing on our part."

"I can see that," I said, kissing her hand. "If we're both going to lose our jobs in shame, I'd like to have been shagging at least more than one night."

"Amen to that." She laughed before continuing. "But actually, that's why Logan doesn't like the idea either. We really haven't done anything grossly unethical yet."

"So what does he want?"

"Well, honestly, Adam, it looks the best for Logan and makes the most sense if you resign, and I stay working at the White House." She looked at me guiltily. "I'm sorry…"

"Don't be. I already told you I'd resign. I meant it."

"Are you sure?"

"Of course. And their political calculus is correct—I wish I'd thought to argue from that angle before. You keep doing what you're doing, and I move on. When it comes out that we've been dating, people will question the timing, but because you're still in your position, it shows the president has faith that nothing untoward happened between us. No state secrets were released, and I didn't go easy on the administration over something. And if I resign now, our relationship is never an issue in the future. It all makes sense."

"But your career…" Her brow knit in concern.

"My career? I don't give a fuck. With Dad so ill and…well, when he's gone…" My throat tightened, so I took a drink to get some composure. After a few seconds, I said, "I'm going to need some time off. I'd take compassionate leave regardless."

I felt the touch of her hand, comforting me as she nudged closer. "I'm so sorry, Adam. This really isn't good timing, is it?"

"I don't think there's ever good timing for something like this." Taking her into my arms, I kissed her cheek. "But considering that I've got you back, I'd say the timing is as good as it gets."

She stroked my hair and kissed me. "I love you."

"I love you, too." It was a lovely moment, but I needed to hear more of her story. I leaned back and asked, "So if you talked to them on the plane, why did it take you so long to get here?"

"I figured I owed it to Juan Carlos to let him know immediately. I went to see him."

"You did? What did he say? What did *you* say?"

"I was honest about everything, and he was angry…really angry." She frowned. "I deserve it—even if he and I were on the outs. I deceived him."

"He must despise me."

"Pretty much. He said something about Felicity being a ruse."

"I assure you, she was not a ruse."

Well, that was a whopper. Yet I wasn't ready to lay it out there that I'd led Nicki on about Felicity. In the end, I was a prideful bastard. Plus, it was true Felicity had her talons in me to some degree, and she was jealous of Nicki. It wasn't like she'd been completely out of the picture.

I took a breath before I said, "She may even be a bloody pain in the arse later, but we'll worry about that when we have to."

"Will she say something?"

I searched for a relatively truthful comment. "Even though we've seen relatively little of each other in the last six months, the break-up didn't go very well. She immediately brought up your name."

"What did you say to that?" she asked fearfully.

"I said, 'Nicki and I are close enough friends that I've realized what's missing in our relationship.' That's it."

"Oh, that must not have gone over well."

"No, it didn't. Felicity has never thought herself lacking in any way. To hear otherwise was quite an insult to her."

"Will she talk publicly about you?"

"I don't know. I hope not." I had two saving graces. Felicity's highborn upbringing dictated silence in matters involving another aristocrat such as myself, and she had a professional duty not to do anything to besmirch the BBC. But I worried about what a scorned, short Latin bloke might do in a situation like this. "Will Juan Carlos?"

"Never. He's too loyal to Logan. If he gossips about me, Logan looks bad. But I also think he'd be too embarrassed by it."

Even I felt a bit badly for JC, but thank God Nicki hadn't been with some apolitical Wall Street arse who'd happily trash her. "I'm sorry about that, but overall, what a stroke of luck."

"Yeah, finally."

"I realize things can still go sideways pretty quickly, but right now I think we're doing okay."

"Right now, yes."

Leaning down to kiss her again, I whispered, "I'm very happy."

"I'm happy, too."

She met my kiss, and we snogged on the sofa long enough that I started to get hard. In response, I murmured, "Let's go to bed."

"I want to, but I shouldn't." She then sat up straight with excitement and began to speak in double-time. "Shit. I'm not done. I need to tell Lisa…and my dad. Before they hear it anywhere else. But I'll call my mom while I'm on the road this week. For any reservations she may have had at the beginning, I know this news will make her very happy, so I don't have to talk to her immediately."

"That's right. There's another trip." I'd forgotten the president was touring the West that week.

"We leave tomorrow night, remember?"

"*We* don't leave tomorrow night. Only *you* now."

She frowned. "No more trips together."

"Hardly." I pulled her back close to me. "Many more trips together. Just the two of us, though. No fucking Dan Roark along."

Giggling again, she asked, "Where should we go first?"

Feeling both joyful and randy, I whisked her into my arms and announced, "To my bed, of course."

"Adam, I just said—"

"The night is young. You'll see Lisa soon enough, and your parents can wait until the morning."

"But you haven't resigned yet."

I smiled at her pathetic attempt at protest. Carrying her back to my bedroom, I said, "No, I haven't resigned yet. I'll do so tomorrow morning, but I'll text my boss right now if it finally gets you in my bed."

"No need for that," she said, kissing my neck.

By the time we reached my room, though, the bed had become obsolete. We kissed along the way, and I couldn't get our clothes off fast enough. When Nicki was naked, I had to listen to her usual nonsense about her body. Women will never learn that men are simply happy that they're naked. After I told Nicki she wasn't allowed to criticize a body I loved, she rewarded me with a forceful kiss. I grabbed her bum, and she kissed me again with a giggle before jumping up and wrapping her legs around me.

She was so close to me that it made the head of my dick feel like there was a homing device in it. The position must've unleashed something similar in her as well. She asked with a smile, "Shall we stand?"

Feeling her wetness against me, I practically hissed, "Why yes, thank you," and my lips met hers for another kiss. As our tongues tangled, it struck me that I now had a far more verbal partner in Nicki than before. I wondered what I could say that would be… inspirational. Sadly, I knew my limitations. I wasn't like my cad cousin. I was far too proper and reserved to talk dirty. So I decided to say exactly what I wanted. "Put me inside of you."

The direct approach seemed to be just as good for her because she gasped, "God, yes." She took my dick and, after a nice rub, placed me right where I wanted to be. I groaned before maneuvering her against a wall. It was the perfect position to watch her unravel, and I loved every second of it.

Afterward, I curled up next to her on the bed and pulled her to me. She placed her hand on my chest and smiled. "Nothing's changed…"

"No, it hasn't. Though I do hope I lasted a little longer than before. I remember not doing too well your first time. I believe you lost your virginity in the blink of an eye because I couldn't control myself."

"Neither one of us was good at controlling ourselves back then."

"Some would say we aren't very good at controlling ourselves now."

We spent the next hour planning out the rest of the week—how I'd resign, how she'd tell her parents, and when we'd see each other again. She wasn't returning from the president's tour of the West until the weekend, but I planned on going back home to see Dad on

Wednesday. And since I wouldn't be working anymore, I realized I should make my trip home open-ended.

When she heard I wasn't coming immediately back to DC, she asked, "Do you want me to fly to see you on Sunday? I could take a few days off."

"You're wonderful," I said, so happy with her offer. "I don't think that's necessary."

"We'll talk this week, though, right?"

"Every day, I hope."

As Nicki got dressed to go home, I threw on my boxers to see her out. I scowled at her buckling her belt. Was she always going to be leaving me?

I grumbled, "I don't like it."

"What? This belt?"

"No. The fact that you're leaving."

"We just discussed this," she said, then kissed my cheek. "I need to talk to some people, and so do you."

"But when we're both back in DC for good, I won't like that you're not here." It was all falling into place in my head. We were finally back together after sixteen years. I'd already told the woman I wanted to marry her. Why on earth would I start dating her like she was some girl I was just getting to know? It seemed like a bloody waste of time.

"What do you mean?" she asked.

I took her in my arms. "Well, I know we haven't been together again for very long—"

"Like maybe a day." She laughed.

"Yes, but given our history, can't we skip the going-out stage?" I gave her a pleading kiss on the forehead. "I know that's where my heart is."

"What do you mean?" she said again.

She was probably bracing for another spontaneous marriage proposal. But even I had to acknowledge there was too much uncertainty in our lives for me to go on bended knee just yet. For all my eagerness, I wasn't any readier for that than Nicki. "Will you move in with me? For now. As a start…"

"We haven't even gone on one date, and you want to live together?"

"Yes."

"Let's get through the drama around your resignation and our relationship first. Let's see how that goes."

I couldn't argue with that. "And then?"

"I agree we need to make up for lost time," she said and sealed it with a kiss.

With sleep still in my eyes the next dawn, I lay in bed as I sent an email to the BBC Washington bureau chief, Ben Keller, and more importantly, to Kent in London. I only told them that I urgently needed to meet with them that morning. They were reporters. I didn't want to give them any hints with which they could start to do their own research.

When I got to work as early as I could, I went directly to Ben's office. He looked up from his computer.

"Adam. Good morning. You wanted to see me?"

"Hello, Ben. Yes. First thing, if possible."

"Fine," he said with a quizzical look. "I'll get Liz to get us set up with Kent on a video conference."

Once we were situated in the conference room and with Kent on the large flat screen, I opened the meeting. "Thank you for meeting with me on such short notice. I appreciate it."

Both men nodded in silence, eager to hear why I'd called such a meeting, so I forged ahead. "I'm resigning from the BBC immediately." I handed Ben the letter I'd written that morning and looked at the screen. "Kent, I just sent the same letter to you by email."

Ben's mouth gaped as he read the short letter. Kent's expression was impassive as he pulled up the email on his laptop. His voice was flat. "This is a surprise."

"I know. And I've given you no time to plan. I apologize for that, but there are extenuating circumstances."

"Is this about your father, Adam?" Ben's head cocked in curiosity. "You know that you can take as much time as you need off. I imagine that with his health and the family estate there are a number of things that must be done."

"No, my father's health isn't a reason for my resignation." I took a breath and said, "I have a personal matter that means I can no longer work here—at least in the Washington bureau—at this time."

"What's that?" Kent asked. He squinted like he knew something was coming.

Kent always was a step ahead of everyone else, so I was quick. "I'm in a personal relationship with Nicole Johnson."

"You'd mentioned you knew her at school," said Ben, leaning back in his chair. "So the old friends are now new friends? A little chummy, are we?"

"Yes," I said sheepishly.

"Well, that would require a resignation. I suppose I should thank you for doing something I would've been forced to do," Kent said with a dark laugh. "Does the White House know?"

"Nicole has told both the president and Matthew Foster," I said.

"How long has this been going on?" Ben scratched head. "I'm so behind. I thought you and Felicity had something going on."

"It's been very recent," I said. "Things have been off with Felicity for a while now."

"So it's only recently that you've become romantically involved with Nicole, but you're willing to resign for her?" he asked with a skeptical eye. "This must be serious."

"It is."

"And the political consensus from the White House was that you're the sacrificial lamb for the relationship," said Kent.

"I wouldn't call it that. Something had to be done. This is the easiest route. And as Ben has pointed out, I need to take some time off for my father and family."

"You've put the BBC in quite an awkward position," Ben said. "You're well aware of that, though. We're going to be accused of going soft on the US president because of their White House correspondent."

"Indeed. It's why I sacked myself."

Ben looked to Kent for guidance as to what the official position would be on my resignation. Kent tapped his hand on the table twice as if he'd just made up his mind. He nodded at me. "We'll get someone to replace you as soon as possible. As to questions about your status, if asked—and only if asked—the BBC will state this was a minor personnel issue that's been dealt with, and though it is saddened by Adam Kincaid's departure, we wish him well and look forward to employing him again if the opportunity arises."

"Thank you very much. Cheers," I said with a smile of relief.

With his hand on the remote to disconnect the video, Kent was warm as he said, "Goodbye to you both. Adam, please keep in touch."

Knowing that I'd have a box of personal crap from my office to take home, I'd driven to work that morning. As I was shutting the boot of my car, my phone rang. It was Sylvia.

"Good morning."

"Morning, Adam. We need to talk."

"Yes, we do. I need to tell you what's going on."

"Whatever it is, it can wait. Mum's just called me. We need to go home."

"Dad is…"

"Fading. It won't be long."

"But I was planning to fly tomorrow. Is that enough time?"

"I asked her the same thing, because I've got a big meeting tomorrow afternoon, but Mum said we should come *now*. I'm leaving this evening. What do you want to do?"

"Well, I'll fly tonight as well, then." It sounded decisive, but really it was an auto-reply. Hearing that Dad was about to die made me feel helpless — it reminded me I had no say in the matter. There were no choices to be made. I was to do as expected.

Sylvia then begged off the phone, and I let her go. It seemed like too odd a time to tell her of my news with Nicki or my job.

Getting in my car, I decided to phone Nicki before I left the car park. It was an odd location for a call, especially since I'd just resigned, but I needed to talk with her. I worried that she might not pick up the phone, but she answered immediately. "Hi, sweetheart!"

Despite the bad news I'd just heard, I smiled hearing Nicki's voice. A lightness had come over her, and you could hear the happiness.

"Are you sure you're still interested in me?" I asked. "I'm just an unemployed bloke now."

"Oh my God. You resigned so quickly."

"Well, my bosses are in London, and they're hours ahead of us. I didn't see any reason not to contact them as soon as I woke up."

"So how did it go?" she said with a quick breath.

"All in all, it went relatively well, but only because I resigned. They asked how long our relationship has been going on, and I said it was relatively recent. They asked about Felicity as well. I was scolded, as could be expected, but since I was quitting, I'd taken away their thunder of sacking me."

"That's true. They don't have much to do now."

As I told her the rest of my story, she took it all in and laughed. At the end, she sounded relieved but said, "I'm really sorry this has turned out this way for you."

"But I didn't tell you the most important part," I answered.

"What's that?"

"They'll hire me back in another capacity in the future."

"Oh, that's great! Especially because we won't live here forever."

"We won't?"

"Well, I mean, I won't have this job forever, and then in the future…if we were still together we could—"

"We're absolutely going to be together. I was just wondering where we might live other than DC?"

"I don't know. I imagine you would want to spend time back in London. Am I right?"

"You are. How do you feel about that?"

"I think it would be nice for a while."

My heart swelled knowing that she'd be willing to move for me. "You don't know how happy you make me."

"You make me happy, too. I love you."

"I love you." The emotion I felt for her gave me the support I needed to tell her what was going on. I sighed. "Things haven't been all good this morning, though. Sylvia called with bad news. Dad isn't doing well at all. I need to go home straightaway."

"It's that bad."

"Yes, I must go so I can see him before…"

"I'm so sorry. When are you leaving?"

"This evening. It just depends on what flight I can get on at the last minute."

Without hesitating, Nicki said, "Would you like me to come, too?"

"No, you don't have to. I'll be okay."

"All you have to do is say so, and I'll be there."

"I know. Really, I'll be fine." I chuckled. "And you already got to talk to him."

"I did. He was very kind."

I wondered again what might have been said between them. I wanted to ask but decided that one day I might learn…or not. As long as Nicki was with me, either would be okay.

I checked my watch. "So, I guess I need to book a flight. Hmm. Funny. I'm unemployed now and without an assistant. I haven't booked a ticket for myself in years."

"Try Orbitz like the rest of us."

"Maybe I will," I said, matching her sarcasm.

Her voice became sympathetic again. "I don't think our travel schedules are going to mesh very well. I'm going to be out-of-pocket a lot in the next couple of days. Please keep in close touch, because I'll want to come later."

"Later?"

It was stupid to question what she meant. As she answered, "The funeral," I quietly said it to myself.

The funeral. There would be a funeral, and she wanted to be there for it. My mind skipped ahead to what it might be like. Visions of a memorial service in Cambridge and interment in Scotland came to mind. I wanted Nicki at my side for both.

I replied softly, "Thank you. Having you there will mean every-thing to me. I'll be in touch."

"I want to be there."

"Then I'll text you when I land in London. I love you, sweetheart."

"And I love you."

Chapter Sixteen

Orbitz served me well. I found an eleven a.m. direct flight out of
Dulles that I could still catch and realized there was no reason
to delay until evening, especially now that I was out of a job.

I arrived in Cambridge late that evening, and when I woke the
next morning, the house was busy. Mum was happy to see me—happier than I'd expected. I soon realized it was because she had a new
friend. A round-the-clock nurse was now stationed in the bedroom,
providing Dad with high dosages of morphine and helping Mum with
his care. Her name was Susan Welch, and she was from Blackpool.
She'd taken a liking to Mum, whose Liverpool accent had become
more pronounced in her presence. The two joked often, and the help
with Dad must've eased a burden on Mum—a burden that she hadn't
wanted her children to see or bear.

Susan didn't have the same rapport with Sylvia, though. Sylvia
found the nurse rough and demanding, and I think Susan had no idea
what to make of my sister. In true Sylvia form, she clacked around the
house in her stilettos, rearranging furniture, photos, and knickknacks
that had been in their locations for decades. She was obviously looking
for some purpose. There was nothing to do, though, besides usher in
the neighbors and friends wanting to pay their respects. Otherwise,
we sat vigil because Dad was barely conscious.

Sylvia warned me before I walked in, "He's really out of it. He
smiled at me but didn't talk."

"Okay. I won't expect much."

"Oh, and that nurse. She says not to talk about him like he's not there—especially about funeral stuff."

"What do you mean?"

"She thinks he hears things—even though he's out of it."

"You don't believe her?"

"Not really, but I'm following her directions. She snapped at me earlier when I said something."

I nodded, deciding I'd also follow those instructions. Perhaps Sylvia thought Susan was superstitious, but surely a hospice nurse knew more about dying people than my sister.

Dad didn't move as I sat down next to him. I held his hand, hoping he might speak to me. His eyes flicked open for the briefest second, only to close again. His mouth gaped, and a scratchy whisper acknowledged me.

"Adam."

Beyond his saying my name, my last real communication with him would be the slightest squeeze of my fingers that he gave me after I told him that I loved him. His hand was cold, paper-thin skin and knotty bones; it was such a contrast to how I knew his body to have been. I understood then that Dad, as I'd known him all my life, had already left us.

Nicki and I kept in frequent contact. When we talked or texted, she was there for me—listening, joking, and overall making me very happy, despite my sad situation.

At one point, Susan pulled me aside, saying, "You should know that your father may pass away without you there. And you shouldn't feel badly. That's how it often happens."

"How on earth will that happen? I'm here all the time."

"I'm simply saying that sometimes people don't want to die with their loved ones around them. They don't want to see them sad."

"Who doesn't want to see whom sad?"

"Either one."

"Huh." I didn't quite get what she was saying. "So he'd choose to die on his own so that it's less sad for everyone?"

"Yes."

I could see how Sylvia thought her superstitious. I nodded and thanked her for the information. Walking away, though, I didn't believe her. *What? Like Dad has any say in the matter of when he dies?*

Yet, what did bloody old Dad do? He died just as he'd wanted to live the remainder of his life—alone with Mum. Late in the day on Wednesday, Sylvia and I had gone to the train station together to pick up David and his mum. We returned, and Dad was gone.

I'd managed to keep the tears back when I was with my family standing in front of Dad's body. It was only when I spoke with Nicki a few minutes later that the emotions pushed through. I cried like a baby on the phone with her.

She listened patiently and was as sweet as ever. When I pulled myself together, she asked, "When is the funeral?"

"Sylvia is in charge. It's a big do on Friday—a memorial service at Trinity College Chapel—but then we'll go to Scotland on Saturday to bury his ashes on the estate Sunday. That ceremony will be small and just family."

"Well...I—"

"Nicki, you don't have to be here on Friday."

"I want to be there. I just need to figure out how."

"Where are you right now, anyway?"

"In Aspen, Colorado. There's a big fundraiser tonight at a swanky house."

"Please, don't cut your trip short. You get back to DC on Friday. If you could make it on Saturday so we could go to Scotland together, that would be wonderful, but, really, that's not necessary either."

"Well, let me see..."

We talked a little more, but she then had to leave. As much as I wanted her there with me, I didn't want to drag her away from what was an interesting trip, just to sit around Cambridge.

After Dad's body was taken away, the initial aftermath of grieving didn't go on for long before organized chaos erupted in the house. Sylvia turned into an event planner, working with the funeral director and handling all the details of the coming days. Mum was the smiling, steadfast widow, dealing with all the guests and callers. The place was so crazy that David and I decided to escape to a pub, where we toasted Dad and watched football.

When I woke up on Thursday morning, there was a text from Nicki.

I'm going to try to make it Friday morning.
I love you. I'll be in touch.

With my first smile in at least a day, I quickly tapped back.

I love you. So very, very much.

As I stood in front of the Trinity College Chapel on Friday morning, I greeted Dad's old colleagues and our family friends, and all the while, I was on the lookout for Nicki. It was silly of me, though, because I knew she'd only landed early that morning. We'd talked, and depending on any delays in arrival, the immigration queue, or traffic getting out of London, she probably wouldn't arrive in time for the memorial service, but she would be at the house for the wake.

There I was, though, looking over everyone's shoulders to see if Nicki had somehow made it. A local newspaper had a photographer there, and he kept trying to get my photo with everyone I spoke with. He thought the new Viscount Adam Kincaid, BBC reporter, somewhat of a celebrity—little did he know I was unemployed and could give a fuck that I now had the family title.

It was almost time for the family to walk down the aisle and take our seats when a hired car pulled up across the way. I could see the passenger handing a slip of paper to the driver. Then the door opened, and a woman's heel hit the ground. I knew it was Nicki.

Ignoring my family, who called me to come back to the church, I walked straight toward her. She saw me and walked faster, though the long, narrow skirt of her black dress slowed her down. When we were close enough, I grabbed her in my arms for a tight embrace.

"I made it," she said with a sigh.

"You did. And I love you for it."

We kissed once and I wanted more, so I kissed her again, and then once more. That one went on for a bit. Nicki pulled away and smiled. "Adam, this isn't the place."

"I don't really fucking care." Then I winked. "And I know Dad doesn't either."

Taking Nicki's hand in mine, I kept it there with no intention of ever letting go. We walked down the aisle with my family, and whilst my eyes were on the altar, I was sure the rest of the church's attention was on Nicki. I smiled inwardly thinking that my father ended up being the person introducing Nicki to his extended family and friends.

As we sat in the pew, rather than pay attention to the vicar's various prayers for the dead, I focused on the eulogy I was about to deliver. I hadn't written any of it down because seeing my thoughts about Dad on a page would be too heartbreaking. Instead, I relied on my television experience to give an off-the-cuff, yet formal speech — with enough sentiment that it wasn't dry, but enough professionalism for no sign of personal emotion. I wanted to keep my feelings for later because I was so confused. It was my father's funeral, for Christ's sake — I should've been devastated. But with Nicki at my side as if she were my partner in life, I was incredibly happy.

After the service, we went back to the house, where Sylvia had organized a proper wake, though the centerpieces were a little artsy for Cambridge. Nicki's hand was still firmly in mine as I introduced her to everyone as "my dear friend," and no one seemed to recognize who she was. When one of Dad's colleagues walked straight up to us and held out her hand, however, I became concerned. Professor Hadley had spent so many years as the sole female in the biology department at Cambridge that she had little time for formalities.

"Hello, I'm Professor Beatrice Hadley. I do believe you're Nicole Johnson."

"Yes, yes, I am," Nicki said with a gracious smile. "It's nice to meet you, Professor Hadley."

Glancing at me, Beatrice commented, "I suppose you know Adam from his work at the White House."

"Yes," I answered on Nicki's behalf. "But actually we knew each other before then."

Nicki gave me a quick look of approval and said, "Yes, we're old friends."

Then another professor joined our conversation. Offering Nicki his hand, he said cheerily, "I'm Graham Schofield—I worked with Professor Kincaid. It's nice to meet you, Miss Johnson."

"A pleasure to meet you, Professor Schofield," she said, shaking his hand.

"So, Adam, how is the BBC these days? Are you still enjoying living in Washington?"

I cleared my throat as I prepared to officially make my resignation public knowledge. "Washington is a wonderful city, but actually, I've left the BBC…for the time being."

Both professors looked a little taken aback by the irrational career move. Thankfully, Mum had overheard it all and interrupted us, saying, "Adam's decided to take some time off so he can be around if we need his help."

As Mum moved on to another group, Nicki added, "I'm also looking forward to Adam spending time on his artwork."

I glanced down at her and smiled. I hadn't really thought about using the time to focus on my cartoons and caricatures, but it was a good idea. Squeezing her hand, I mumbled, "I suppose I'll have time for that."

"Artwork? What would that be?" Professor Hadley was curious.

"Oh, political cartoons. It's just a hobby of mine." I shrugged.

"Really? Do you know Richard Lawrence at the *Financial Times*?"

"Only his work. I've never met him. His work is brilliant, though."

"He's a very good friend of mine from school days. We go way back; we were at Stowe together. You know, he's retiring soon. He'll still contribute to the paper, but not daily. If you want, I can introduce you two."

Nicki gave my hand a hard squeeze. I didn't need her prompt, however, to readily answer, "That would be wonderful, Professor Hadley. I'd really appreciate that."

By midafternoon, I could see that the jetlag had caught up with Nicki and she was flagging. When I thought she might fall asleep standing up, I whispered, "Nicki, let me take you upstairs. You're knackered."

Her eyes popped open, and relief spread over her face. "Thank you. I haven't had much sleep."

"I just need to tell Mum."

On my way to inform her, I bumped into David. "I'm taking Nicki upstairs for a kip. Can you help out down here if they need me?"

"A kip? Like you're going to let her nap." David smirked.

"Yes, I'm going to let her nap. Do you really think I'm taking her to my room to shag her brains out during my father's wake?"

"Seems like as good a time as any, mate." His smirk widened. "Everyone's sorted down here."

After telling Mum and grabbing Nicki's bag, I led her upstairs to my room.

"Will your mother be okay with this?"

"I'm pretty sure she had cottoned on to the fact we were sleeping together sixteen years ago. I doubt that she'll be upset today." Kissing her forehead, I added, "Besides, with David and his mum here, the house is full. There's no other space. You're stuck with me."

"I like that," she said happily.

Walking into the room, Nicki looked around and laughed. "This is quite a collection."

I smiled. She had to be remarking on my Liverpool obsession. I placed her suitcase on my desk chair and glanced up at a giant football poster from 1989. "I always meant to change it, but never got round to it."

"Oh please. Like you'd really want to take any of this down."

"You're right about that." Smiling at her, the bed caught my eye. I'd forgotten it was a single. "Bugger, I only just noticed the bed. We might be a little uncomfortable in this small space tonight."

"Never," she murmured, wrapping her arms around my neck. After a long kiss that changed from loving to highly erotic, she pulled back. "Don't you remember? We've only ever slept together in a twin bed. That's what was in my room in high school."

"Ah! That's right." I touched her hair. "I never wanted to leave."

"I never wanted you to leave." She rose up to kiss me. "And I still don't."

Her mouth and body were so tempting that I gave in to her kiss.

Damn it, David. Now all I can think about is how much I want to fuck her.

Just as I felt myself getting hard, I begrudgingly broke off our embrace. "I should go back downstairs."

"I know. I'm sorry about that." She smiled sheepishly. "I got carried away."

"Believe me. I want to get carried away with you. I just can't right now."

After leaving Nicki with a towel and an introduction to the loo down the hall, I went back downstairs. David stood at the bottom, chatting up Professor Hadley. She had no idea what to make of him because he was at least thirty years her junior, yet he kept calling her "love."

When she wandered away, I asked him, "Do you often chat up old-age pensioners?"

"She's lovely…for her age. I probably made her day."

I shook my head at him. Realizing that we hadn't talked about women in a while, I asked, "So how are things with Lisa?"

"Lisa?" David grinned wickedly. "She's my never-ending challenge."

"What happens if she gives in?"

"Oh, she has, and she's still a challenge." He raised an eyebrow. "It's fantastic. For now."

"For now?" I leaned back in alarm. "You can't just toss this one aside, David. She's Nicki's best—"

"Good God." He laughed. "I'll be the one who's tossed on the rubbish heap when she moves back to Houston. She's already told me that."

"She's planning on dumping you, yet she still wants to see you." I shook my head in disbelief. "How do you do it?"

"Charm," he said with pure self-satisfaction. He then patted his chest. "And of course, I have other…physical…attributes and abilities that keep the ladies interested."

I held up my hand. "That's enough."

He chuckled and gently slapped my back. "You know I'm taking the piss. It's just because I'm jealous you've found your lady for this life."

"Thanks, but I doubt you really want to settle down."

"Fuck no," he said with a derisive snort. He looked off outside a window. "God help me if I ever do find the one."

Talking with him only made me want to be back upstairs with Nicki. As soon as the last guest left, I made sure that Mum was happy with her sister and a glass of brandy before I hotfooted back up the stairs.

I'd promised Nicki that I'd wake her before it got too late so that her body clock could adjust. When I found her still asleep, though, it seemed cruel to disturb her. She was in a deep sleep, so I thought I'd rouse her gently. Stripping down to my boxers, I got in bed with every intention of easing her out of her slumber. But as I lifted the covers, I saw she was wearing a lacy pink camisole with her pajama bottoms.

The sexy sight stuck in my mind as I leaned in to give her a kiss on the cheek. She didn't stir. Then I got an idea. Maybe I'd coax her out of her sleep.

I slipped my hand beneath her pajamas and between her legs to very gently stroke her over her knickers. At first, her body didn't react. Eventually, though, she spread her legs slightly wider, offering me better access. I took the liberty of sliding her pants to the side, which caused her to unconsciously mew and roll onto her back as if offering her body up to me to play with. When I finally touched her skin, I concentrated solely on that one spot and watched as Nicki came to life. She squirmed and moaned a while, then opened her still-drowsy eyes for a moment and mumbled, "Don't stop."

"Then I won't."

So I continued tormenting and pleasing her only with my finger. It was amazing to watch one small, consistent motion on a tiny spot of flesh wreak such havoc on a body. Arching her back, she clutched the sheets and attempted to stifle her sounds as I increased the circular pressure. She was soon shuddering and coating my hand with her wetness. It was all I could do not to mount her like a dog in heat.

I let her go at her own pace, though. Blinking a few times, she opened her eyes and shyly smiled. "That was nice."

"It was nice to watch."

"Was it, now?" She snickered and found my erection waiting for her. "Well, it appears it was."

With her hand on my rock-solid cock, I leaned in for a kiss. "I get off watching you get off. Call me old-fashioned."

"You're old-fashioned, and I like it," she said and pulled me on top of her.

I went after her like the randy bastard I was. No thoughts of Dad or his memorial or my family members downstairs entered my mind. She was the one who made sure we were quiet.

Afterward, I caught my breath and kissed her hair, and she looked up at me and grinned.

"You're smiling."

"I am?" I asked, though I obviously knew she was right.

"You are."

"Probably because I'm so damn happy."

"Good," she said, following up with a kiss.

I kissed her back, but guilt eventually pulled me away. I stopped smiling. "It's odd though…feeling this way. I don't think I'm supposed to be cheery after my father has just died. It's very confusing."

Her eyes softened. What I thought was sympathy coming from them was actually empathy. "I know. I remember that feeling."

"What do you mean?"

"Way back…when we first started dating. I thought my heart was going to burst. I was so elated…such a giddy teenager. But even though everything felt right between us, I felt like I was doing something wrong—like I'd forgotten about Lauren. Like I should've been in mourning. I couldn't be in mourning, though, not with you around."

"That's exactly how I feel." I squeezed her, enjoying the shared experience, but then I remembered Dad and winced. "Maybe if I'd been able to give him a proper goodbye, it would feel differently. Why did he have to go while I was away?"

"Oh, Adam." She ran her fingers through my hair. "You can't think about it like that. Lauren and I were bickering over something stupid when she died. Why would I want to focus on that? You're not supposed think about the end. The end is full of regret that you can't do anything about." Her voice quavered. "You need to remember them living—when they were really alive—not sick or dead in a car."

Seeing Nicki become emotional about her sister always touched me, but this time was different. Now I understood what she felt.

I started to tear up as I confessed, "I think I'd miss him too much if I thought about what he was like before he was ill."

With her own eyes glistening, Nicki helped wipe my tears away. "You'll always miss him. You just won't miss him all the time, if that makes any sense."

"It does." I smiled.

Kissing my cheek, she whispered, "I love you, Adam."

"I love you." My hand went beneath her chin, and I raised her face so I could see my sweet, smart, and sexy woman. "You know, you're making me smile again."

"You make me smile, too. I'm even happier than I was back then."

"I'm happier as well." And just before another kiss, I said, "Because this time we're together for good."

Chapter Seventeen

Nicki and I were packing our luggage for Scotland the following morning when Sylvia greeted us with *The Cambridge News* in her hand.

"Morning, Nicki. Morning, Adam. I thought you might want to see this."

I grabbed the paper from her. "What's that?"

"Look right here," Sylvia said as she pointed to a few photos accompanying an article about Dad's memorial service. The first photo depicted mourners in front of the chapel. The second photo was of Mum and me greeting Dad's colleagues. Then there was the third photo. The room fell silent.

Sylvia shrugged. "It's a darling photo of you two. It would be lovely to frame."

I gave my sister a look that conveyed she was completely insane.

After taking the newspaper from me, Nicki studied the photos, lingering on the last one — the one of her standing in front of me with my arms encircling her as she stared into the distance.

She read the caption aloud. "'Cambridge-born BBC White House Correspondent, Viscount Adam Kincaid, consoles himself over the loss of his father with Ms. Nicole Johnson.'" Looking up, she gave her professional assessment. "This is going to be picked up somewhere. There are probably other photos, too. Let me call Matt, and you should warn the BBC."

I nodded. "I'll call Kent after you talk to Matt. I need to know what the White House might say."

Trying to brighten the day, Sylvia said, "I knew you two would want to see this, but isn't the bright side that it's a lovely photo?"

"It is a nice one." Nicki smiled, succumbing to Sylvia's optimism. "Now let me wake up Matt."

Ten minutes later, Nicki returned from making her call in a private room. She grimaced as she walked in.

"How was it?" I asked.

"He wasn't happy, and he won't be for a while, but we came up with a good statement."

"What is it?"

She read from a piece of paper, "If asked, the White House will say that 'Deputy Press Secretary Nicole Johnson was given a few days off to support her old friend Adam Kincaid at his father's funeral. The BBC notified the White House on Tuesday of this past week that Adam Kincaid had resigned.'" She looked at me. "That's it. I think it sounds all right. Now go find out what the BBC will say."

"It does work." I wrapped my arms around her. "Just give me a moment to track down Kent."

"Oh, and Matt and I agree it's important that I show up at work on Monday morning. You know — give everything a sense of normalcy."

"That *would* be the best thing. If you stay here, it looks like you're hiding out."

She cringed. "Unfortunately, that means I'll need to leave tomorrow, after the interment."

"You know, I think David was planning on flying back to the States on Monday. I'm sure he would change his plans to head back with you tomorrow. It might be good to have someone with you in case there are photographers."

"That would be great if he could."

"You know he'd be happy to." I gave her another kiss. "This is going to work out. Now, let me call Kent."

Sitting in Dad's quiet office, I leaned back in the antique oak swivel chair that only professors seemed to own. I was sure that you needed a PhD to find them comfortable. After only one ring, Kent picked up the line. "Good morning, Adam."

"Morning, Kent."

"My condolences. I'm very sorry for you and your family."

"Thank you. I appreciate it."

"So what can I do for you?"

"Well, Nicole Johnson is here with me. She was at my father's memorial service yesterday. *The Cambridge News* has published a photo of the two of us together at the service. It identifies both of us and says I'm the BBC correspondent at the White House but doesn't say her title."

"It's a local paper. It wouldn't do more research than find out her name from one of the attendees."

"I'm sure that's what happened."

"So, I suppose the photo shows some public display of affection between you two."

"Yes." I couldn't stop a chuckle. "Not too bad in this one, but there are others, I'm sure."

"Others that I'm sure someone will pay dearly for." Kent laughed. "This local photographer didn't know he'd stumbled on a gold mine."

"If things work as Nicki and I suspect, I wouldn't be surprised if this shows up in the Sunday tabloids tomorrow morning."

"Oh yes. Someone will put two and two together." His tone became more formal. "I presume she's spoken with the White House about it."

I relayed the White House response on the matter. Kent took a moment before declaring, "The BBC response is only slightly modified from the one we talked about earlier. It now reads something like, 'Adam Kincaid resigned from the BBC last Monday. We look forward to employing him again if the opportunity arises. The BBC will permanently fill its White House correspondent position shortly. Our condolences go out to Adam and his family as they mourn the loss of the former Viscount Kincaid.'"

"Thank you," I said as relief and gratitude overtook me. "Thank you very much."

"Not a problem. Frankly, I think if everyone is forthright, this should blow over relatively quickly. I'm guessing you're heading to Scotland soon."

"Yes, we are. Shortly."

"Well, when the hacks call for the BBC response, I'll give them my unsolicited advice that it will appear unseemly to stalk the young viscount during this period of mourning—especially at the Kincaid estate in Scotland."

"Like they'll heed your advice," I said with a laugh.

"Wait a moment." I could tell that he took the phone from his ear because I heard him say, "Hmpf," in the background. When he came back, he said, "Speak of the devil. It's my counterpart over at the *Daily Mirror* ringing me right now."

"Damn, they act quickly. Maybe they've hacked my phone."

"I wouldn't put it past them. I should take this call to get our response out there. Take care, Adam, and please give your mother and sister my sympathies."

"I will. Cheers, Kent. Thank you for everything."

By the time we arrived at the family home in Scotland, my phone had rung no less than ten times—all London numbers, none of which I knew, all of which were surely the tabloids. I didn't answer any of them.

Sylvia kept looking over my shoulder with concern. "Shouldn't you say something?"

"Absolutely not." Nicki frowned and shook her head. "Don't give in to them. No one in the general public will expect him to return a reporter's call when he's burying his father."

"It's true." I laughed. "I always knew revealing our relationship would be controversial, but Dad's death is giving it an air of dignity that it wouldn't otherwise receive."

As our driver pulled onto the long road toward the estate, Nicki's voice went flat. "That's your family house?"

I looked up from my book to acknowledge the collection of ancient stone buildings, tucked in a glen. "That's it. Since the fourteenth century."

Sylvia rolled her eyes and said, "I hate it. Everything smells like wet rock—even in the family quarters, even if it hasn't rained for a month." She looked at the car behind us, which David was driving with Mum and his mother. "Poor David. I bet he's having to listen to them gush about it. He hates it, too. He says being here makes him feel like a serf."

"I can see why," Nicki said, gawking at the property. "I'm feeling very inferior myself."

"Ridiculous," I said. "It's not like we earned this place or the title. There's no merit involved."

"That's very egalitarian of you, *Viscount* Kincaid."

"I won't be using the title, and you know it." I nudged and kissed Nicki as she giggled.

Stepping out of the cars, we all walked around a bit, weary from the hours of road and air travel but happy to be upright. Nicki surveyed the surroundings with amazement. "It's hard to believe that you own this."

"Well, we don't really anymore." I winked. "The nation is kind enough to let us squat."

She looked off at the water and trees in the distance. "It's a stunning place to squat."

Impulsively, I pulled her to me and whispered, "Maybe we could live here for a bit. Raise some wee ones with thick Scottish accents that neither of us understand."

Nicki's mouth dropped open while her cheeks burned red.

Grinning, I asked, "You'd like that wouldn't you? I know I would."

"Do I get to see you in a kilt?"

I tousled her hair. "Naturally."

Despite me ignoring their calls, the tabloids wrote their stories. Nicki kept in contact with Matthew, who confirmed that the White had fielded numerous inquiries about the photo but offered nothing more than the official statement.

First thing the next morning, we checked all the tabloids' websites. Sure enough, the *Daily Mirror* had bought all the photographs from the Cambridge photographer.

David looked at the computer screen over my shoulder and whistled before remarking, "That's quite a lip-lock you two have in that picture."

"I think it looks sweet," said Sylvia.

"*Sweet?*" Under his breath, he mumbled, "Maybe sweet in an 'I'm gonna fuck your brains out later' kind of way."

I laughed. David knew me too well.

Apparently, Nicki didn't agree it was funny. "I'm never going to hear the end of it from Matthew."

"If all you're worried about is being made fun of by your boss, I think we're okay." I squeezed her hand.

"Thankfully, there's not much to their story. It's pretty thin." She smiled. "If the coverage continues this way, I think you're right."

After the Sunday morning church service, the vicar, who had been friends with my father since childhood, ushered us to the family crypt to inter Dad's ashes. Even with someone so close to my father leading our way to Dad's final physical resting place, the moment felt less emotional than the memorial service. As we walked back to the house holding hands, I mentioned it to Nicki.

"Well, that's because he's still alive in a way when we talk about him," she said. "There's not much sense of him as a person in a spooky crypt."

I let go of her hand and, grabbing her by the waist, stared at her appreciatively. "I wouldn't be getting through this without you."

"Oh yeah, you would."

"No, I wouldn't."

Pressing her forehead into my suit jacket, she said, "Well, if that's true, I'm glad to help you because you helped me so much. I love you."

My heart leapt, and I lifted her chin so I could kiss her. Before I could, David called out from behind us, "That'll be the last one of those for a while. I need to get Ms. Johnson to her chariot."

I saw him walk past us, but he stopped to give me a punch in the arm. "Don't worry, cuz. I'm a pro at taking care of her."

"Hey!" Nicki laughed in dismay. "That was a long time ago."

"You're a dead man," I snarled.

David didn't look back as he strode ahead laughing. "No worries. I'll safely deposit her, untouched, at my bird's door."

Saying goodbye to Nicki was difficult, but we knew we would be in constant contact. Still, I wanted her in my bed again that night, and it would've been nice to have time to show her around the place and the region more.

That would have to be saved for the future.

Chapter Eighteen

After Nicki and David left for their return journey to the States, Sylvia and I spent a fair amount of time monitoring the media coverage. The *Daily Mirror* story continued to repeat over and over again. There wasn't any new information until that night.

Nicki was still on a plane when the piece hit. As soon as she landed, we talked and I gave her the update. Beyond the regurgitated stories from the original tabloid trash, we'd suffered a direct hit by someone we knew.

"That complete arsehole, Dan Roark," I said. "He wrote a few sentences on his blog about us."

"He did not!"

"Yes, he did. It just proves I was right about him all along."

"Why would he do that?"

"Because he's a twat, that's why." With a guilty groan, I added, "And unfortunately, he had a little help from Felicity." I'd always thought Felicity was a crap reporter, but she had a nose for this type of news—or maybe it was just female intuition about a man she was involved with.

"Oh no. Read it to me, please."

"All right." Clearing my throat, I read the drivel, imitating Roark's irritating American accent. "'There's lots of gossip among the White

House Press Corps. I don't know if anything inappropriate happened between Nicole Johnson and Adam Kincaid while he was at the BBC. I do know they used to talk a fair amount while at work. I never saw anything out of the ordinary, but some people said they believed things started between them at the White House Correspondents' Dinner.

"'Then they were seen dancing together rather closely last Saturday night when the president was traveling in Istanbul. It was at a restaurant with many people around, including other members of the press. Kincaid resigned on Monday, and now there are photos of them together. Word on the street is that they knew each other in high school and never got over one another. We'll see what pans out this week.'"

"Asshole," she said. "How do you know Felicity was involved?"

"The part about never getting over you. She accused me of that when I first started seeing you outside of work."

"I love how he walks a line of not being too accusatory of me. Maybe it's because I did those shots with him."

"Maybe, but I bet it's more that he doesn't want to poison his relationship with the White House in case you stick around."

"His blog is just crap, but unfortunately someone will read it. I'll call Matt to see what he says. Tomorrow is going to suck." She sighed in frustration.

"I know. I'm very sorry about that. Here you thought I was going to be the sacrificial lamb for our relationship, but you're the one who will take the public beating."

"Yes, I will. But I'll take it if I get to finally be with you."

"That's exactly what I want to hear."

That Monday morning, Nicki was the central issue of the White House press briefing. The press corps clamored for answers on our relationship and whether or not the BBC had special access at the White House because of it. In an effort to show its impartiality, even the junior reporter for the BBC joined in the heckling. Of course, Matthew said no and repeated the official statement.

Nicki stood off to the side with the same blank look she had every day at the briefings. Yet now the subject matter was her personal life, which particularly steeled her expression against any emotion or interest. As a television viewer, I found it effective.

At one point, Matthew turned to her and smiled. "Nicole, would you like to answer any questions?"

They must've rehearsed the exchange, because she smiled and, in a poised voice, said, "No, I won't comment on my personal life."

"There you have it," Matthew said. "Now, on to more pressing topics."

Yet the media wouldn't let it drop so quickly. For the rest of the day, the cable news ran God-awful pieces on us, even dredging up ghosts of girlfriends past like Meredith Daniels. That set Nicki off.

The following day, President Logan took questions after making some remarks on events in the Middle East. The first question came from Dan Roark, asking, "Mr. President, I'm sure you've heard about the relationship between Nicole Johnson and BBC reporter Adam Kincaid. Has your presidency been compromised in any way because of it?"

The president shook his head in amused dismay. "Of all the things going on in the world, you ask me about that?"

The briefing room exploded with laughter. I tried to see Nicki on the screen, but she was hidden behind a phalanx of staff and security.

The president waited for the room to die down before he continued. "Pardon the joke. But no, of course not. My presidency hasn't been compromised at all by their relationship. Nicole has worked for me since she was in college. She's like a daughter to me and has kept me informed of things. Adam is no longer with the BBC. Nothing has happened to compromise the integrity of any of the parties involved. I don't really see the intrigue — other than it's a nice story."

In the end, it was fitting that utter arsehole Dan Roark had been the one to finally ask President Logan about the scandal — and sweet revenge for me that his question killed the story altogether. Logan had pronounced the matter dead, and after that, for the most part it was. The questions and articles about us had almost dribbled to their end by the time Mum, Sylvia, and I left Scotland the following afternoon. We'd planned on staying longer, but Mum declared there was too much of Dad and the Kincaid family at the house for her to bear being there.

On the car ride back to the airport, Mum and Sylvia talked about everyone who needed to be thanked for their help over the past few days. I stared out the window at the Scottish moors, fixated on my own life and how much it had changed in the last few days. I imagined how differently the story could've played out if the news hadn't broken during my father's burial.

In the end, Dad had made sure Nicki and I could be together.

I silently thanked him for that.

Epilogue

Nicki Johnson
Malaysia
2011

Wiping the sweat dripping from his brow, Adam took a sip of water. I peered at him through my sunglasses and said, "You're wilting. I don't think Brits are supposed to be this close to the equator."

"I'm getting used to it." He smiled. "Bloody steamy, though. I don't think I could've been an early explorer, at least not in Borneo."

"No, it's not like you to dominate and pillage. At least that's what your kind did in America."

"You're still holding that against us?" He laughed. "You wouldn't be alive today if we hadn't come to America hundreds of years ago."

"Well, I'm very happy that one Brit came to America a few decades ago." I wanted to throw my arms around him, but remembering we were in a Muslim country, I gave him a quick peck on the cheek instead.

"I am ready now," a male voice called in choppy English.

We walked up to the rickety booth, and Adam asked for two tickets for the ferry. The dark man's finely groomed mustache twitched as he studied us. I guessed he was trying to figure out if we were married. I took a step closer to Adam, and he gave me a possessive touch.

Counting out the change in ringgits, the man asked, "Where are your children?"

"Oh…uh…we don't have children." Adam fumbled the words.

"Why not?" the man asked incredulously. He looked at our hands and saw no rings. He pointed to the jeweled ring on his right hand, common for married Malaysian men. "Aren't you married?"

"Um…no…we aren't."

I avoided the man's eyes, which I was sure looked at me in judgment. I knew I shouldn't feel as I did. I was a Western woman who'd led an independent life with a very successful career. Why shouldn't I be proud of that? Yet I felt the man judged me inferior in some way—like I was a tramp or barren. Otherwise, why would a thirty-five-year old woman be unmarried? I shuffled my feet a few times in awkwardness.

"You should be married," the man declared. "You are too old not to be married and have children."

Adam's eyes widened, and I peeked at the ticket man warily.

"You will like it," he exclaimed with a grin.

Adam and I smiled in return, but neither one of us looked at each other. The man continued to speak, "Children are God's greatest gift. They will bring you joy even when there is no joy to be had."

"That's what my dad used to say," said Adam.

"You should listen to your father." He then pointed to a man untying the boat from the dock. "He is ready for you now." Without another word, he returned to counting his prayer beads.

Later that afternoon, we trekked out of the rainforest and onto a secluded beach. The South China Sea lapped lazily on the sand. It was our reward after an oppressively hot hike through the jungle.

After tossing his backpack to the ground, Adam took off his shirt. "If it weren't for the authoritarian government, I'd say we should skinny dip."

"I know," I said, adjusting my bikini top after taking off my shirt. "No one's here, but I don't want to take a chance."

"Though you might as well be starkers in that." He admired the scraps of cloth constituting a swimsuit.

"Pfft." I rolled my eyes. "I'm still covered."

"That's a shame." He winked and extended his hand. "Let's go in."

The ocean was warm, but the wetness still cooled us down. We swam and played in the water until we were so tired we simply bobbed on our backs in the buoyant sea.

After a period of blissful silence, Adam asked, "So…what do you think about what that old man said?"

"What man?" I asked without breaking my concentration on the clouds.

"The man who sold us the tickets."

"Oh. Him."

"Well, what do you think?"

"Why? What do you think?" I didn't want to be the one to start the conversation.

Adam swam closer to me and stood in the sand. That was a good sign, I thought, and an even better one was when he took my hand. He declared softly, "I think he's right."

"You do?" I stopped floating and stood next to him, wanting to hear everything he said as clearly as possible.

He nodded but was quiet. Damn it. He wanted me to speak first.

"I do, too," I replied, squeezing his hand.

"Why haven't you said anything?" he asked, his face beaming brighter with the moment.

"I don't know." I shrugged with a big smile. "Isn't the man traditionally the one who brings it up?"

"But I did…a few times, and you told me you weren't ready."

"That was right after I moved in. I told you I just needed time. It's been two years."

It was true. After being apart for so long, I'd thought we should simply be a normal couple for a while. A part of me also hadn't wanted to rub it in Juan Carlos's face that he'd been permanently replaced so quickly. Now things had changed. I was going on thirty-six and thinking of children, but more importantly, I wanted a sign from Adam that our time together had arrived.

"Yes, you asked for time, but it sounded like you wanted a lot of time—you wanted things to stay the same for years. I stopped talking about it because I thought when you were ready, you'd let me know."

"Really? You were waiting for me?"

"Yes, but…" With a tentative hand, he touched my salty, sandy hair, and I wished I looked a little better for a proposal. My regret turned to fear when he said, "…I've also wanted to come clean about something from a few years back. I did something to you that was wrong, and it was self-serving, but also a little Machiavellian."

My mind tried to race through possibilities, but none came up. It was an odd description. "You wronged me where the end justified the means?"

"Yeah." He shook his head in what had to be self-disappointment. "It seems silly now. Water under the bridge, you know? But I should tell you that back when you were with Juan Carlos, I lied to you a bit about Felicity."

"You did?" I hadn't heard her name in so long it took me a while to remember what I knew of their relationship. Now I wasn't threatened by her in the least, but back then, she'd really irritated me—not just because of her relationship with Adam, but she also embodied British perfection, something I'd never be. So it would've been bad enough if it was just simple jealousy, but she'd also been a royal bitch to me.

What on earth had Adam done with her? My heart caved as dread engulfed me. With a wavering voice, I jumped to the worst conclusion. "How so? You made it sound like you two were on the outs. Were you actually sleeping with her the whole time? Did you lie to me about it?"

Adam flinched for a moment before he burst out laughing, which made me flinch in turn. That wasn't the response I'd expected. He then put his arm around me as some indication I was dead wrong. Still, I wasn't sure that I welcomed the gesture.

He chortled. "Fuck no. Not at all. Just the opposite, in fact."

"Huh?"

"I *did* lie to you. Remember how old Juan Carlos thought Felicity might be a ruse? Well, he was sort of right. Things fell apart with Fel even before the White House Correspondents' Dinner, but I didn't tell you. Because you had Juan Carlos, I felt the need to save face. I also suspected you were jealous of her. I thought Felicity might be useful in making you want me again."

My shoulders stiffened under his touch, and I crossed my arms. I realized it looked a little silly to pose like that while wearing a bikini top, but whatever. Though I wasn't mad at him—because it was sort of sweet even if he had played me—I was annoyed to have been kept in the dark about it for so long. "Wanker. You're a wanker, that's what you are."

Holding my rigid body tighter, he laughed. "I am. I admit it, and I'm truly sorry I lied to you, but all is fair in love and war, right?"

"I suppose…" My body softened and my indignation began to subside as memories of that crazy time flashed back to me. Then one jumped out that made me give him a stern look. "So were you playing Felicity, too? Is that why she was such a bitch to me? Is that why she gave information to Dan Roark for his blog?"

His mouth guiltily twitched. "Possibly. It all worked out okay, though, right?"

For a split second, I was annoyed again, but that boyish grin of his always melted my resolve. "You know, you're more like David than you care to admit. How do you two get away with this shit?"

"Don't ask me why David gets away with his antics. That's for you women to explain." His expression became more serious as he wrapped his arms around me in a full embrace and rested his forehead against mine. "As for me, it's because I've loved you so damn much, that's why."

With our faces still touching, I looked into his eyes. "And I've loved you so much. That's why I forgive you."

"Thank you."

We were both quiet, and as I realized a marriage proposal might very well come next from his mouth, the healthy, modern woman side of me shouted a damn good question to my heart. I knew the answer, but for good measure, I took a step back and asked it aloud. "But how do I know you won't lie to me again?"

He shook his head with a smile. "Because I'll never lie to my wife."

And I believed him. We'd lived together for the last couple of years, plus I'd known him since childhood. For all his faults, and God knows I had plenty of my own, I knew *that* one wasn't going to be repeated.

I kissed his forehead. "So you want to get married, do you?"

"Hell yes. Last weekend in Houston, I almost got down on bended knee when I saw you holding Rachel's new baby. I thought you might be receptive, but I wasn't sure."

My mouth fell open. "You're ready for kids, too."

"You could stop taking those silly pills right now for all I care." He kissed me and murmured, "I've *been* ready, sweetheart."

"I'm sorry it took me a while." I kissed him back. "But I'm here now."

"I'm sorry," he said, pulling away so he could look me in the eye, "for not asking you sooner."

"You haven't actually asked me to marry you yet."

"Shouldn't I have a ring?"

"You know I don't care about things like that." I raised my eyebrows in hope. "I just care that you mean it."

"Oh, I bloody well mean it." Taking both of my hands in his, his face became somber, and he waited a moment to collect his thoughts. Finally, he said, "Forgive me if I fuck this up. I would've practiced had I known I'd get the chance, but there is one line I've always wanted to say."

"What's that?"

"You've always been my one true love." He seemed to smile with all his heart, and then he took a deep breath. "Will you do me the honor of spending the rest of your life with me? Will you marry me?"

"Yes," I said. The easiest question I ever answered. "Absolutely. I'm never letting you go."

Later that afternoon, we made our way to the shade of a banyan tree on the beach. As Adam pared an apple for me, he asked, "So where should we have the wedding?"

"I'm not sure."

"Maybe Kuala Lumpur?" he joked.

"No, we can't do that. My mother will kill me if she doesn't get to buy a wedding dress."

"You want a big wedding, then? And when? I'll do whatever you want."

"Small. Very small." I grinned. "And I want it as soon as possible."

"Sounds brilliant. Where's the honeymoon?"

"I don't know. Let's pick a place we've never been."

"And after?" he asked hesitantly. "Where should we live?"

"You want to go back home, don't you?" I already knew the answer, and I took his hand to tell him it was okay.

"I do. But we don't have to do it immediately."

"Well…" I kissed him behind his ear. "After you knock me up, we can move wherever you want."

"Promise?"

"Of course."

"But what will you do? Won't you miss your job?"

"You know I've only wanted to work for the administration for one term. I've been there three years. It's time to let someone new take on the role, especially because I don't want to kill myself during the reelection campaign."

"That's true."

"And I can always do PR consulting." I shrugged. "Matthew already sold out, and his firm is huge. He'd hire me, and I can do that anywhere in the world, just like you've been doing your work from DC."

"And it hasn't been a problem for me. In fact, the time alone let me build up a portfolio and get better before I sent my stuff out there."

"It worked, too. Look how well you've done." I smiled, leaning back on the small blanket.

He looked at my almost naked body extended before him. With a smile, he stretched out beside me and nuzzled into my neck. "I have a very supportive fiancée."

"And I have a very supportive fiancé."

I kissed his hair as he kissed around my neck. When his hand traveled down to my stomach, I knew what he was up to.

"Um…remember where we are."

"I don't fucking care where we are," he replied, trailing his hand up and down my curves. "I want to make love to my fiancée where we got engaged."

Acknowledgments

Does an acknowledgment in a book suffice for a formal thank-you note? I don't think so, but it's a start to pay down my debts to the wonderful people who've aided and abetted in the writing of this book. Those ladies include:

My beloved fan fiction community, who a few years ago helped with the beginnings of this book, especially Catherine Waring and Corey Ward.

Azucena Sandoval, Dana Lam, Daisy Prescott, Liv Morris, Michelle Kannan, Ruth Clampett, and S.L. Scott, who gave me daily encouragement.

Omnific Publishing—Elizabeth Harper and Enn Bocci, who put up with me, and most importantly, my editor Colleen Wagner for her wonderful ear and heart when it comes to words and people. The fact she lives in London and helped me with the voice of all my Brits is just icing on the cake.

A thousand thanks to you all, and that still doesn't seem like enough.

About the Author

Even before she graduated from law school, Mary knew she wasn't cut out to be a real lawyer. Drawn to politics, she's spent her career as an organizer, lobbyist, and non-profit executive. Nothing piques her interest more than a good political scandal or romance, and when she stumbled upon writing, she put the two together. A born Midwesterner, naturalized Texan, and transient resident of Washington, DC, Mary now lives in Northern California with her two daughters and real lawyer husband.

＊——＊New Adult＊——＊

Three Daves by Nicki Elson
Streamline by Jennifer Lane
The Shades series: *Shades of Atlantis* by Carol Oates
The Heart series: *Beside Your Heart* & *Disclosure of the Heart* & *Forever Your Heart*
by Mary Whitney
Romancing the Bookworm by Kate Evangelista
Fighting Fate by Linda Kage
Flirting with Chaos by Kenya Wright
The Vice, Virtue & Video series: *Revealed* & *Captured* by Bianca Giovanni

＊——＊Erotic Romance＊——＊

The Keyhole series: *Becoming sage* (book 1) by Kasi Alexander
The Keyhole series: *Saving sunni* (book 2) by Kasi & Reggie Alexander
The Winemaker's Dinner: *Appetizers* & *Entrée* by Dr. Ivan Rusilko & Everly Drummond
The Winemaker's Dinner: *Dessert* by Dr. Ivan Rusilko
Client N° 5 by Joy Fulcher

＊——＊Paranormal Romance＊——＊

The Light series: *Seers of Light, Whisper of Light* & *Circle of Light*
by Jennifer DeLucy
The Hanaford Park series: *Eve of Samhain* & *Pleasures Untold* by Lisa Sanchez
Immortal Awakening by KC Randall
The Seraphim series: *Crushed Seraphim* & *Bittersweet Seraphim*
by Debra Anastasia
The Guardian's Wild Child by Feather Stone
Grave Refrain by Sarah M. Glover
Divinity by Patricia Leever
Blood Vine series: *Blood Vine* & *Blood Entangled* & *Blood Reunited*
by Amber Belldene
Divine Temptation by Nicki Elson
Love in the Time of the Dead by Tera Shanley

＊——＊Historical Romance＊——＊

Cat O' Nine Tails by Patricia Leever
Burning Embers by Hannah Fielding
Good Ground by Tracy Winegar

Romantic Suspense

Whirlwind by Robin DeJarnett
The CONduct series: *With Good Behavior* & *Bad Behavior* & *On Best Behavior*
by Jennifer Lane
Indivisible by Jessica McQuinn
Between the Lies by Alison Oburia

Anthologies

A Valentine Anthology including short stories by
Alice Clayton ("With a Double Oven"),
Jennifer DeLucy ("Magnus of Pfelt, Conquering Viking Lord"),
Nicki Elson ("I Don't Do Valentine's Day"),
Jessica McQuinn ("Better Than One Dead Rose and a Monkey Card"),
Victoria Michaels ("Home to Jackson"), and
Alison Oburia ("The Bridge")

Singles and Novellas

It's Only Kinky the First Time (A Keyhole series single) by Kasi Alexander
Learning the Ropes (A Keyhole series single) by Kasi & Reggie Alexander
The Winemaker's Dinner: RSVP by Dr. Ivan Rusilko
The Winemaker's Dinner: No Reservations by Everly Drummond
Big Guns by Jessica McQuinn
Concessions by Robin DeJarnett
Starstruck by Lisa Sanchez
New Flame by BJ Thornton
Shackled by Debra Anastasia
Swim Recruit by Jennifer Lane
Sway by Nicki Elson
Full Speed Ahead by Susan Kaye Quinn
The Second Sunrise by Hannah Downing
The Summer Prince by Carol Oates
Whatever it Takes by Sarah M. Glover
Clarity (A *Divinity* prequel single) by Patricia Leever
A Christmas Wish (A *Cocktails & Dreams* single) by Autumn Markus
Late Night with Andres by Debra Anastasia